PENGUIN BOOKS

STONE RIDER

David Hofmeyr was born in South Africa and lives between London and Paris. In 2012 he was a finalist in the Society of Children's Book Writers and Editors Undiscovered Voices competition and in 2013 he graduated with distinction from Bath Spa University with an MA in Writing for Young People. He works as a Planner for Ogilvy & Mather in the UK. *Stone Rider* is his first novel.

Books by David Hofmeyr

STONE RIDER

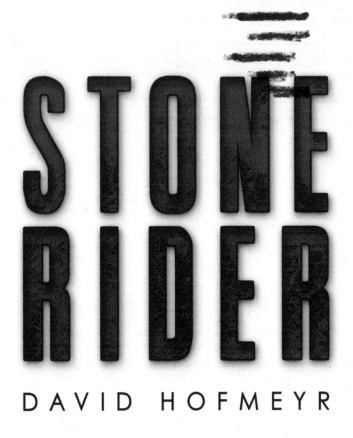

STONE RIDER

DAVID HOFMEYR

PENGUIN BOOKS

PENGUIN BOOKS

UK | USA | Canada | Ireland | Australia
India | New Zealand | South Africa

Penguin Books is part of the Penguin Random House group of companies
whose addresses can be found at global.penguinrandomhouse.com.

Penguin
Random House
UK

First published 2015

001

Text copyright © David Hofmeyr, 2015
Map by Tony Fleetwood
Map copyright © Penguin Books Ltd, 2015
Lines from *The Waste Land* on page 1 © Estate of T. S. Eliot are reprinted by
permission of Faber and Faber Ltd.

'The Rider's Code' illustration copyright © ShutterStock, and Tony Fleetwood, 2015

Set in 10.5/15.5pt Sabon LT Std
Typeset by Jouve (UK), Milton Keynes
Printed in Great Britain by Clays Ltd, St Ives plc

British Library Cataloguing in Publication Data
A CIP catalogue record for this book is available from the British Library

ISBN: 978-0-141-35443-9

www.greenpenguin.co.uk

MIX
Paper from
responsible sources
FSC™ C018179
www.fsc.org

Penguin Books is committed to a sustainable
future for our business, our readers and our planet.
This book is made from Forest Stewardship
Council™ certified paper.

For Delphine. I love you.

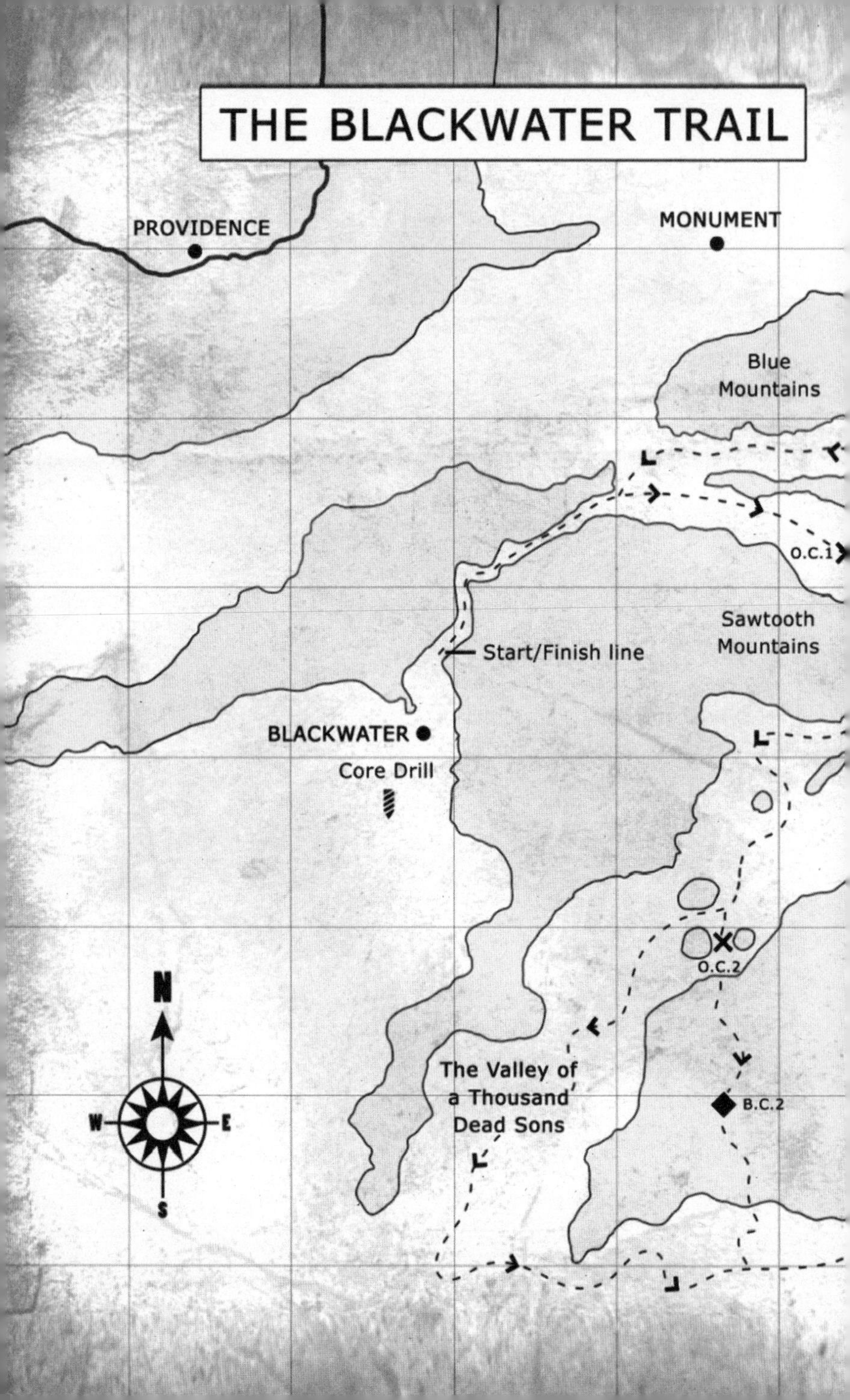

THE BLACKWATER TRAIL

PROVIDENCE

MONUMENT

Blue
Mountains

o.c.1

Sawtooth
Mountains

Start/Finish line

BLACKWATER

Core Drill

O.C.2

N
W — E
S

The Valley of
a Thousand
Dead Sons

B.C.2

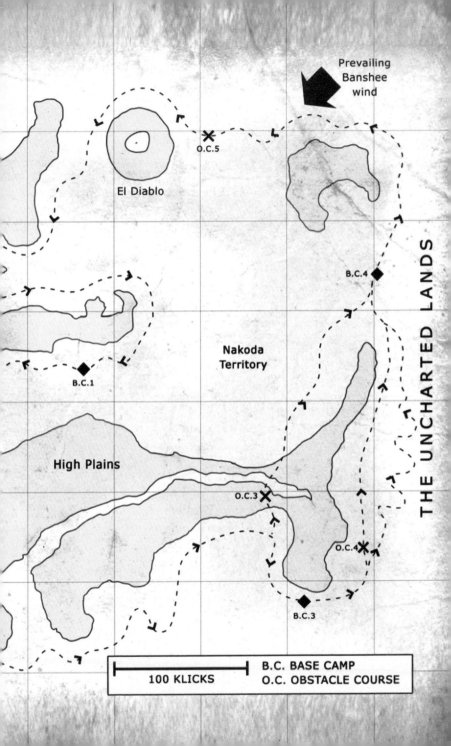

(Come in under the shadow of this red rock),
And I will show you something different from either
Your shadow at morning striding behind you
Or your shadow at evening rising to meet you;
I will show you fear in a handful of dust.

T. S. Eliot, *The Waste Land*

Here for blood. Three dark Riders. In single file.

They ride with bursts of speed, angled back in their seats, arms shaking as they steer their wild machines. Three Riders on low-slung, otherworldly bykes that catch the sun and bristle. Dirt clings to their gold-mirrored sun visors and their gleaming riding suits. They muscle across a wind-hammered landscape, riding up the slope of a dark mountain.

A volcano.

The lead Rider reins in his posse with a raised right hand and they slide out behind him in a snarl of black dust. When the dust clears, they see what he sees.

In the valley lies the course. A steep affair with furrowed lanes, fierce turns and six massive jumps. Alone below, a Rider on a byke of pale silver leaps skyward. He turns his front wheel in mid-air, floats and then plunges down the far side of a tabletop.

It's an impressive jump.

The lead Rider, above on the hill, acknowledges the feat with a smile. No one sees it. The smile is concealed behind his visor.

3

It's an hour after dawn. The sun is behind them, low against the black hills. Their shadows – lean and long – strike out down the slope, pointing the way.

'That's *him*!' Wyatt exclaims, flicking up his visor. He's the tall one, pale and thin. He looks at his companions and rocks back in the saddle of his black Shadow byke.

'The hell you say,' Red spits, with his visor up. 'We busted him.' Red is bull-necked and broad-shouldered. Mean-looking. He sits lower on his blood-red Chopper than the others.

'I don't know . . .' Wyatt pauses. 'The way he rides . . .'

They watch the Rider slam on his brakes and skid into a corner. He swerves, accelerates hard and throws himself into the next jump – a fluid move – all finesse and grace and perfect balance.

'It can't be,' Red insists. 'It's not possible.'

'It's him,' Levi says, his voice muffled behind his visor. 'Look at the byke.'

'How the hell . . .?'

'I can take him from here.' Wyatt's hand moves to his sling. 'One clean shot.'

'You think he's seen us?' Red asks.

'He's seen nothin, dumb-ass. We're uphill, against the sun.'

He's right. The dirt valley Rider sees nothing but the track. His concentration is fixed on the next turn, his next jump. His silver byke flares in the morning sunlight. The Riders above watch him duel with the dust. He completes another free-floating jump, cool and sleek.

4

'Lemme do it. I swear I can take him.' Red swings off his byke, sling in hand. He squares his shoulders and takes aim.

'No,' Levi says, removing his helmet, placing it in the crook of his arm. He speaks out of the corner of his mouth. His eyes are narrow slits.

'No?'

'He means you couldn't hit a tree from two yards.' Wyatt kicks out his byke stand and swings a long leg over his seat. 'I'll do it.'

Red throws Wyatt a defiant glare.

'I said *no*,' Levi repeats. 'We fix him right this time. Up close and personal.'

'How close?'

'Close enough to get his blood on your face.'

'Hell, yeah!' Wyatt hoots.

'Damn straight!' Red yells.

He pulls up at the top of the last ramp and sits on his pale silver byke – a customized Drifter. He breathes hard and pellets of sweat stream down the small of his back. His riding suit is grey and caked in dirt. Gold sun goggles shield his eyes and an air-filter mask covers his mouth.

He turns his head, listening. A chill crawls up his spine. He concentrates on three Riders coming out of the sun, careering down the lava slope like the devil's on their heels.

He knows them. The one on the white byke in particular. He can't see his face, but there's something in the way he rides, angled to the right. You get to know the way a person rides in the Race. That's the way you beat them. By anticipating their next move.

The other two are dangerous, but the one on the white byke . . .

They keep coming.

Nothing stops them.

Time to haul ass.

With a last glance, he kicks down and flies. He zooms down the jump and he's away. Flicks a look over his shoulder, sees nothing but dust. He flips a gear and the byke grinds. He's tired. He can feel the lead weight of his legs.

The byke will have to do the work.

He pulls off the track, strikes out for the Badland. He looks back and sees one of them at a standstill. Nothing like the speed of the Drifter. He smiles. He'll outstrip them, dead legs and all.

ZZZLICK!

Something shoots past his ear. He swerves and ducks down. He's riding like a demon. Going as hard as he can.

ZZLICK! SSSHNICK!

Stones.

He looks back over his shoulder and there they are. Still coming. Still flying. Except the tall one, back on a rise, sighting him with a sling.

*

That's the last thing he sees before the pain hits. And then the world spins upside down and the sky turns black.

He moans. Crawls on the ground. His byke lies in a heap, wheels spinning, handlebar jutting. His goggles, incredibly, are still strapped to his head. But his mask is gone, ripped from his mouth. He knows he may have broken something. A rib. Possibly cracked. The pain is fierce. His temple throbs. Blood drips into his eye. He can feel the hot pulse of it running down his forehead, down his cheek. But it's OK – head cuts bleed. He's seen it all before.

That one guy can sling a stone – must've been a hundred yards out.

He looks up groggily.

Three Riders circle him. One tall. One muscular. One on a white byke. He tries to think. Tries to order his thoughts, but he can't. His vision is blurred. A ringing noise jangles in his ear. Pain throbs at the base of his skull. It feels like his bones have turned to rubber.

The one on the white byke, obviously the leader, comes to a sliding stop with a back-wheel break. The others follow suit. The lead Rider lifts his visor and squints down at him. His eyes are dark brown. There is no mistaking this face – these brown eyes.

'Who are you?' the Rider says.

The kid coughs and winces with the pain.

'Man asked you a question,' the muscular one says, lowering his red byke to its stand. With sling in hand, he approaches. There's a hint of a tattoo at his neck, hidden by his riding suit.

'Nobody,' the kid croaks, finding his voice.

'Well, that's all wrong,' the Rider on the white byke says. 'I know you. And you know me.' He swings off his Stinger. With steady hands, he unclips his goggles.

The kid knows what's coming now.

Vengeance.

PART 1

BURIAL OF THE DEAD

PART 1

BURIAL OF THE DEAD

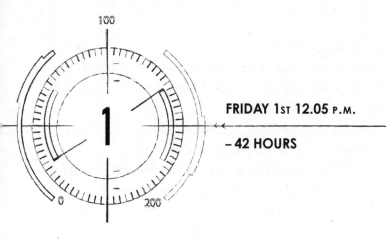

FRIDAY 1ST 12.05 P.M.

– 42 HOURS

Adam Stone empties the bucket of rotting vegetables into the trough and then he stands back to watch. Dried mud hangs in clots from the pig's coarse, hairless skin. The pig shovels its nose into the muck, squeals and looks up with a dumb expression. As though it's surprised to be alive.

Which it ought to be, given it's the only one left.

He likes the pig. It's tough. Has to be, to survive when all the others got sick and died.

But he hates the pig too. He wonders what drives it to endure the foul-smelling sty. A prisoner, dependent on a food supply outside its control.

He thinks about releasing it sometimes, letting it free into the wild. But where would it go? And how long would it last?

As he watches the pig, he thinks about the Race. The Blackwater Trail. Just two days away. Less than forty-eight hours. It dominates his thoughts. Each day. Every day.

How long will *he* last, out there in the desert?

'What are you doin in that barn? You black out again?'

It's the old man. Adam shakes his head and makes for the door. He steps outside, bolts the door fast and turns into the glare of a noon sun.

'Finish with the hog?' comes the old man's thin voice.

Adam squints in the harsh light. 'Yessir.'

Old Man Dagg. Oldest man in Blackwater. Seen more than fifty summers. He stands in the sparse shade of a charred cedar tree, leaning on his stick. He's wearing a grey-white vest with yellow sweat stains and a pair of ancient jeans blackened with dirt. Same thing he always wears. His face is hidden in the shade of a battered wide-brim hat. He leans to the side and spits.

'Goddamn hot,' he says and limps into the house.

No kidding. Old Man Dagg always says the obvious. Always about the weather. It's hot. Looks like rain. Gonna be freezin come winter.

'Need me for anything else, Mr Dagg?'

He follows the old man, steps up on to the cool porch. The stone floor is worn smooth and flakes of grey paint peel from the walls. He moves to the door and looks into the gloom. Hears nothing but the squeak of a mosquito door on busted springs.

'Mr Dagg?'

Adam is hit with a strong reek. Stale sweat and boiled vegetables – cabbages and turnips, something else he can't place.

He shifts his weight and the floorboards creak underfoot. Then he hears the tapping of a stick. Emerging from the shadows, the old man comes with his pale, sightless eyes. His face is drawn and grey and the bags under his eyes are dark, almost green. His O2 mask, with its clear airpipe, dangles loose at his neck.

Old Man Dagg pushes past Adam, draws the back of his hand across his mouth and clears his throat. The rattling sound doesn't bode well.

'You're bleedin me dry, boy.' Old Man Dagg pulls a yellowed note from an open billfold. 'S'pose you think it's fine stealin from an ol' man?' His breath could peel paint.

'No, sir.'

The old man turns his head to the side, the way a dog listens to distant sounds. He doesn't move. Now Adam hears the muted roar. He looks to the horizon and he sees a white jet stream and the tiny, metal glint of a solar rocket.

'You fixin to ride the Race?' the old man says.

'Yessir,' he answers, watching the distant rocket climb into the sky.

'Yessir; no, sir; three bags full, sir. Don't you never say nothin else?'

Adam looks at him. 'No, sir.'

Old Man Dagg's eyes are rheumy and red-rimmed. Adam wonders if he can see anything. Shadows maybe. Shapes.

'You ain't afraid?' the old man says.

'Nope.'

Old Man Dagg sneers. 'You *will* be afraid. Mark my words. You *will* be.'

He massages his neck and pulls it to the side. Adam hears the bones click.

'I seen kids like you come and go,' the old man says. 'All the same. Think you don't belong here with the Left-Behind. Think you belong up yonder with the Watchers. But you're wrong.'

Adam says nothing.

'Figure you're some kind of special case? That you know *how* to win?'

He shrugs. 'Reckon I got a chance.'

'Hell. You don't know nothin. Nothin about before neither.'

'I know things were different.'

The old man nods, but not in agreement. 'Things were more'n different. How many summers you got . . . fourteen?'

'Fifteen.'

'Hell. Had myself a full head a hair when I was a boy. Goddamn toxic sky. My grandpap lived to a full sixty summers, if you'd believe it. But not him or any damn one of us had enough cash money to get his ass up to Sky-Base.'

'Maybe he should've learned to ride. Could've earned a ticket.'

Old Man Dagg's top lip curls. He shuffles past Adam. With his right hand, he drags a metal cart that supports his O2 canister. It looks like a bomb, a chipped silver tube with a red base and a tap for the O2 at the top end. Old Man Dagg lifts his face to the sky, arches his neck, twitches and sniffs the air. Then he turns his head to the side and spits. 'Rain comin.'

Adam looks up. The sky is a brown haze.

The old man must be addled with booze, because Adam can't see a hint of rain. Not a storm cloud in sight. Just a chalk-smudge of white jet stream, a reminder of the rocket's upward thrust.

The old man holds out his hand. The yellowed note flutters between the stubs of his dirt-stained fingers. It's the last note Adam needs to enter the Race. The note that will fly him away. He grabs it with a shaking hand, stabs it into his back pocket before the wind can snatch it.

Old Man Dagg pulls up his O2 mask and sucks in a ragged breath. Adam stares at the dripping beads of condensation on the transparent plastic. He watches the old man's lips pull at the cloudy air. When he lowers it, there is something else in his look. A sadness maybe. He turns and limps back to his door. The wheels of the O2 cart make a wretched squealing noise.

'You gonna wish me luck?' Adam calls after him.

Old Man Dagg turns at the door. 'Luck?' He tilts his face to the sky and shakes his head. 'What's comin is comin. Not a damn thing in the world you can do about that.'

Adam climbs on his byke, claps on his goggles and suctions on his air-filter mask. He takes the money from his pocket and transfers it to a secret chamber in his boot, knocked out of his heel. Then he rolls back the throttle, loving the vibration in his hands.

Everything is different on the byke. It's the only place he feels free.

The engine thrums. The hot westerly cuts into his face. The sun burns his neck. All thoughts of crazy Old Man Dagg drift away.

He takes the lake towpath. Past the deserted woodcutter's lodge, down through the burnt-out cedar tree forest to the old jetty. The way he always goes on hot days like this when the air is choked with dust and everything moves in slow motion.

Everything but the byke.

The Longthorn is a thing of beauty. A wonder-machine.

She elongates on the flat, reducing air resistance for speed. On the dirt jumps, with a slick gear shift, she cinches up, providing maximum control. The byke borrows her power from the elements – the wind and the sun – trapping and storing energy through air ducts and solar panels, concentrators and photosensors. A control panel, set between the handlebars, has a gauge showing cumulative charge capacity and another indicating bursts of charge, delivered by a flash of sunlight, a strong wind or even movement.

The byke works in sync with him. Feels him, feeds off his movements.

If he takes evasive action and swerves, the byke remembers, she *learns*. And the next time he leans for a sharp turn the byke is one step ahead, keeping him safe, keeping him alive. From the byke he draws what he always does. Resilience. A cold resolve. Frank told him never to ride for too long. It will take over, this hardness. It will engulf and it will corrode.

He glances at the Longthorn's dashboard.

His digital timer is set to countdown mode. Just forty-one hours.

His capacity gauge blinks seven bars. Maximum charge. This gives him another seven or eight hours of riding, depending on how he rides and where he goes. The byke will carry her charge into the dark, losing power after the sun dies when the wind is still.

But night is a far-off thing. Now there is only blazing heat.

He rides with a keen sense of instinct. A sixth sense. He could ride blind he knows the byke so well.

The gears click and take and Adam feels resistance in her shocks as they career down a hill. The byke wallows and floats. She needs a tune-up.

The Longthorn isn't new. She isn't anywhere close. Father to son, brother to brother, mother to daughter – bykes are passed through the family line. He knows they were gifted to the planet by Sky-Base back when the Races were first conceived and that each byke carries an echo of her previous Riders – all of them through the bloodline – fading as time passes.

He can sense his brother's echo now, running through the machine. He can *feel* him. And, further back, a residue of someone else. Pa.

Adam powers forward, eyes on the road. Bony tree limbs point the way and he follows, as if in a trance. This is how riding makes him feel. In *the zone*. A different dimension. That place he goes when he rides. The road is a tunnel and he floats along it, without consciousness.

He's free. Free of this dead place.

The cracked white cement comes at him and his tyres grip. He plunges on to a gravel path. He carves through a rutted track. He knows it by heart. Every stone. Every turn. He comes sweeping full tilt up the trail, pulling wheelies and charging tree stumps. He swerves at the last second. Rubber burns as he brakes. Then he belts it round a bend, exploding out of the turn, towards the jetty. One false move and he's in the scrub.

He smells the silt now and feels the air cool. Blackwater Lake.

He thinks of the money in the sole of his boot and he feels a wild excitement build. But then his thoughts turn to Frank. And Sadie. Beautiful, determined and dangerous Sadie. Adam feels something altogether different. A dull ache in his stomach.

Guilt.

He's free. But he's not free at all.

He strips to his underwear, folds his clothes into the dry grass. Now he stands at the end of the jetty and watches the dark water. He knows what lies beneath the surface. But he runs to it anyway. He gulps a breath, and leaps feet first.

Cold grips him. He pinches his nose to equalize the pressure, then he jackknifes and down he goes. Down deep where it's quiet and dark and green weeds drift.

Frank taught him how to swim. Taught him the mean way. Swung him round by an arm and a leg . . . and let go. Adam remembers the feeling. The frantic panic in his chest. The water in his mouth, in his nose. Thrashing his arms and his legs. He kicked and he pulled and he screamed. Somehow, he made it back to the bank and his brother stood over him, watching him suck air. Adam didn't speak to him for weeks after that.

He floats now, hanging limp, arms outflung, head spinning. He'd sink to the bottom if he could. Down to the lake bed. He can see it beneath his pale feet, out of reach, shimmering like a face in the darkness. A ghost face. A cold feeling stirs in him. Colder than the water.

Frank warned him. Told him never to come back. But if he didn't want him coming to the lake then he shouldn't have taught him to swim.

Bubbles rise from his nose. He feels a movement in the water and turns. Fast. His heart hammers. He pushes himself through a one-eighty arc.

He's alone.

The burning in his lungs is fierce.

He can feel the Blackness rising.

Up through his legs. Deadness in his calves. Spots of light in his vision. A tiny dart of pain in the back of his head. He feels tired. Bone-tired. His eyelids droop.

No! Pass out now and I'm dead. Just like Pa.

He stares at the warping surface. Cranks himself out of the stupor. Rises with slow and steady kicks. He bursts out of the water with a showering spray and a gasp. He throws up his arms, shouts at the hazy sky, at the white sun with its rainbow halo in the blurry light.

That's when he sees him.

At first, just a vague outline. A shadow.

Then a kid. Sitting on his haunches. Looking at *his* byke.

'This your byke?' the kid says in a flat tone. Head down, eyes in shadow.

Adam blinks and wipes the water from his eyes. He looks up the trail, through the skeleton trees. Then glances at his boot, where he hid the money. 'Who's askin?'

The kid shifts on the balls of his feet and looks down at him. 'Nobody else here.'

Adam makes him out to be near the same age as him. Maybe a summer or two older. Seventeen most likely. Darkly tanned skin. Crazy wolf-yellow eyes, quick and calculating. And low on his skull, behind his left ear, a jutting metal tube.

Adam feels his jaw tighten. A twinge of panic in his gut. *A Circuit Rider.*

'She's a nice byke,' the kid says.

'I know. She's mine.'

Stupid. I should've been watching.

Adam treads water, playing it cool. 'Who are you?'

'They call me Kane,' he says, rising off his haunches.

He wears a black riding suit, frayed at the seams. He's tall. Maybe five eleven. And well-built with broad shoulders. His face is handsome, regular ... if not for the ugly scar running up his cheek, from his lip to his eye. Adam wonders what left him this terrible memento and what he might have looked like before.

Kane's eyes are impossible to read. These are eyes that miss nothing and hide everything.

'Just Kane?' Adam asks. 'Nothin else?'

'Nothin else.'

'You from Monument?'

'Nope.'

'Providence?'

'Hell, no.'

Adam hesitates. He's running out of towns. 'What are you doin here?'

Kane undoes the zip on his suit and peels it from his shoulders. 'Come to swim.'

Adam watches him pull off his boots, one by one. 'This is where *I* swim.'

Kane dumps his riding suit in a heap, flings down his underwear. 'It's a free world, right?'

He stands buck naked on the jetty edge.

His body is lean and toned and his skin is tanned. His dark hair – like every other Rider Adam has ever known – is shorn close to the bone. But this is normal. What sets him apart are his amber-coloured eyes ... and the scars. He's covered in wounds and welts. A mean-looking suture, long healed, runs under his shoulder. Another traverses the left side of his abdomen, under the ribs. But he's clean of ink. No crude tattoos.

He's a loner. Just like Adam.

Kane glares down at the glittering water and there's something in his look that makes Adam feel a spurt of fear. The way he scowls at the placid lake as though its dark water has done him some injustice and he's come to exact revenge.

'How far down does it go?' he says.

Adam looks at him. 'To the bottom, I guess.'

Kane smiles. 'How deep?'

'Deep enough.'

Kane stares at the water. His face – with his yellow-coloured eyes, his high cheekbones and his straight jaw – has an alarming, fearsome beauty. Despite the scar. Maybe because of it.

'Dive down and see,' Adam says. 'I dare you.'

Kane turns and walks back down the jetty. His back is criss-crossed with scars.

Adam spits water and laughs. 'Whatsamatter? Chicken?'

But it's a forced laugh. He paddles at the surface, feeling the panic rise. He's taking risks, but he *has* to. He has to show he isn't scared.

Keep it steady. Don't lose it.

The jetty rumbles and the planks rattle. Kane comes slamming down at a hard run. He leaps off the edge. Dives right over Adam – a flash of bronze flesh – then a sucking sound, not even a splash, and the black water swamps him.

Adam spins round. He's gone.

He gulps a breath and ducks underwater. He searches through the roiled sediment, but he can't see a thing. He surfaces, climbs the jetty stairs, streaming water. Stands on the edge, hands at his crotch, shivering. The water churns and ripples, then slowly turns flat calm.

Nothing moves.

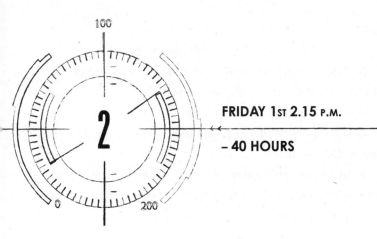

FRIDAY 1st 2.15 P.M.

– 40 HOURS

How long can someone hold their breath? One minute?

Adam checks the money in the sole of his boot. All there. He shucks on his jeans and sits on the jetty edge, dangling his bare feet. Nothing disturbs the surface of the lake. Not even bubbles. Whenever he times himself, all he can manage is forty-five seconds.

He checks his watch. It's a solar-powered antique – but it works. He shakes his wrist. Two minutes.

Two minutes without breathing. Adam stands up. A sick feeling churns in his stomach. He can't see a thing beneath the black surface. Not a thing.

He paces, wondering what the hell to do. But he does nothing. He waits. You don't survive long in Blackwater by sticking your neck out. Not for Outsiders. Not for anyone.

The sky has turned overcast and the water is darker. Like oil.

Maybe he's stuck in the weeds. Tangled up. Maybe he's down there, kicking and fighting.

Then the water explodes, and a figure bursts out.

Kane gasps and waves his fist in the air. His yellow eyes are wild and defiant. Pale sand spills through his fingers, runs down the side of his forearm.

Adam comes to the edge and looks down. 'No way you reached the bottom.'

Kane throws the clump of sand from his fist. It hits the jetty stairs, slides and drops into the lake. 'How you figure on that sand, then?'

'Took it with you.'

'Saying I'm a cheat?'

'Nobody swims that deep.'

Kane shrugs. 'Just did. Sand's the proof.'

He's calm. Composed. Breathing easy. Not at all bothered by his descent into the black lake.

Adam leans forward and offers his hand, despite himself. 'Name's Adam.'

It's a stupid gesture, and he knows it, but it's too late to pull his hand back. And, when Kane ignores him and hauls himself up the stairs and out of the water, Adam feels like an idiot. His cheeks burn as Kane brushes past him, utterly naked.

He watches him stamp down the jetty, leaving wet footprints that fade quickly. Kane pulls on his black riding suit and stretches. There's danger in him. Maybe it's the way he moves – light on his feet, lithe and strong. Or the weals and scars on his body.

Hoping Kane won't see his scrutinizing, he approaches their bykes. 'You ride a Drifter.'

Kane nods, without turning, pulling on his boots.

Kane's byke is lightweight and powerful. Streamlined. Built for speed. A Drifter is one of a kind. No byke can touch her on the flats and she can generate massive acceleration, like a rocket. Adam notices evidence of soldering work. The byke is scarred and dented. This is a byke grown accustomed to long, hard roads. But nobody owns a new byke.

Adam admires the lines. 'Sky-Base don't make 'em like this any more.'

'That's a fact.'

'Your pa's?'

'Nope.'

'Brother? Sister?'

'Them either.'

'Where'd you get her, then?'

Kane takes a step towards him. 'From someone who won't be needing her any more.'

Adam feels a twinge of panic again. 'Why's that?'

'Broke his back coming down a big jump.' Kane stoops to lift a smooth stone. He flips it up and down in his hand. 'It happens.'

Adam stares at him. 'You *stole* her?'

Kane shakes his head. 'He gave her to me, 'fore he died. Got the script of sale.'

'It's not possible. Not to ride someone's byke who don't have the same genes as you.' Adam points at his own byke. 'No one but a Stone rides the Longthorn.'

Kane smiles. 'It can be done. Just gotta deal with the Rider's echo running through the machine. Gotta understand him. Think like him. Move like him. Then the byke will let you ride.'

'I'll stick with the Longthorn.'

Kane nods. 'A person can ride a good race on a byke like that.'

Adam's byke – a beat-up, dark blue Longthorn – is solid and durable. A dinosaur by comparison to the Drifter. But she's *his*, and Adam rides nothing else.

'She's no Drifter, but she's tough,' he says. 'She can take a knock.'

'Yep. Saw you riding in on the towpath. Got some skills.'

Adam looks at him. He doesn't like the idea of being watched.

Kane hurls the flat stone and they watch it skim across the lake surface, hopping one . . . two . . . three, four, five, sixseveneightnine times.

Adam bends to collect a pebble and follows suit. He flings it low across the surface, but it only manages a disappointing four hops before splashing into the lake, disappearing from sight. He tries another, and then another, but the most he manages are six feeble hops.

Kane watches him without saying a word.

Adam rounds on him. 'Where you from?'

'Other side,' Kane says, waving his hand in a vague way.

'Other side the lake?'

Kane shakes his head. He stoops to collect more stones and places them in a leather pouch tied to his waist. Adam watches him. He sees the sling. A braided cord hanging loose at his belt.

'*Where*, then?'

'Other side the desert,' Kane says, as though it's the most obvious thing in the world.

Adam feels himself clench and unclench his fists. 'There's nothin other side the desert.'

Kane looks at him. 'You know why I'm here, don't you?'

Adam knows. There is only one reason a Circuit Rider comes to Blackwater.

'Sure,' he says. 'You've come to swim.'

Kane smiles and says nothing.

It's the last thing he needs. More competition. Especially someone who rides a Drifter. Adam wishes Kane *had* drowned in the lake. He puts dark thoughts to bed as they ride into Blackwater.

The town is built in a basin carved by ancient glaciers.

Blackwater Lake is wide and long, running north to south for ten klicks. It looks like a hand from the top of the escarpment wall, contouring its western shore. A dark hand, reaching out, holding nothing but dust. No river feeds the lake. It's cut off. The water seeps up from below.

The town is crescent-shaped and it pincers the lake.

The two boys cruise through Blackwater's Outer Ring on one of six roads that cut through to the core. This is where the Freemen live, those too old and infirm to work the mines. And Riders, past and present, who win the right – through racing – not to work the mine. A Blackwater Law. You race, you get to stay clear of the mine. A strong enough incentive for most.

Here, in the Outer Ring, the houses are low and flat-roofed, covered in a grey dust. Smallholdings mostly. A scattering of homes bent against the wind. Some of them with banks of sand heaped up against their sides, as though their occupants have long ago grown weary of fighting the desert.

Blackwater. A town adrift in the sand.

The boys ride past lines of furrowed earth. An assortment of resilient crops are grown here and they wither in the sand-choked soil, yielding a meagre offering.

Old Man Dagg's place lies on the Outer Ring, on the western arm of the crescent. Adam's place is far outside the town, on the eastern shore of the lake. But he's not riding home. Not yet.

Every house they pass lies in ruin. Collapsed porches lean on creaking stilts. The ghost face of a child pressed against a cracked and mottled window watches them pass. A mongrel dog, all skin and bone, skitters across the road.

Adam watches the dog lift its leg on an ancient lamp post. He stays alert for any sign of the gangs. But the streets are quiet.

They ride easy down the crumbling main road, dividing at a sinkhole, rejoining after it. Kane rides in the sun. Adam slips into the shadows of huge, looming apartment blocks that line the Inner Ring. This is where the miners are housed, living stacked up, one on top of the other.

They pass a block-wide, two-storey brick building. Billboard posters hang from the storefront, advertising sundry Sky-Base goods – mostly hydro-pills and nutrient biscuits.

Above the store, a beetle-black supply drone hovers.

It's small – about fifty yards in length, ten yards in depth and five yards in width. Ugly – like a flying insect – with a central rotor column, a flight control head, and a fat abdomen from which a ribbed umbilical cord extends, docking the drone to a metal receiver in the building's roof. The drone delivers supplies to the store this way every day, like a ritualistic feeding.

Grover Jackson exits the store at street level, pushing a broom. Been his place of business for two summers, ever since his pa died. Seventeen and the town's only storekeep. There was trouble back when his pa got turfed in the dirt. Some kids bust into the place. Thought they could take what they wanted. It didn't go well for them. Grover has Levi on his side.

And Levi has the Colonel.

Grover leans his chin against the broom handle and eyeballs the two boys. His worn clothes are filthy and his apron caked with dirt. There's something wrong in the way he leers at them with his gap-toothed grin. Grover's never been right in the head since his pa passed on.

Adam glances at Kane. Sees him staring at Grover, fearless as a wolf.

By the time they reach the deserted gas pump, there's a hot, dense wind blowing. Adam looks up and, sure enough, the clouds are dark and brooding. Electricity zings in the air.

The instrument panel on his byke flashes an amber weather-warning light. He glances at Kane's panel. Same signal.

'No threat,' Kane says.

Adam nods. He knows amber isn't life-threatening. In most amber cases, he can leave his air-filter mask on his neck and he might get his lungs a little scorched or he might get drenched – it depends on the type of storm. A red light is more serious.

A paper flyer flutters through the air and sticks to Adam's byke frame. He uncurls it and flattens it out. A picture of the Colonel stares at him.

Absolutely bald. Skin pulled tight over his bones. He wears mirrored silver shades and a crisp, military-cut black uniform. Deep and grizzled scar lines mark his brow and cheeks. The Colonel points a finger at him, inviting a challenge in the stencilled lettering above:

ENTER THE BLACKWATER TRAIL. WIN A TICKET
TO SKY-BASE.

Underneath the picture of the Colonel, more words:

HAVE YOU GOT WHAT IT TAKES TO BE FREE?

A bright splash hits the flyer and Adam looks up.

Rain.

A torrent comes down in sheets. A sudden brute of a storm. Huge drops slash through the sky and dance on the ground like oil on a hot skillet. Blue lightning cracks and the world turns dark.

Adam releases the flyer to the wind and takes off. He pulls up at a shapeless grey building in the rain and leans his muddy byke against the wall. Kane shadows him and they skip up the wooden stairs to the porch, three at a time.

They stand side by side under a creaking Bykemonger sign – sodden clothes stuck to them, foreheads dripping – and they watch the storm lurch through the town, picking up scattered flyers, throwing them, windmilling, to the sky.

The rain abates as suddenly as it came, like it always does, and leaves them wet to the bone and Adam wondering about Old Man Dagg and forces beyond his reckoning.

'You again.'

The voice behind them belongs to Blackwater's best Bykemonger. A girl. She wears a red bandanna tied round her head. Streaks of black grease are smeared across her cheeks. She's lean and long and she holds her body upright, like a stick of dynamite.

Sadie Blood.

She has a way about her, Sadie. Makes Adam feel hot and cold head to foot. Sometimes he gets so twisted up he can't think straight. He nods and runs a hand over his scalp. He can feel the skin itch.

'How goes it, Sadie?' Adam points at a faded poster tacked to the wall, anything not to look at her. He tries to say something else, but no words come to his lips.

'It's fifteen to enter,' Sadie says, wiping her hands clean on a blackened cloth. 'Same as always, Adam.' She flicks her eyes from him to Kane. She lingers on Kane's face, the scar. Then she turns back to Adam. 'Got the dollars this time?'

'I got the dollars,' he says, feeling his cheeks colour. Sadie is sleek as a panther. Her hair is pixie-short and coal-black. Almond-shaped hazel eyes. Confidence and resilience in them.

Eyes that burn holes in him.

'Only two days left,' she says. 'You like cutting it fine.'

He stares at the porch floorboards.

'The Race doesn't leave room for doubt,' Sadie says.

Adam shifts his feet and glances at Kane.

Kane is staring at Sadie. Looking at her with a quiet intensity, as though he's trying to place her. Studying all her quirks and mannerisms. The tilt of her small mouth. The curve of her lips. How she stands, one leg cocked, the other straight. How she moves her hands when she speaks.

Adam knows these things. He knows everything about the way her body moves.

Same way he knows the Longthorn.

Kane turns his head away and leans in to read the poster.

THE BLACKWATER TRAIL

SUNDAY 3RD. STARTS AT 07:00. ENDS WHEN THE LAST RIDER CROSSES THE LINE. A 2,500-KLICK CIRCUIT. FIFTEEN DOLLARS ENTRY PER BYKE. SLING WEAPONS PERMITTED. NO KNIVES. NO

SHOOTERS. ANY INJURY OR DEATH SUSTAINED IS NOT THE RESPONSIBILITY OF THE COLONEL. TOP THREE PLACED RIDERS WILL RECEIVE $1,000 IN PRIZE MONEY EACH, 200 BASE POINTS AND AUTOMATIC ENTRY TO ANY CIRCUIT RACE. THE FIRST RIDER OVER THE FINISH LINE WINS A ONE-WAY TICKET TO SKY-BASE.

RIDERS CAN PURCHASE ENTRY AT BLACKWATER BYKEMONGER SHOP. LAST DAY OF PLUGGING WILL TAKE PLACE SATURDAY 2ND AT THE TOWN HALL.

GOOD LUCK AND MAY YOU LIVE TO SEE THE SKY.

'Twenty-five hundred klicks through the hardest country known to man or beast,' Kane says.

Adam feels a knot of fear. Fear mixed in with excitement. The Blackwater Trail is a big deal. He knows all the Tribes will come. It will be hell. A week of hell. *At least* a week.

Kane looks at him. 'Think you'll win?'

Adam shrugs to hide his thrill and his terror. 'Wouldn't enter if I didn't.'

Injury or death. Why are those the words that jump off the poster?

'Forty per cent mortality two summers back,' Sadie says. 'One hundred Riders. Sixty survived.'

Kane smiles. 'I like those odds.'

Adam feels his body clench. Two summers back. Longest Blackwater ever ridden. Lasted fifteen days, thanks to a bank of bad weather. Adam tries to recall who won that year. Every Race winner achieves folklore status. Adam can recite each one from the past twenty summers. Maybe thirty. But for some reason he can't remember the winner from just two summers back.

Then he does remember.

It was the summer the Outsider, Finn Ankar, won. It was also the summer Frank lost his leg.

Sadie looks at Kane, points a slender finger at the jutting Plug low down on his skull, behind his left ear. 'You're a Circuit Rider.'

'That's right.'

Sadie looks him up and down. 'Ride any of the Big Four?'

'Zuckerberg Drop. Last winter.'

'You place?'

'Came in third.'

'So you've got money.'

Kane shakes his head. 'Spent it on the byke.'

'Well. Placing gives you automatic entry.' Sadie wipes her forehead with the back of her hand. 'But the Blackwater is meaner than the Zuckerberg, or the Southern Deep, or the Silvermine.'

Kane says nothing.

Sadie glances down the stairs at Kane's Drifter. 'Nice byke.'

'She can move.'

Sadie stands in the doorway and juts her hip. 'I can fix any to ride as fast.'

'I'll bet you can.'

She flashes him a look. The kind of look that would have Adam searching his pockets and staring at the floorboards. Kane holds her gaze.

'I've seen you somewhere before,' Sadie says.

Kane shakes his head. 'I don't think so.'

She looks at him. And it feels to Adam that something passes between them.

'*They'll* know,' she says. 'You can't hide who you are. They know everything about you, soon as they Plug you.'

Kane's hand reaches up to feel the metal tube in his head.

Adam watches him. 'Does it hurt?' he asks. 'When they Plug you?'

He knows it hurts. He *wants* it to hurt. He wishes he could find words to inflict the same pain on Kane right now, in front of Sadie, to expose a weakness, *any* weakness.

Kane looks at him. 'You *will* feel it,' he says with a crooked smile.

Sadie turns to Adam. 'Well, if you're not paying, I'm not standing here waiting.'

She swivels on her heel and walks into the building. Adam watches her without speaking.

God. The way she moves.

He wants her. Craves to run his fingers across her collarbone. Wants her smooth skin touching his. But he knows the only place he's ever going to feel her skin is in his dreams. It's never going to happen. He's not the kind for Sadie Blood. Not him. An Outsider maybe.

Adam forces himself to think of something else. The money, burning a hole in his boot.

Just give her the dollars.

'Got juice, that girl,' Kane says.

Adam wants to call out after her, but he doesn't. Instead he stands there, doing nothing.

It's the same every summer. He saves up, comes here with his cash in his boot, but he can't do it. He can't bring himself to enter. How can he? How can he leave Frank? How can he leave Sadie? He's never told her how he feels – she barely acknowledges him – but what can he do?

She's Sadie Blood.

'Best fixer in town,' he says aloud. 'There's nothin on a byke she can't set right.'

He watches her. He can't keep his gaze from her, the way she walks with a cool sway. On anyone else he would call it a swagger, but on her it's something else. It's catlike.

'Whatsamatter? Chicken?' Kane says, mimicking Adam's own taunt. 'You didn't pay her.'

He smiles and mooches across the porch, leaving a trail of mud. Puts one booted foot up on the railing. Adam stares at his back. He feels a spike of jealousy, a scattershot of anger.

'Who the hell are you to say . . .'

He drifts off, mid-sentence. Looks over Kane's shoulder.

Six silhouetted Riders move on the main street. Behind the Riders the sky is blood-red and their distorted shadows travel spiderlike up the road before them. Each one rides low and the slings at their hip are easy to see.

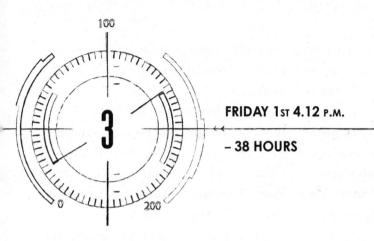

There's no escape. They've seen him.

Adam glances up the main road in the opposite direction, but it's too late. A worm of fear turns inside him.

'Best stay quiet,' he hisses, coming down the steps with Kane at his side.

The lead Rider, on a white Stinger byke, drifts alongside. His opaque goggles reflect the red sun. He wears a gleaming riding suit, still dripping from the rain. Adam has seen a Voddenite suit before, but never owned one. Too expensive. They are made from a woven composite of the miracle-stone Sky-Base mines from deep in the Earth. Light, flexible and incredibly strong, a Voddenite suit moves fluidly with a Rider. If the Rider falls, the suit tenses and becomes rock-hard, protecting the soft flesh and the bones beneath.

Its colour is fluid and changeable, like the surface of a lake. Black, then silver, then gold.

The lead Rider stops and the gang rolls into a threatening horseshoe around him. They look impressive. Adam can see their eyes, but not their mouths under air-filter masks that clamp to them like claws, each with eight breathing pipes feeding them clean air.

Two Riders – his lieutenants, also in Voddenite suits – take up position either side of him. One sits astride a black Shadow, the other a red Chopper. One tall. The other muscular.

Adam knows them. The strong one is Red Stetson, a bruiser and tough as nails. You don't rile Red and get away unscathed. The tall one is Wyatt Dawson, hot-headed and mean as hell. Can fling a stone further and faster than anyone.

Anyone except maybe Levi, the lead Rider.

'You boys entering?' Levi asks. He speaks in a quiet voice, muffled by his mask.

Adam says nothing.

Levi removes his goggles and dusts them down with his hand. His fingernails are long and stuck with dirt. He pulls down the mask to reveal a mouth curling into a smile.

Without looking up, he says, 'Stone. Is that right?'

Adam nods. 'That's right. Adam Stone.' He scans the gang with a hammering heart. They're Scorpions. Ranged between the ages of thirteen and nineteen. Most of them wear scorpion tattoos on their neck. Others have shaved scorpions into the sides of their cropped hair.

Adam weighs up the prospect of outriding all of them. No chance. They sit on their bykes as though their bodies are moulded to the seats. All of them are Plugged.

'And your acquaintance?' Levi says, still smiling.

Acquaintance. Levi's family are home-schooled with the kind of private tutors that most people don't have the means to afford. Levi likes to remind people of their place in the world.

He looks up and sets his goggles atop his head.

Pale circles ring his dark brown eyes. Intelligent eyes. White crow's feet fan out from the corners. The rest of his face is dark from the sun and caked in dust.

Adam glances at Kane. Kane's alarming amber eyes are lit up. He's staring hard at Levi.

Levi looks Kane over. 'What are you riding?'

Kane doesn't answer. It doesn't look like he's about to say anything.

'Drifter,' Adam says, wondering why he feels the need to speak for Kane, whom he hardly knows. Who just *appeared*.

'Drifter, is it?' Levi looks at Kane with his head cocked to the side, as though listening to distant voices. 'I know you.'

'He's not from here,' Adam says.

'No. I see that.'

Levi is good-looking, in a traditional way. Strong jaw. Sculpted bones. Wide-set eyes. But he's ugly too. It's what lies behind his eyes. The malice and disdain. A torrent of insecurity.

'That's a fearsome-looking scar,' he says. 'Must've hurt.'

Still Kane doesn't speak.

Levi's eyes laugh. 'Lost your tongue?'

Kane looks at him. He doesn't move.

'Doesn't speak much, does he? Savvy. Less you say, less trouble you land yourself in.' Levi jerks his thumb at Wyatt on his left. 'Something associates of mine would benefit from learning.'

Wyatt, hostile on the black Shadow, pulls a sling from his belt and plays with the cord.

Levi sucks air through his teeth. 'So ... I assume you have the entry fee? The full fifteen?'

Adam feels the worm twist. He knows what's coming. He knew from the start.

'Assuredly these are tough times,' Levi says. 'Times like these you need protection.'

Wyatt flicks the sling's cradle with his thumb. Red rocks back and forth in his saddle and punches a fat fist down on his handlebar. A mindless thing to do, observes Adam, silent in his thoughts. Mindless is the right word. Red's eyes are a dull mud colour. Not much going on in his skull. Wyatt isn't a great deal smarter, but there's a warning light flickering in his eyes. Not a rational kid, Wyatt. Not the sort that thinks too much. Prefers action.

'You understand, don't you, Stone?' Levi says.

'Well, I ...' Adam's mind ticks over. This situation is tricky. Maybe even lethal. He has to be careful. You don't survive long in Blackwater if you make mistakes. Adam isn't particularly big or strong. But he's street-smart. He knows about survival.

'I'm not asking for it all, mind,' Levi says. 'I'm not the devil. Though I am acquainted with him.' He smiles. 'No. I'll kindly only accept ten. Let's call it tax.'

Adam shuffles his feet. His palms begin to sweat.

Breathe, Adam. Breathe.

His hands are trembling. His arms feel heavy. Now the curl of pain at the back of his head. It's starting again.

Why now?

He knows the feeling. The rising Blackness. Spots of light in the fringe of his vision. A weight on his shoulders. His muscles caving. He tries to fight. But he's powerless.

It happens fast.

One second he's standing and the next he's on his knees, blinking at the dirt, like some giant bug leapt up and bit him in the leg and filled him with paralysing juice. It happens so quick he can't tell if there was a lapse in time between standing and falling.

He clenches his fists in the dirt. Runs them through the ground until his knuckles bleed.

How much time did I lose? Minutes? Seconds?

He looks up and sees faces, too close for his liking. Bulbous and dirt-ingrained. Wild eyes and jagged teeth. A sound comes warping to him. A laugh.

'I forgot you were the kid who blacks out.' Levi's voice. 'Have you recovered, Blackout Boy? Need some shade? Some water? A hug?'

The Scorpion kids slap each other and grin.

Adam doesn't answer. His mouth feels dry. A vague, lingering pain dances at the back of his skull. He stumbles to his feet and looks around.

Must've been a few seconds only. Nobody's moved. One of the quick ones.

Levi shakes his head. 'Look here, Stone. Let me paint this picture clear.' His tone hardens. 'I aim to take that cash money. I aim to take it and move on. It's business, understand?'

Adam stares at him, trying to regain composure. 'I . . . I worked for this money.'

Wyatt laughs, loud and hard. He spits into the sand. 'You kidding me? Call that work? Feeding a pig? That's nothin but kid's play. Now hand it over, 'fore things go bad.'

Adam hates the way everyone knows everyone's business in Blackwater. He stands his ground, shaking, saying nothing. Kane says nothing either. *Still* nothing.

Levi tilts his head, the slightest of gestures, and Wyatt loads a stone the size of a pig's ball.

Adam is filled with panic. It's taken six months of hard grind to build up the princely sum of money hidden in the sole of his boot and he can't bring himself to hand it over. He can feel nerves jumping in his legs. His thigh muscles contract. A blackout residue.

Wyatt holds the release cord between thumb and forefinger. The stone hangs down, neatly encased in its diamond-shaped cradle. He steadies himself and takes aim at the metal Bykemonger sign, creaking on its rusted iron chain. He swings the sling in a lazy arc above his head – once, twice – then whips it round once more, a quick, powerful swing, and . . .

CRACK!

A sonic boom. He releases at the top of the arc. The stone zings through the air.

KE-TAANGGGG!

It ricochets off the metal sign in a shower of raindrops, and disappears somewhere behind them.

Wyatt fetches another stone from his shirt pocket and it's pouched and drawn back in one fluid movement. Now he aims at Adam and silence falls on the group.

'I wouldn't do that, friend,' comes a cool, steady voice.

It's Kane.

His sling conjured from his belt. A river stone pouched and held back in his left hand, high above and behind his head. With his right, he holds the release cord and his arm points at Levi.

Adam wonders how Kane managed to pull it off without making a sound. Not even the ghost of a sound.

The gang looks equally stunned. Every last one of them. In particular, Wyatt. His sling falls slack and he looks at Kane, his face puce with anger.

Adam sees the gang go for their weapons, but Kane's voice brings them up short.

'Best leave 'em be, else your boy here loses an eye.' He says it without a smile, eyes on Levi. There is no emotion in his voice.

Wyatt gawps at him. A purple vein pulses on his temple.

Levi says nothing. He looks at Kane with dark eyes, narrow as slits.

Kane, without a trace of fear, returns his gaze.

Impasse.

Then another voice cuts the tension.

'Go on, get lost! Beat it!'

Adam whirls round and comes face to face with Sadie. She grips a sling in her right hand. Her eyes are hard and her stance is all business. Adam shifts his gaze from Sadie to Kane to Levi.

Levi doesn't take his eyes from Kane. He looks tight as a coiled spring. Then his shoulders relax and a slow smile spreads on his face. The easy charm of the smile makes liquid warmth run through Adam's body, fear combined with helplessness.

Levi flicks his eyes to Sadie. 'Taking sides, Sadie?'

Sadie doesn't flinch. 'Protecting my property, is all.'

'*Your* property?'

'That's right. *Mine.*'

'Bykemonger Station is Colonel property.'

'You know he gave it to me, Levi.'

Levi points at Adam and Kane. 'These boys your property too?'

The Scorpions laugh nervously.

Sadie stands there, looking at Levi. 'You've said what you came to say. Now clear out.'

'Watcha gonna do?' Wyatt says. His teeth are crooked and yellow in his sunburnt face. 'Take out your claws and scratch us up?'

She swivels on him, gripping her sling. 'Try me.'

'I figure she will, Wyatt,' a scrawny Scorpion kid pipes up. His skin looks raw and cracked, taut across his cheeks – another victim of airborne toxins. 'She's crazy as a panther,' he says.

Sadie looks fierce. Her eyes blaze.

Levi smiles and holds up his hands in mock submission. 'All right. All right. Wyatt ... put your sling away.' Wyatt shakes his head and, with cheeks reddened in mute rage, he returns the sling to his belt. He shifts his gaze to Kane, keeps his eyes on him. Nobody says a word.

Levi clamps on his riding goggles. 'I'll be seeing you boys,' he says in his dry, whispered voice. Then, with a last glance at Adam and Kane, he pulls his byke round and heads back the way he came. The Scorpions throw mean looks and do the same.

Adam, Kane and Sadie watch the Riders until they're out of sight.

Sadie turns to look at Adam. 'You'll need a weapon,' she says. 'Now more than ever.'

'I don't believe in 'em.'

Sadie snorts. 'Yeah. I forgot. You don't like violence.'

She shakes her head and returns to the gloomy dusk of the Bykemonger Station. Adam can see by the way she walks – tight, upright, and the way she clenches hers fists, the whiteness of her knuckles – that she isn't as cool as she wants them to believe. He wonders then if she saw him black out. She *must* have.

Must think I'm a coward.

Kane looks at Adam and grins. 'Don't *believe* in 'em?'

Adam shrugs to hide the hotness of his cheeks. 'Longthorn's all I ever needed.'

Kane smiles. He replaces his sling in his belt. 'That girl is something, right?'

There isn't a hint of concern in his voice.

'Don't you realize what you've done?' Adam says, turning on him.

'*Me*? I ain't done nothin.'

Adam shakes his head. 'Levi's no joke. They'll come. They'll come find us.'

Kane just smiles. His eyes are wild and bright. 'Let 'em come.'

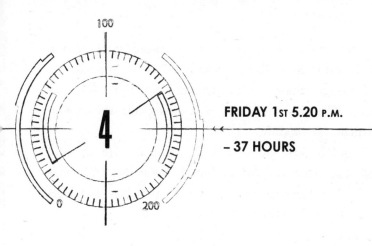

On the western shore of the lake, the water is dark and deep. An obsidian cliff surges up five hundred yards or more – a precipitous wall of rock exposed to the wind. On one side, a plateau escarpment stretches into the desert and on the other . . . a sickening drop to the lake. At the top, the view to the west is staggering. Nothing but desert haze into the distance.

It's the place Adam feels most vulnerable. But, when he needs to think, something inside him, some unnameable force, pulls him here to an abandoned railway track right up against the cliff edge. Parts of it have fallen away, down into the lake. Great chunks of metal and rock rise twisted from the surface, far below. Adjacent to the rail line is a gravel path that skirts the edge.

It's here he brings Kane.

They ride slow, inches from the drop, sending stones and rocks skittering over the lip. They come to a rocky ledge where a sheer canyon cuts into the lake and obstructs their ride. The other side of the canyon is a whole klick away at the widest point – where it meets the lake – and it narrows into a jagged channel inland, a giant crack, ripping into the desert. The only way forward is down, into the canyon, through a steep gully.

Adam brakes and swings off his byke. He feels the pull of a lonely wind behind him, buffeting him, billowing his jacket. He narrows his eyes to the dust and faces away from the desert, towards the lake and the town beyond.

Blackwater looks perfect from above. Peaceful even. A silent crescent of buildings. Like a secret sign for the gods, stamped out in the desert sand. There is grandness in the neat perfection of the shape, a measure of what Blackwater might have been. But the effect of the concentric rings and straight roads is also disconcerting. A paradox of order and technology in a world governed by whim and terror.

'Welcome to hell,' Adam says, under his breath.

On the far side of the lake, a grey, windowless tower rises up from the earth. At the top of the tower is a platform over five hundred yards into the sky. More or less the same height as the escarpment. Adam sees tiny figures, like termites, moving on the platform, hustling between industrial structures. And far below, at ground level, a constant stream of miners flowing in and out of a brightly lit entrance. Hundreds of them, changing shifts. A human tide.

Adam feels a sudden and powerful sense of estrangement. Of not belonging.

'One of them drills in every town I been in,' Kane says. 'Pulling up all that Voddenite like it'll last forever. Death traps all of 'em. Suck a person's soul right out.'

Adam doesn't speak. He remembers the dim, predawn light. The front door creaking open, closing with a soft click. His pa's footsteps, scraping the dirt outside. Fading away. Every day. An early rise to catch the drone and march into the mine.

A turbine throb carries to them. Adam feels it in his legs first, shuddering up through the byke into his spine. Then an airship descends from the haze. Cylindrical and grey, powered by four turbines, two each side. It makes a series of neat adjustments to bring it horizontal with the platform. Then it sinks behind the structures that crown the platform, and is lost from sight.

The throbbing sound cuts out and the jarring in Adam's spine fades to a murmur.

'Voddenite carrier drone,' Kane says.

Adam steps to the cliff edge, feeling reckless, and staggers back. The height makes him dizzy. He watches sunlight shimmer on the lake surface. Then he stares at the drill and pictures his pa traipsing into the towering edifice. Each day, every day. Until his last day.

An *accident*, they called it. Adam hates the word. *Accident*. It doesn't begin to cover the turmoil, the fractures left behind. Just an accident – that's all – a *mistake*.

Sorry, your pa was alive. Now he's dead.

They say he came up here for the view one evening. And he slipped. That's all. Lost his footing. *It happens*.

But Adam doesn't believe the official story.

He jumped is what he did. He filled his pockets with stones and he jumped.

Kane hauls out his sling, loads a stone from his hip pouch and shoots it – with an astounding bullwhip *CRACK*! – into the air. They watch it arc through the sky and fall . . .

Down, down, down.

Not even a muted splash.

Kane contemplates the drop. 'These blackouts you get. Might be a problem when you ride.'

Adam picks up a stone, lobs it into the air. Watches it disappear. He turns to face Kane, aware of the cliff edge a pace to his right, a yawning chasm, tugging at him. 'It's nothin. Things go dark. It just happens. I wake up after and don't remember. Doc says I need meds, same as my brother Frank.'

Kane nods. 'All kinds of sickness going around. Sky-Base got meds for that. Cure it all.'

They stand and watch the wind whip the surface of the lake. Adam feels uneasy. He's not accustomed to speaking his mind. He's the quiet one. The one in the shadows. The one no one sees.

'Reckon Sadie's OK?' Kane says.

Adam flashes him a look. He doesn't want to talk about her. Not with *him*.

Kane smiles. His amber eyes burn. 'You gonna go back and give her the cash?'

Adam shakes his head.

'I've got something to show you,' Kane says, wheeling his byke round. 'Some place I went yesterday. You'll like it.'

'I don't know. It's getting late . . . and the bykes –'

'Don't be scared your entire life. C'mon!'

They descend the gully path into the canyon. It zigzags along a steep ravine wall, down to the dry river, and they slide and skid on a slope of scree. Kane leads. Adam tails him, sweating with the effort.

He thinks about Sadie to steady his nerves. He feels deflated. Heartbroken. He saw the look she gave Kane. He feels split in two when it comes to Kane. Part in thrall to him. Part hating him.

Adam's back wheel slides and he turns his attention to the task.

It takes them twenty minutes of hard, technical riding to get to the bottom. They stand off their seats all the way down, fingers pressed to their brakes.

Now they follow the stony river, leaving broad tyre tracks winding like ribbed snakes on soft sand. They ride through a terracotta canyon. Above them the sky is wild vermilion. Everything comes afire with the setting sun. There's no sound of water from the riverbed.

Gotta move. Sun's gonna set. The cold will come soon.

Adam motors hard. The byke throbs under him. He overtakes Kane and rides out front. Kane catches him quick – lightning-quick – and he's past him in a flash.

Adam watches the lithe form ahead. Kane rides effortlessly, smoothly. Up and down over rises – a stone skipping water. Adam guns hard after him, swerving and skidding and leaping ditches. But Kane is too quick. He fades to a shadow ghost in the rising dust. Then disappears.

'WAIT UP!' Adam yells.

Exhausted, he pulls up. His lungs are on fire. He's covered in grime and sweat.

'KANE!'

The canyon walls throw back his voice. KANE ... Kane ... Kane.

Adam drives the Longthorn forward and works up a fresh sweat. He rounds a bend and Kane is there, three hundred yards ahead, standing astride his byke.

'IT ALL BEGINS HERE!' Kane calls. And then something else, but his voice is snatched by the wind and Adam hears nothing more.

Painted white stones are placed equidistant from one another, about ten yards apart, in long parallel lines that follow the contours of the canyon. Either side of the stones are flags. Bits of red and white ribbon stuck on tall poles. They snap and gust in the wind.

Adam feels excitement and fear build in him. He knows this place.

Blackwater Trail starting line.

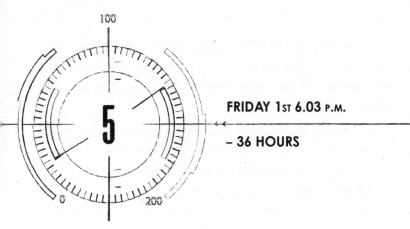

FRIDAY 1st 6.03 p.m.

– 36 HOURS

It's cold on the starting line. They gather a pile of driftwood and build a pyramid. Adam brings out his sparker and sets the pile ablaze. They watch a nest of spiders scatter.

Kane unfolds out two silver sheets from his supply pack. He hands one to Adam. It's light, almost insubstantial, but large enough to drape over Adam's entire body. More than just a cloak or a blanket – an enclosed, thermal shelter.

'Heatkeeper,' Kane says. 'Waterproof. Can survive extreme temperatures.'

'You always carry two?'

'Sky-Base supplied 'em. Last two Races.'

Adam wraps himself up and immediately feels the difference.

They huddle close to the fire, crouching, watching sparks skitter. Each boy wrapped in the silver cocoon of his heatkeeper.

Stars blink above them. It's always this way. The storms come, the haze cloud lifts and, for a brief respite, the sky is clear and the night drilled with stars. It doesn't last. Not more than a day or two. Then the haze returns, often thicker, and Adam soon forgets about the blueness of the sky.

He stares at the gathering darkness beyond the fire. Listens to the bykes ticking as their Voddenite frames contract in the cold and he feels a sick thrill.

'What's out there?' he whispers.

Kane, on his haunches, pokes the fire with a stick. 'Dust mostly.'

Adam watches him. 'S'pose that desert track won't be easy.'

Kane narrows his eyes against the heat of the fire. 'Desert aims to spit you out. Dead or alive. It doesn't care. You don't just ride against other Riders. You ride against the sand. Against the heat of day and the cold of night.'

A log collapses. Sparks swirl.

Adam looks at him. 'How many Races you seen in all?'

'Enough,' Kane says.

'Then why race the Blackwater? It's the toughest. Isn't it smarter to keep building up your base points on some easier Circuit Races? Get to Sky-Base that way?'

Kane shakes his head. 'I'm done with that. I'll take my chances on the biggest. The ultimate challenge. I'll ride the Blackwater. Then I'll ride no more.'

Adam shakes his head and looks up at the night. He searches the sky for a cluster of lights. And sees them. Three blazing stars, bigger than the rest. But they're not stars. Not plancts cither.

Space stations. Three great ships that make up the Ark of Sky-Base.

Balthazar, Gaspar and Melchior.

'What do you think it's like?'

'Sky-Base? Aim to find out.'

Adam fans the sand with his boot. 'I heard stories. They say it's a place where food isn't pills and biscuits. Where people aren't dying. They say they got endless supplies of fresh water.'

Kane shrugs. 'Maybe. Maybe not. People say things aplenty.'

'You don't believe it?'

'I will when I see it.'

'They say people live to a hundred and fifty up there. Lose a leg and they grow you a new one. Got no disease. No sickness. Nothin. Like you say, they got the meds.'

'That's what I heard.'

Adam wraps himself up tight. 'I believe the stories. Things are different up there.'

Kane says nothing, stirs the glowing embers with his stick. His face floats in the light of the flames and his yellow eyes are ablaze, amber stones woven through with threads of fire.

A full moon comes up, the colour of fish scales. It's eerily quiet and the night is cold.

'I like the quiet,' Adam says. 'Hardly any sound out here.' He pauses and looks up. 'It's something though, right?'

'The quiet?'

'The moon.'

Adam considers the pearl disc. Earth's companion. Aloof and impossible to fathom.

'No matter what we do down here, she just sits up there all peaceful, floating in the middle of all that darkness, watching us.'

Kane faces the fire. He reaches a hand to his shoulder, massages the muscle, arches his back and rolls his neck to click the bones.

'Some nights you feel the moon can save you,' Adam says with his head flung back. 'You know. Protect you. The sun . . . that's another story. But the moon is different.'

'You're wrong,' Kane says, flicking a red-hot coal with his stick. 'It ain't.'

He stands and he hurls the stick into the flames, watching it burn. Adam looks up at him and a cold wind gutters the fire.

Kane stares at the flames. 'It's just a hunk of rock, messed up with scars and craters. Don't be fooled. The moon is dead. Stone dead. Dead as Blackwater Lake.'

For a second, Adam sees Frank's face, swirling in the woodsmoke, and he feels a sudden pang in his stomach. The familiar ache of guilt. Then it's gone.

'My brother raced the Blackwater,' he says.

'That a fact?'

'Took an arrow on El Diablo. Never raced again.'

Kane looks at him. 'Racing's the only way for people like us. We're lords of dust and gods of dirt. There's nobody and nothin gonna save us but ourselves.'

Adam feels a chill rise up his neck. He looks up at the night sky, at the scudding clouds and the silver moon. Then he remembers where he is and the kid he's with. An Outsider.

Said he was from other side the desert. Hell does that mean?

All thoughts of the moon turn to dust.

He stands and kicks earth on the fire. 'We gotta go. Bykes won't have much charge left.'

He looks at Kane. He's dangerous. There's no mistaking it.

It's like Frank says. Trust no one. You're on your own.

But Adam understands people, even better than Frank maybe. He's spent his life watching, deciding who to trust, who to fear, who to run from. Kane might be dangerous and complicated and he might also be the one Sadie wants, but Kane has another side to him. Adam can sense it.

Besides, it never hurts to keep your enemies close. Frank says that too.

'Don't reckon you got a place to stay,' Adam says.

'Don't reckon,' Kane says.

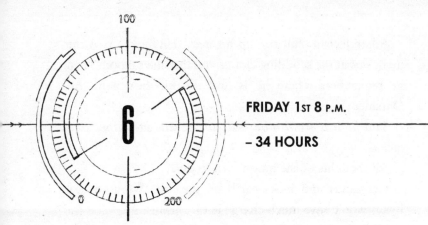

Steep cliffs rise behind the farmhouse, maroon against the dark sky. The cabin squats in their shadow – a simple, three-room, cedar-wood structure. More a shack than a cabin. Wreaths of smoke rise from a leaning stone chimney.

The place has a sour smell. It comes from the chicken coops out back.

Frank Stone emerges from the cabin as they roll to a stop in front of the well.

'Hey, Frank,' Adam says, dismounting. His breath clouds in the chill air.

Frank is bone-lean. He's nineteen but looks older. Tough as leather. Tall and stooped at the shoulders. His clothes – a denim work jacket and jeans – are ragged and they hang on him. His cheeks are gaunt. His skin is dry, burnt teak by the sun. His eyes bloodshot and lined with crow's feet. He walks with the aid of two crutches, favouring his good leg, the right one.

Frank lifts his chin at Kane. 'Who's this?'

Adam glances at Kane, who sits astride his bike, one boot anchored to the ground, the other resting on a gear pedal. 'His name's Kane.'

Frank snorts. 'He doesn't speak for himself?'

Kane doesn't move. He remains silent.

'Where's he from?' Frank says.

'Other side the desert.'

Frank narrows his eyes. 'There's nothin other side the desert.'

'Can he stay?'

'Got enough mouths to feed.'

'It's just us, Frank.'

'That's a fact,' Frank says, looking at Kane.

Kane leans his byke against the well. 'Good to meet you,' he says with a small nod.

'He can bunk down in the shelter, can't he?' Adam says.

Frank massages his chin and turns his gaze on Adam. 'You're late. Where've you been?'

'Rode the canyon some.'

Frank shakes his head.

Adam leans his byke – his *kin's* byke – against the well, next to Kane's.

'He's got nowhere, Frank.'

Frank mutters under his breath and sighs. 'Maev brought us potatoes. Got chicken soup and fresh bread.' He turns and hobbles into the shack, making a clanking sound on the wooden porch.

'Chicken soup,' Kane says. 'Been a while.'

'I'll get the shelter set,' Adam says.

The cabin has a sweet smell of woodsmoke and baked bread. Maev, a neighbour with kind and otherwise intentions, has delivered a bounty of food in exchange for eggs, and to win his brother's affection, no doubt. Bartering for Frank's love. Not an easy task.

Adam's mouth waters as he circles the kitchen table, ladling steaming soup into clay bowls. Strings of chicken meat cling to the ladle. The room is small and Adam has to shuffle sideways in the gap between chairs and wall. He serves Kane and sits opposite him.

Kane unfolds his hands on the table, breathes in the aroma of the soup and glances up at Adam. Adam nods and Kane lifts his spoon and makes a loud slurping noise as he tucks in.

Frank leans back on his stool and watches them wolfing down their food. Then he sets about his own bowl.

Frank wipes his mouth with the back of his hand. His fingers are flat and crooked, the fingernails chipped. His joints are bruised and swollen-looking. These are hands that have seen harsh weather. Working hands.

He fixes his eyes on Kane. 'Got skills?'

Kane shrugs and spoons up his soup.

Adam bites into a hunk of bread. 'He can skip stones better'n anyone I ever seen.'

'Not exactly a skill a Rider needs.'

'He can dive too. Dived right down to the bottom of . . .' He stops speaking, mid-sentence.

Frank looks at him, his spoon poised mid-air. 'You dive with him?'

Adam says nothing. He pretends to focus on the food.

'You got no business diving to the bottom of that lake.' Frank glares at Adam. 'Dammit, Adam! What are you doin swimming when you ought to be working?'

Silence falls on the room. The only sound is the slurping of soup and the slow boil and spit of the pot. Frank pushes away his empty bowl, takes a ragged breath and digs his thumbs into his belt.

Kane keeps spooning up his soup, eyes down.

Adam runs his hands along the table edge and notices how the wood is worn and chipped. He looks at the empty bowl in front of him. The clay is scratched and rough. His eyes travel to the window and the ripped and stained curtains pulled shut against the darkness.

'Well,' Frank says. 'S'pose you boys ain't thinking about work anyhow.'

Adam stares at the window and says nothing.

When the meal is done, Adam leads Kane to the shelter. They unbolt the trapdoor and descend the stairs with a lit candle. Adam first, Kane following. The air smells musty and it carries the sharp, unsettling tang of chicken shit from the coop. A smell that lingers on every part of the property. But down here it smells different, tinged with the odour of earth.

The shelter is little more than an underground hovel. There are no bales of hay, or any kind of farming gear. Dust-covered seed bags slump against a bare wall next to a twisted roll of wire. In a dark corner, an empty O2 canister complete with a set of hanging masks. They cast weird shadows high on the wall. Shelves, running along the wall, are littered with tinned food, boxes of supplies. The floor is cement, polished with wear. It's a brutal, functional place. But it's warm and when the winter descends and grips the land they come down here to ride it out.

'Frank's not as mean as he thinks,' Adam says, placing the candle on a barrel. It makes a hollow knocking sound as he sets it down. The orange flame flowers a pool of yellow light and the corners of the shelter disappear into gloom. A draught comes from under the door and the flame gutters. A night wind rattles the bolt.

'He's a good man,' Kane says, throwing his sleeping roll on the floor. He sits to remove his boots. With a grunt and a sudden jerk, he manages to free his right foot. He rests his elbows on his knees – one foot booted, the other in a blackened sock.

'You can see it in the eyes. Eyes don't lie. Not ever.'

Then he pulls off his other boot and flings it across the floor. Adam watches it skid to a stop.

'Helluva thing,' Kane says. 'To lose a limb.'

Adam perches on the barrel, trying to fathom the stories Kane's wolflike eyes hide.

Kane strips off his suit and Adam gets another view of his welts and scars. The air duct throws a rhombus of moonlight on Kane's back. Adam has never seen a body so bruised and battered. Not even his brother's.

It's like some creature got its teeth into him.

The trapdoor creaks and they both look up the stairs, but no one comes. The door moans, bracing against the wind.

Kane hangs his sling and his leather bag of river stones from a hook hammered into a support beam.

Adam looks up at the wooden beams holding up the roof of the shelter. There used to be owls up there. They must have found their way in through the air duct somehow and they shared the shelter with the Stone kin during the storm nights. He spent days staring at them and they stared back at him with their quiet eyes. He still finds their pellets sometimes, but the owls are long gone. There used to be mice too, but not any more.

Kane eases himself down on to his makeshift bed, then props himself up on his elbows. He looks at Adam and his eyes gleam. 'When you last see the Colonel?'

'Couple of moons back, maybe. Why?'

Kane shrugs. 'Maybe I'd like to see him before the Race.'

'That's unlikely.'

'Why? Because of who he is? A Warlord?'

'He's protected. Sky-Base pays him to put down mine strikes and any rebellions. Like them past ones about solar-rocket tickets being too expensive.'

'Rebellions don't happen that often any more. So he's not really a Warlord. He's a tyrant.'

'Yeah. Reckon so.'

'Scorpions his thugs?'

Adam nods. 'Most of my cash would have landed up in his pocket some way or another.'

Kane looks hard at him, as if mulling something over.

Adam slides off the barrel. 'Less you see the Colonel the better. But he'll be there come Race day. You can bet on that.' He makes for the trapdoor stairs.

'Adam!'

He half turns. It's the first time Kane's used his name. The sound of it startles him.

'You gotta ride to earn a ticket to Sky-Base,' Kane says. 'No way out but up.'

Adam looks at him and – for no reason he can fathom – he feels fear slide up through his gut. He climbs the stairs and fumbles with the bolt on the door. 'Lock it from the inside,' he mumbles. Then he steps up into the night and shuts Kane inside.

'He's dangerous,' Frank says. 'I told you. Stay alone. Stay safe.'

He stands hunkered in the doorway to his room, a dark silhouette against the amber light within. There's only one bedroom in the cabin and that's always been Frank's. Adam bunks down on the couch. His ma's desert-flower print faded to a uniform grey, the fabric worn and threadbare.

Adam says nothing. He punches his pillow.

'You shouldn't have brought him here,' Frank adds. 'Nothin good will come of it.'

Adam looks up. Stares at Frank's metal leg, jutting from his jeans. 'He's just some kid.'

Frank shakes his head and coughs. 'He's not. He's different.'

He releases a crutch and supports himself with one hand on the wall. He coughs until his face is blue and his eyes bloodshot.

'You OK?' Adam says, rising.

Frank wheezes. He shakes his head and waves Adam away. 'You're different too.'

'How's that?'

'The way you help people. You've got a generous heart, Adam. It's liable to get someone killed some day.'

Adam says nothing.

Frank leans on the wall and looks at him. 'He really swim to the lake bottom?'

Adam sees verdigris weeds drifting through dark water. The flat calm. No bubbles rising to the surface. He sees Kane shoot up in a sudden spray, his eyes wild and yellow, the silver sand running down the length of his outflung arm.

'I don't know. I guess he did . . . after I showed him how.'

Frank shakes his head. He shuffles to the cabin front door, the metal of his left leg and the two crutches making an uneven knocking on the wood floor. He checks the lock, rattles the door handle, lifts the grey curtain and looks out at the night. He stands for a while, saying nothing, staring out towards the old oak tree. He looks troubled.

'Another rooster died today,' he rasps. 'Fourth one this month.'

Roosters dying is bad news. When you breed chickens, you keep your roosters alive. You feed them well. You protect them. If all your roosters die, *you* die soon after.

'Add that to the others stolen for the fights and . . . well, do the math.'

'So I'll work the mine. Get more dollars than working for Old Man Dagg. Buy us more wire for the coop. Maybe get us some meds for . . .' Adam's voice trails away. He knows money won't buy what Frank really needs. A flesh-and-blood leg.

'You're just like Pa,' Frank says. 'Know that?'

Adam watches his brother, the line of his back, the narrow shoulders. 'I'm nothin like him.'

Frank shakes his head. He turns and looks at Adam. 'Wish you'd be generous with Pa too. I know you think he jumped, but he couldn't have. He was the best Rider alive back then. But he chose the mine over racing. To be with *us*.'

'So what happened? If he loved us so much?'

'You know what happened. Ma died . . . and he just . . . Well, he got lost, is all. And –'

'I'm nothin like him,' Adam repeats.

Frank sighs and watches him. 'People break, Adam. It happens.'

Adam looks away. He notices a fluttering shadow dance against the cabin wall. A moth. It circles the candle in erratic loops. Then it turns too close to the flame and, with burnt wings, flounders in a pool of hot wax. Adam flicks the singed moth and watches it stick to the floorboards.

A wind tunnels under the door. Adam gazes at the gusting candle flame, lost in thought.

No. He's nothing like his pa. It occurs to him maybe he and *Kane* are the same. Maybe they both belong on their bykes, drifting through desert tracks, not stuck underground. Maybe Kane only makes sense when he speaks with his byke, and his sling, and his stones.

'You see that boy use his slingshot?' Frank wheezes, as though reading his thoughts. 'I'll bet he uses it pretty good.'

Adam says nothing.

Frank lets the curtain fall. He moves towards Adam and reaches out his hand. He winces. Grips the crutch again. 'Damn leg.'

'It'll be OK, Frank,' Adam says. But he can feel the space fill with his lie.

Frank shuffles across the floor to his room. He stops at the door and turns. 'If I could go back, I would. I'd get my name off that Race ticket. I shouldn't have gone. Shouldn't have left you.'

'It was fine at Maev's. Besides, you had no choice. Race and live how you wanna live or work the mine. That's Blackwater Law.'

Frank shakes his head. 'I could've won. I *should've*. Lost my concentration, is all. Stupid mistake.' He points his crutch at him. 'But *you* won't make mistakes.'

Adam looks at his brother and his stomach churns.

'Listen to me, Adam. You're important. Don't ask me how I know that. I just do. I *feel* it. You matter. You'll make a difference. But I've been holding you back. We put in those hours training for a reason. Not for you to stay here and let 'em go to waste.'

'Frank, I –'

'You won't be alone. I'll be with you. In the byke's echo. You'll never be alone.'

'But –'

'What happened to me won't happen to you. You can ride, like Pa. We both know that. Chickens won't last and then the mine's for you.' He shakes his head. 'But that's not your path.'

Adam regards the outline of his brother. His features are hidden in the dim light, but Adam knows he's looking at him, waiting for him to say something. Anything. But it's Frank who speaks again.

'I love you,' he says. Then he turns and enters his room, leaving the door ajar.

Adam looks at his brother's door. Listens to his uneven step beyond. Hears the rasp in his breath. Sees the light blown out.

And that's when he knows he can't do it. He can't leave Frank behind.

He licks his fingers, snuffs out the guttering candle and plunges the cabin into darkness.

He knows he'll never be on that starting line again.

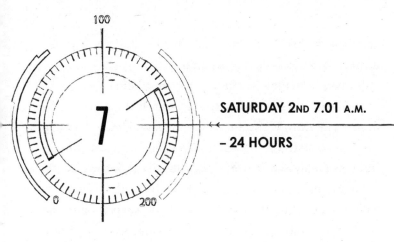

He glides through a desert, infinite in all directions. The
sun rides high with him, a blazing white disc. Heat waves
float from the ground. Then a cry goes up. He turns. Wild
animals flank him, either side. To the left, a lupine shadow.
To the right, a sinuous panther. The animals lope beside
him, quick over the ground.

Adam! Adam, wake up . . . ADAM!

There's panic in the sound of the voice in his head. It
conjures a figure and, for a brief moment, Sadie sits in the
room beside him. He can smell her dusty skin. He can feel
the warmth of her next to him.

A hand to his shoulder. Shaking him.

GET UP, ADAM! GET UP!

A crash and the shatter of glass. A rapid-fire succession of
hard objects hitting the walls. *RAT-TAT-TAT. RAT-TAT-
TAT.* A scream outside. Wild-throated and high-pitched.
Adam sits bolt upright, covered in a cold sweat. His heart

hammers in his chest. He's half awake, half sunk in his dreams. A bitter taste fills his mouth.

It takes him a few seconds to realize where he is.

His head jerks from side to side, eyes flicking across the room. The drawn curtains allow a bar of mote-swirling sunlight to spill into the cabin. He vaguely recalls animals from his dream. Then everything comes crashing in on him.

Something small and dark explodes through the window with a loud crash. It zings overhead and smashes into the clay plate stand against the wall. Adam ducks his head, throws up his hands to shield his face. The stand comes crashing down in a cloud of splinters and glass. He coughs in the choking dust.

A whoop and a holler, outside in the half-dark.

Another window smashes and another missile, dark and fast, zips through the air. Adam cringes and hears the whine of it above his head. It clatters into the wall, rebounds off and bounces down on the couch, resting at his naked feet. Adam kicks it away. A stone – round, smooth and hot from flight.

Slingstones!

He's wide awake. Wide-eyed and fumbling for his jeans and his shirt, draped over the back of the couch. He rolls off the sofa bed with his clothes bunched in his fist.

Not fast enough.

A flash of pain flares on his shoulder. A deafening smack and a white-hot blow to the side of his head. Adam is slammed sideways. He hits the floor hard, sprawling. His hand flies to his temple and comes back sticky with blood.

It's just a graze, though. It has to be. A direct slingshot to the head is a kill. Every time.

He leans against the seat back, breathing hard. His head throbs. His right shoulder throbs. He feels dizzy, disorientated. He turns his chin to his shoulder and sees a raised welt and the rapid bloom of a purple bruise.

More missiles come zinging into the room. He pulls on his jeans in a cold sweat.

Voices screaming. Growing louder and louder. Then another fusillade of stones comes flying through the shattered windows. The room is full to bursting with incessant din. Timber splintering. Glass crashing. And, all the while, laughs and curses and cries from outside.

Adam hunkers down, back pressed to the fabric, knees tucked to his chin, trying to think.

Where are you, Frank?

And Kane? Where's he? Still in the shelter?

A horrible tearing sound and dust and plaster rain on him. Adam throws up his arms to shield himself. Part of the ceiling collapses.

'FRANK!' His voice is hoarse with panic.

There's no answer from the room next door. Another crash and the shatter of glass. Another hail of stones flies through the air. They rattle into the couch, like bullets. Blood drips into Adam's eye.

'WHAT'S GOING ON?'

Nothing. No response. He blinks and wipes away the blood with the back of his hand.

'FRANK! WHERE ARE YOU?'

A vase implodes. The stone slices through the middle of it as though it were made of paper. A picture explodes into hundreds of glass shards and the wooden frame clatters from the wall, rolling drunkenly on the floor.

The violent cacophony goes on and on. Adam clamps his hands to his ears and tries to drown out the sound. But it keeps building. On and on.

Stones fly. Shrapnel fragments pelt the walls. The half-light of a rising sun makes everything a play of red shadows. Then one last smash and all he hears are the whoops and screams outside.

Now he hears the front door swing open.

The onslaught of stones must have torn the bolt clear off. Adam feels the presence of someone in the room with him. He can hear breathing. Outside the shouts die down and there's silence. Adam's heart is in his throat. He's outraged by his own cowardice. He wants to stand to confront the intruder, but fear pins him to the floor.

He thinks he's hidden but he isn't sure.

Footsteps crunch through the debris. Breathing and footsteps. The slow creak of floorboards.

Adam wants to scream, but he makes no sound. Instead he listens to the crunch of the footsteps as they make their way through the room. They stop. At what he thinks is Frank's door. Silence. Adam sweats and holds his breath. Time drags.

The intruder's footsteps scrape and then fade to the front door, and exit.

Adam waits. His cheeks burn hot with the embarrassment of his fear. When he hears the cries take up again outside, he moves. He crawls over the debris and his knees are sliced as he goes. He winces with the sharp pain. The sound of the scraping is loud. He trails crimson blood.

When he reaches the window, what used to be the window, he raises his head, real slow. Shreds of curtain flutter in the breeze. Shards of glass cling to the metal frame. It's been blown to pieces. Torn apart.

Dark figures move in the red dust outside. Silhouettes against the low sun. The light catches their goggles and throws flares at him. Riders. Their mouths are covered by masks, but he can hear them laughing under them. They sit on their bykes and set themselves to riding in a crazed circle, flinging up spumes of dust and crying out, whooping and hollering.

One of them, on a white Stinger, sits astride his byke, not moving at all. He looks at Adam. Right at him. Then he calls something out, something sharp, and the Riders circle him.

The lead Rider, alien in his gold goggles, salutes Adam with a raised right hand and then they turn and they ride out, one after the other.

The last Rider, a skinny kid, carries a flagpole in his hand. The flag whips back and forth as he rides. Adam sees the black marking on the cloth, clear as day in the red haze.

Scorpions.

Adam hobbles back to the couch, staunching the bloodflow from his head with his bundled shirt. He picks his way through jagged rubble and his feet are cut and bleeding by the time he reaches his boots. He lifts them from under a pile of smashed bits of wood and glass and he pulls them on, slides into them, blood and all. His head throbs and his heart hammers.

He doesn't speak. He hardly breathes. He doesn't call his brother's name. Instead he surveys the wreckage. A table, scarred and broken. Ornaments, smashed to pieces. A carpet, ripped and torn. Every surface strewn with debris. And stones. Stones everywhere. Hundreds of them. Too many to count.

Bastards. Bloody bastards!

Only then does he move to his brother's room. His hands shake. His guts twist into painful knots. At the door, he sees what he knew he'd see. What the intruder must have seen.

A thin stream of blood runs in the gutter of the wooden floorboards. It comes from a wound in the side of his brother's cracked skull. The body lies inert on the floor, unmoving.

'Frank,' Adam says. It's more a puff of sound than a word.

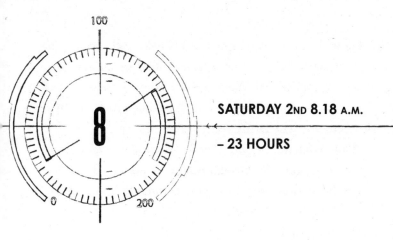

Adam feels his legs carry him to the porch. He stares at the sun, hands limp at his sides. He takes a spade from where it leans and he walks out to the one tree left standing, the wild oak.

He looks at the two headstones already there, blinks at them. A single white feather floats across his vision. It lands on Pa's headstone, catches a gust and whirls up into the oak's bare branches.

Something grabs his attention.

Throughout the attack a sound was missing. A sound that marks every dawn, regular as clockwork. Roosters crowing. He doesn't bother going round back to check the coop. He knows in his gut what they've done to the chickens. The dead quiet tells him.

The silence builds to a roar of accusation in his ears.

Adam glances across at the mound of the shelter. The door is shut. Stillness hangs about the place as if no one's been near it for months.

He looks at the well and sees his byke still propped up against the wall. The Tribes have a kind of honour with bykes. A convention. Never touch someone else's byke. Not ever. His Longthorn is still there, but there's no byke alongside her. The Drifter is missing.

Why? What happened? Where'd Kane go? And when?

Questions tumble through Adam's head.

But he knows only this with certainty: Kane up and left . . . and Frank is dead.

Dead. Dead. Dead.

The word repeats itself inside his skull, each hitting like a hammer blow.

He digs with quiet fury. Slamming the spade into stones and dirt. Digs a ditch big enough to sink a man in. Digs without thinking, shutting his mind off, chopping through roots and hauling out rocks. It takes him hours, even though the ground under the oak is porous. He goes down so deep he has to throw the spade up and haul himself out with his hands.

Breathing hard, he stands with his thumbs dug into his back pockets and looks into the hole. Sweat pours from his forehead and drops into the dust. He rolls on the balls of his feet, back and forth. His cut feet burn inside his boots. A weight presses on his chest and his throat is tight.

He turns and makes his way back to the ruin of the shack. His boots drag through the rubble with a muted noise. Adam feels a million klicks away. Somewhere else. Somewhere above, looking down. This isn't him. This isn't his life.

Adam lifts his brother under the arms and struggles backwards with him, inch by inch. It startles him how heavy the body feels. Even a body as thin as this.

'Dammit, Frank.'

But Frank isn't Frank any more. His body is waxy. It looks nothing like him.

Adam takes up the arms again. He leans back and heaves the body along the wooden floor. The feet – one flat metal, the other flesh and bone – roll outwards, making two parallel drag marks through the rubble. The arms spreadeagle. The head slumps to a shoulder and nods against a jutting collarbone. The worn jeans hike up and the prosthetic leg is exposed, grotesque and alien.

Adam pauses at the front door to rest. His eyes scan the room in a mist. He picks up a slingstone smeared with blood. He rolls it in his hand and drops it in his pocket. Then he stoops to take up the body again.

He pulls it through the doorway. Bumps it down the steps. Averts his eyes at the sound. Across the yard he jerks the body. Through the weeds and through the dust. It takes forever to reach the ditch.

He looks down at the body that used to be his brother.

Frank's immutable laws of survival run through his head. His seven mantras:

1. Keep your head down. Stay low. Say nothin. That's how you survive.
2. If you fall, roll when you hit the dirt. And you get right back on your byke.

3. Keep looking for a way out. And, when it comes, ride like hell.
4. If you have to fight, fight dirty. No kind of clean fighting left.
5. You gotta keep trying. Never give up. Not ever.
6. You gotta be hard to survive. A Stone Rider. Hard as the desert.
7. Trust no one. You're on your own. Stay alone. Stay safe.

'What happened?' Adam says aloud. 'Why didn't you listen to your own rules? Why didn't you keep your head down, like you told me?'

There's no answer.

Adam returns to the house. He comes out with a ripped sheet and he tips the body over and rolls it into the sheet until it's wrapped tight, head to foot. He doesn't look at the face before he covers it. He can't.

It's just a body. It's not Frank.

He gives it a hard shove with his boot and it falls into the grave. It makes a dull *thump* against the earth. The vibration shudders up through Adam's boots, runs through his limbs and his stomach, straight to his heart. A sob escapes his throat. He leans forward, hands on his knees, gasping, feeling sick. He stays this way a long time, concentrating on his breathing. One shuddering breath at a time.

Breathe ... Breathe ... Breathe ...

He recovers enough to collect the spade and he starts filling the hole. Slow. Methodical. Mechanical. He doesn't pause. He doesn't rest. He digs in the spade, kicks it down with his boot, scrapes on the soil, lifts and then scatters it. One load after the other. He doesn't make any sound, apart from the occasional grunt as he works.

Something hard and cold turns inside him as he pats down the soil with the curved back of the spade. A bitter taste fills his mouth.

He throws the spade aside. Presses his fist into the small of his back and arches. His body aches all over. Every sinew and muscle. His hands drop to his sides. He rocks back and forth.

'I'm sorry, Frank. I should've given Levi the money. I wasn't thinking.'

No answer. Adam reels under the weight of the silence.

He brought the Scorpions here. It was *his* fault. All because of his bloody-minded fix on racing. But what good is guilt? Frank is dead.

A sound vibrates the air. The low growl of bykes. Adam looks up.

Two of them, approaching from the direction of Blackwater. And he can tell in his bones, with absolute certainty, that there is nothing human about them.

Adam watches them bear down and doesn't move. They *look* human – or humanoid at least – two arms, two legs, a body, a head. But they're not. They are metal and bolt and rivet. There is no flesh on them. No blood and no bone. No soul. Their metal suits are pitch-black and polished. Strapped to their thighs, are bulky fusion shooters. They ride modified Cobras, dark and sleek, fast as thought. Built and supplied by Sky-Base, controlled and deployed by Warlords like the Colonel, these are Ground Roving Utility Bots. GRUBs.

They come to a grumbling stop in front of him and sit while the dust settles.

'Blackwater citizen,' the GRUB on the right says, dismounting. 'State your name.'

A Talker. Third generation.

Its speech is clipped and to the point. The voice sounds metallic. Hollow. Its head has been moulded to resemble a human skull, encased in a helmet, with mandible-like jaws and an oval speaker disc for a mouth. Its black visor is opaque. Adam sees himself reflected.

He looks small and misshapen.

The dismounted GRUB carries a computer tablet in its hand and stands upright, like a gunfighter, legs apart. The second GRUB – silent and deadpan – remains seated.

Second generation.

Adam knows they were designed by Sky-Base to keep the core mines running. Engineered with singular purpose. To curb rebellion. To defeat the will of the Left-Behind. And – when required, with efficiency – to apply uncompromising force.

Their state-of-the-art, muscular design is an obvious display of might. Adam knows that. He also knows not to mistake bulk for lack of speed.

He stares at the GRUB's holstered fusion shooter and feels his palms begin to sweat. He's never seen them blast, but he's heard stories. Riders vaporized into red mist.

The GRUB speaks again. 'State your name.'

'Adam Stone.'

The GRUB consults its tablet. 'Our data indicates the death of Frank Stone. Verify.'

Adam feels a surge of animosity. 'You know it's correct – why ask me to verify?'

'Comply, citizen. Confirm the data.'

'Why don't you check for yourself?' He nods at the freshly dug dirt.

The GRUB looks at the mound. It returns to its byke, lifts an object from a concealed compartment panel. A scanner gun. Then it walks to the grave, its articulated parts making soft motor noises and clicking sounds. The GRUB passes the gun over the raw earth and takes a reading. Adam hears the fizz of static. Then it stops.

The GRUB replaces the tool in the byke and turns to Adam again. It pauses, almost human. Then comes the mechanical voice, dull and even-pitched.

'This property is no longer the abode of a Freeman. Your byke is no longer registered to a family with a living Freeman. You have one day to purchase a Race ticket or new accommodation will be assigned and you will register with the mine. Do you understand?'

Adam looks at the GRUB. 'You aren't gonna ask me how he died?'

'Trauma to the head,' the GRUB retorts. 'Do you understand the order?'

'Does it matter?'

'Do you understand?'

'Yeah. I understand. I get it.'

The GRUB retakes its seat, starts the motor and the two of them, side by side, wheel round and cruise back the way they came. Adam watches them until they are out of sight.

Now he's got nothing left. Nothing left to lose.

Now he's the last one standing. Just like Old Man Dagg's hog. The last Stone.

Now he will do the one thing he was born to do.

Ride.

He looks at the grave. 'I'll beat 'em, Frank. I'll beat 'em all. I'll ride, like you taught me. And I'll find him. The one who killed you. I'll take blood for the blood he spilled.'

He pauses, feels the sting of tears. It's not like him, this feeling. This *need*. It's new. It stirs something in him. A darkness he's never felt before. He's appalled. But – most frightening of all – part of him *likes* the feeling.

It's a dry, calm morning. Windless. Still not too hot. The sky is a hazy indigo, filling up with dust. A few wispy cirrus clouds float high, where the sky is so dark it's almost black. It's going to be a perfect day.

Adam falls to the ground and lets the sobs come.

PART 2

BADLAND

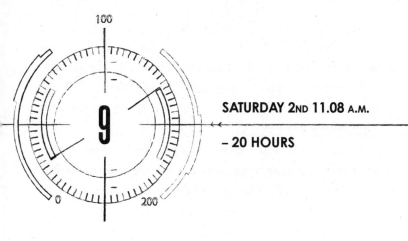

He rides wild and fast. He flies along the track. His tyres are filled with air and he feels the road hard under him. He stands off his seat as he comes down a steep hill and the wind pulls at his jacket. He knocks his goggles into place, thumbs down a gear and soars.

Adam opens his mouth and screams into the wind. Screams, until his tongue is dry and his throat is on fire. The screen of dead trees either side of the road flashes past him in a blur of grey.

Here comes the wind farm. Hundreds of turbines, chopping the air. Interspersed between them, flat solar panels angled to the sun. Then the power station, enclosed by a tall fence. A sign shouts at him. FORBIDDEN. KEEP OUT. His passing sends Race flyers scattering.

Here comes the lake, black and wide, hiding its dark secrets. A smell of silt and damp.

Here comes the core drill – hammering, plundering – rising to the sky.

Through the Outer Ring he goes. The low houses and their furrowed fields, studded with the shells of wrecked and burnt-out machines. Through the Inner Ring. Looming apartment blocks – grey and bleak – housing the miners, the destitute, the dying.

He passes two more patrolling GRUBs. They police the street in unison, their heads swivelling in perfect synchronicity. Left, right, left, right. They stop and watch him pass.

He doesn't stop. He keeps going. Alone in the sun.

It's noon by the time Adam rides into the town centre, right up the main road.

His head is filled with noise: the crashing of glass, the smashing of plates, the crunching of debris under his feet, the dragging sound of heels – and a metal leg – on the wooden floorboards, the sickening *whump* of a body hitting the dirt and the sound of the spade dumping soil.

He takes a long swig of water from his flask to clear his head, but his ears keep buzzing. He can't escape the noise. And it's not just inside his head.

One full day before the Race and a dark tide is rolling into Blackwater. It's not the same town he and Kane rode through yesterday. The main road is choked. Riders travel up and down, looking for trouble. And most find it. Fights are breaking out. Skirmishes everywhere.

Adam is watchful. He knows how it works. The Tribes of Blackwater are legion and loyal to their own creed. Through the winter they remain circumspect, operating in the shadows, allowing the dominant Tribe – the Scorpions –

to rule the streets. Until the summer, when the Blackwater Trail comes around, and all that changes. New Tribes emerge, like cockroaches from the cracks.

Every summer it's the same. They crawl in from all parts. Local and beyond. Outsiders from places Adam's never heard of. Towns with names as mean as the kids who come from them. All of them demonic with their mirrored goggles and their bristling armour. Packs of malefactors, looking for a fight.

Here are the Deads now, with their alabaster-white skin, dyed teeth – coal-black – and their plum-coloured lips, painted eyes and long nails.

Here are the Crows in their dark hoodies, with their red eye lenses and their faces hidden in shadow. Silent as the grave. They are known, at best, as artful pickpockets and, at worst, assassins.

Here are the Dog Soldiers. Crazy, wild and barbarous. They're easy to spot with their evil grins. They have a gory and bizarre tradition, the Dogs. They remove both their front teeth on induction and file their canines to sharp points – signs of brotherhood to the pack. They ride close together, churning the dust. The Riders leer and crack loose shots with their slings.

Here the vainglorious Hawk Nation, with their crimson jackets . . .

Here the Daggers . . . Here the Snakes.

Riders form alliances to survive. They stick together for safety in numbers.

But not all of them.

Adam can sniff out the loners and the rejected ones. Those affiliated to nothing and no one. They radiate a palpable brand of self-awareness. Visible in every movement, every action. Stealth and wariness, more akin to solitary animals than humans. Adam knows them well. He *is* one.

Now he rides through a pool of black shadow and looks up. The sky is dark with resting airships.

The Watchers have arrived.

The vast ships are grey and oval-shaped, each powered by four giant, circular turbines. Eight of them drift above the town. Despite their size – at least three hundred yards in length and one hundred in width – they move with the finesse of dragonflies, floating and jostling for space. Surrounding the body of each ship are huge extending decks, sealed in behind invisible force fields.

The ships are low enough for Adam to see figures on board, standing at the edge, trading telescopes, lounging in observation chairs. Watchers, in their flowing robes, groomed and calm.

The elite of the elite. So close. So out of reach.

A shuttle – small, light in tone and sleek – banks away from one of the airships and swoops down to street level, sending up a flurry of dust. It hums about ten yards up in the air. The noise it makes is soothing and rhythmic, like a purr. Adam can see several occupants through convex viewing panels, darkened against the sun. Most of them are trussed up in protective gear – high-tech, expensive-looking filter masks and Voddenite bodysuits – even inside the shuttle. They take every precaution. No skin exposed, no threat of infection from Earth's atmosphere.

But one of them isn't covered head to foot.

She's a girl, Adam sees. Beautiful. Serene. She looks directly at him as they pass. Large eyes. Blue or green, it's difficult to say. High cheekbones. Young-looking, but not a child. Anywhere from fourteen to twenty. Light-skinned and luminous. She radiates health.

Beautiful, long blonde hair. Like spun silk. This being the chief physical difference between the Watchers and the Left-Behind. Long hair.

Adam runs a hand over his own spiky-short dark hair. No one knows why hair growth is stunted on the planet, but, like most of the widespread degenerations and diseases, people point to one thing. Toxic skies. The reason they all left in the first place.

Frank says Watchers are descendants of the first Leavers. They are human, definitely. But there is – both in their manner and their appearance – a suggestion of evolution to something . . . *else*.

The girl's face shows no emotion. She stares at Adam with curious indifference. No expression, malevolent or otherwise. Perhaps forming an opinion, deciding whether he's worth his salt. Or whether he's destined for the dirt.

He will never know her decision.

The shuttle blasts a warp of heat from its wide exhaust and shunts up the road, leaving him with no more than a lingering impression of her, like a handprint on cold glass.

*

89

Adam passes an O2 saloon he knows well. He remembers the feeling: the tension leaching from his bones and easing from his muscles. Two dollars for an hour stretch, jacked to the wall. He's heard they exist in most towns, as an antidote to all the toxins.

He has no reckoning of the truth to this rumour. Never in his life has he ventured to a single town outside of Blackwater. *Too dangerous*, Frank always said. Tribal fights kick-start when Outsiders come to town. Adam has seen it happen in Blackwater. There's only one time when Outsiders are tolerated.

Race time.

He passes a heaving bar spilling drunken Riders, tanked up on Jhet Fuel. He used to wonder what compelled them to do this to themselves, to rip apart their lives.

He doesn't wonder any more.

He keeps riding. Veers down an alley and takes the backstreets. It's all about survival now.

Stay out of trouble. Get Plugged. Make it to the starting line.

Adam snakes his way to the Bykemonger Station, staying alert, nerves on edge. There's no sign of Kane. And no Scorpions either. But why would there be? Kane wouldn't show his face, and the Scorpions only turn up when you least expect them. When you least *want* them.

Adam is glad he doesn't see them. He's not sure how he'd react. He's not sure he could trust himself. Not any more.

Keep your head down. Stay low. Say nothin. That's how you survive.

Frank's old mantra is starting to wear thin.

'You again,' Sadie says, looking at him behind a dark pair of shades. She stands at the entrance of the Bykemonger Station, leaning on the door frame. The light from within outlines her sinuous body and she looks ethereal. A spirit being. Less real somehow.

Adam stands on the porch before the sign, the way he did the day before. Only this time it's different.

'You've come to pay,' she says. It's not a question.

He *has* come to pay. But he's come to pay for more than just the Race. He's come to pay respect for the dead. For justice. For revenge.

Adam holds out the money.

Sadie looks at the cash. She takes it without saying anything. Doesn't count it. Removes a billfold from her pocket and slips the notes inside.

Close up, Adam sees the reason for her shades. A dark coloration under her right eye, the skin puffed up and swollen. A bruise. She must notice, because she moves from the door and brushes her hand over her cheek, concealing the mark.

'Your byke needs fixing,' she says. Then she turns and heads back into the station, lithe and sleek. 'Follow me.'

Adam wheels the Longthorn after her, watching the way she moves.

That Scorpion kid was dead right – she is a panther.

He's seen one before. It was back when a travelling circus came through Blackwater. They set up a makeshift tent and Frank held Adam up in the crowd to see. He remembers the painted clowns with their twisted smiles – he didn't like them – and the high-wire trapeze artists who performed daredevil byke feats high above the ground, and a cat-tamer with his whip and his skin-and-bone panther. The panther's amber eyes blazed with quiet fury. She prowled the tent as though she alone were the authority in the land, despite her ragged appearance.

Adam follows Sadie and thinks about the panther. She had dignity, that cat.

He shakes his head. He knows he has to let Sadie go. Leave her behind. It's like she said after all. He made a choice. He chose to pay. Besides, Sadie isn't his to leave behind anyway.

He thinks of the way she looked at Kane and darkness falls on his heart.

The Bykemonger Station is built like a warehouse. An open space, the equivalent of two storeys in height and almost a hundred yards in length. It is one of only a handful of buildings in Blackwater supplied with electrical current from the turbine field. Long, flickering tubes run the length of the ceiling and flood the place with an almost blue artificial light.

At the far end is a small, semi-enclosed office. This is where Sadie leads Adam.

The station is full of activity. Customers – most of them kids about Adam's age, some a few years younger and not many older – traipse across the cement. The rigours of the Race are suited to the young, not the old. Adam can't remember anyone over nineteen ever winning.

He watches the young byke owners wheel their prized heirlooms across the cement floor. Sidewinders, Blackthorns, Rockhoppers, Snakecharmers, Scorchers, Duneblazers, Sunblazers, Backtrails, Diamondbacks, Sandtrackers, Desertcrawlers . . . and more.

Adam avoids looking at their owners. He keeps his eyes down and follows Sadie.

The space fills with an echo of hammering and clanging. Three Greasers sit on low wooden stools and ply their trade to spinning spokes and dismantled gears. Byke parts strewn everywhere and the whole place smells of rubber and oil. Adam lets the sounds and the smells wash over him.

Sadie takes the byke from him. Her hand brushes his thumb, but she doesn't seem to notice. She turns the Longthorn handlebars and squats to inspect the gears. Frowns and sucks her teeth. She straightens, wipes her brow with the back of her hand and looks at him. A smear of grease remains on her forehead.

'Your byke's a relic,' she says. 'Shot suspension. Cracked gear mechanism. Loose brake pad. I could go on and on.'

Adam blinks. He isn't sure what he's supposed to say. 'Can you fix her?'

'Course I can fix her. She's a byke.'

A clanging and hammering rings out against the walls. The warehouse throbs and bangs.

'You'll need gear,' Sadie says, over the noise. 'This way.'

Against the far wall is a padlocked cage. It runs the length of the wall, about ten paces deep and is filled with all manner of byke gear. Seats and wheel spokes and gears chains. Inner tubes and treaded tyres. Chrome spikes, long and hard and pointed sharp. Drawers spilling an assortment of bolts, washers, Allen keys, cable ties. There isn't anything a Rider needs that Sadie doesn't have. Goggles by the dozen, hanging on mean-looking hooks. Supply packs. Gaffer tape. Helmets. Air-filter masks. Heatkeepers.

Further along, an open metal cupboard with an assortment of wind-and-waterproof flak jackets, then rows and rows of riding suits. None of them new, Adam can see that. All second-hand. Most of them torn and frayed, some of them with dark smears that can only be one thing. Old blood.

'Take your pick,' Sadie says. 'It's all we have left.'

He looks at the gear. He knows that, according to the rules of the Race, Riders are free to kit themselves up the way they please. And because the Colonel runs the Race, and owns Sadie's workshop, she gets a cut to cover her losses.

Adam glances at the Longthorn and, out of nowhere, he thinks about Frank and is paralysed by a sudden wave of grief. He stares up at a ceiling fan chugging the air and he clenches his jaw.

Sadie watches him. When she speaks again, her tone has softened. 'Anything else you need? *Rider's Code*? I've still got a few, I think.'

The *Rider's Code*. A manual for Riders of the Vodden Circuit. Some say the experts wrote it. Slingmasters, Race winners and Bykemongers. But others say Lord Kolben Vodden himself is the author. The man who conceived the Circuit Races. Adam thinks about the old, heavily thumbed *Rider's Code* back at the farmhouse. He remembers Frank reading to him. Technical tips – how to patch a wheel or slide a gear sprocket, the best type of suspension fork. A breakdown of byke families, their worth and history. Circuit guides. An entire chapter on slingshots.

'Hello? Earth to Adam. Need anything else?' Sadie repeats.

'Yeah,' he answers. 'I'll take a weapon.'

Sadie looks at him. 'Thought weapons weren't your thing.'

Adam says nothing. Sadie shrugs and moves to a wall, lined floor to ceiling with shelves. Each one is stacked with small, leather pouches. She selects one, then replaces it and retrieves another. Sadie turns and unfurls something from the pouch. A braided sling.

She holds it out to him. 'It's made of hemp, woven through with Voddenite. Allows you to generate incredible force. Use it in the right way and it'll bring you what you need.'

Adam takes it from her. He follows two fine strands, threaded together – one dark, the other light. He runs his fingers over the tightly braided knots. They feel cool to the touch.

Sadie watches him. 'I'd look out for that friend of yours. I know his type.'

He turns the sling angrily in his hands. Even when he's alone with her, Kane's there at the fringes, with all his danger and mystery.

Adam hooks the sling into his belt, trying – and failing – to look like a pro.

'He's not my friend.'

'But you're riding with someone, right?' Sadie asks. 'You've got back-up?'

'I ride alone.'

She looks at him with her shades reflecting the light. He's sure he can see a trace of hurt in the angle of her shoulders. Just for a moment, and then it vanishes.

'Suit yourself.' She jerks her head at the gear room. 'Tell them what you want and they'll mark it for collection in two hours. Your byke will be ready same time.'

Then she wheels it away, without another word. The Longthorn's tyres make a woeful squeal on the cement.

Adam's stomach lurches and his cheeks burn as he walks to the gear. He feels stupid, ashamed for blurting out he rides alone. But it's too late. He said it. He has to live with it.

It takes every ounce of willpower not to spin round and beg her to forgive him. To thank her for yesterday. To see if she's OK. To ask her about the bruise. Instead he keeps walking and says nothing. Besides, Adam knows, with *her* kin, bruises are a dime a dozen.

Life would be easier if Sadie weren't the most beautiful girl in Blackwater. But the trouble with Sadie Blood isn't her beauty. It's her bloodline.

She's Levi Blood's sister.

And, worse, Colonel Blood's daughter.

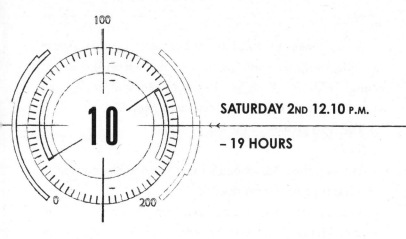

'Will it hurt?' Adam asks the man.

The man looks at him. 'Why ask if you know the answer?'

Adam sits strapped to a metal chair inside the Plugging clinic, a bare room in the town hall. The man before him has a face like carved rock. His eyes are dark blue, almost black. He wears a surgical mask and gloves. In his right fist is an electric scalpel, attached to a bleeping machine. His white coat is freckled with dried blood.

'Every Rider asks the same question,' he says. 'And every Rider knows the answer.'

Adam feels an involuntary shiver. The room is cold. His hair has been shaved right down to the scalp. Another condition of the Race. Every Rider must have their hair sheared. Even the girls.

'Your Tribe?' the man asks, holding his head at an angle, studying Adam with manic interest. His eyes are intense. 'Not a Dead. Not pale enough. Dog Soldier? Crow?'

Adam shakes his head and looks away. He sees a glass jar filled with a yellow liquid and recognizes the curled thing inside it. A snake. Red-coloured and fat in the formaldehyde. He jerks his head back round.

The man glances at the jar. 'Snake?'

'No.'

'A loner, then. Never had a loner win the Blackwater.'

'First time for everything,' Adam says.

The man points to Adam's neck with the metal scalpel in his fist. 'I'll make an incision quick. You won't feel it, not at first. The pain comes after.'

It's a line Adam remembers from Pa. One phrase. He'd bang his toe or fall and Pa would smile at him. *The pain comes after*, he'd say. Adam has no idea why most memories elude him, but this one remains.

He controls his breathing and tries not to care about the metal bonds on his wrists and ankles. The man sees this and puts his left hand on Adam's thigh to settle him. A gesture that has the opposite effect. A cold thrill of terror runs up Adam's leg and he feels his hands begin to shake.

'It's the Plug that hurts,' the man says. 'Not the knife.'

'Please. Just make it fast.'

The man's eyes darken. 'Relax, boy. I know what I'm doin. Done it a million times.'

He removes his hand from Adam's leg and places it on his head. He turns his skull so Adam is forced to look at the snake in the jar. Adam knows he does this on purpose, puts the snake there to strike fear into the Rider. It's a rite of passage, the Plugging. It's not meant to be enjoyed or even tolerated. It's meant to be feared. Meant to be *felt*.

A whining noise starts up. The man has flicked the motor switch.

'Don't remember a kid who didn't cry,' he says over the drone. 'Hard as they try.'

He pushes Adam's head down and Adam squeezes his eyes shut.

It's nothin. Just pain. I can deal with pain.

The man wipes Adam's skin, under the bone behind his left ear. Adam can smell ether and some other anaesthetic probably. He feels a sudden scratch and burn. The scalpel. He grits his teeth, clenches his fists and he breathes in shallow gasps.

In his left fist is the blood-covered slingstone. He feels the smoothness of it, the comfortable weight of it in his hand.

Pain is nothin.

Pain is nothin.

Pain is nothin.

But he's wrong. Pain *is* something. Pain is scaled and writhing. Pain slides in hungry loops. The tongue flicks, licks the air. The head rears. The eyes are blood orbs. It snatches. A blur and smack of speed. A madness of razor teeth. A white-hot, mindless shock. Pain coils and spirals round him, clamps down, snaps his bones. He screams inside. He begs for the end, but it goes on and it goes on until he feels the Blackness rise and he releases, slides with relief into the abyss.

*

He staggers across the street to the Bykemonger shop in a daze. He raises an unsteady hand to the back of his skull, under his left ear, and touches the metal tube there, the spiky stitches in his skin. He feels dizzy and disorientated. The worm twists in his gut.

He is deep in thought, trying to steady his emotions as he steps up the ramp, when a dust-stricken figure comes lurching out of the door. The figure falls towards him, cursing as he goes. He barrels right past Adam, barging him with a shoulder.

Adam wheels out of the way and the figure half staggers, half falls down the ramp, all the way to the bottom, where he trips and sprawls in a tangled heap.

Adam looks down at him. That's when he sees the silver byke at the foot of the stairs and a red anger stirs in him.

Kane!

Kane licks his lips and blinks. A smear of blood comes from his nose and mouth. He raises his head. He looks up at Adam with bleary eyes. His shirt is soaked in sweat and Adam can smell his breath from the top of the ramp. He's high, or drunk, or both.

Adam shakes his head. 'Where were you?' he demands.

Kane doesn't answer. He rolls on to his knees and forearms, sways and dry-retches. Adam watches him. Does nothing to help.

A group of kids rides past. One of them yells out something incoherent and the others laugh.

Kane wipes his mouth with the back of his hand and smears the blood on to his chin. Still on his hands and knees, he looks up at Adam. His yellow eyes are glazed. He opens his mouth, as though he wants to say something, but no sound comes. Then he lifts a hand and waves and this small gesture brings his entire body tumbling down. He rolls on his shoulder and flops on to his back and he belches.

'You're not worth a damn,' Adam says.

Kane rolls his head to the side and looks up at Adam. He blinks and spits blood. 'Took you a while to figure,' he croaks.

Adam turns on his heel and marches into the afternoon gloom of the Bykemonger Station.

He wipes out everything but one line of thought: to fetch his Longthorn and his riding gear, to find some place to sleep . . . and then to race.

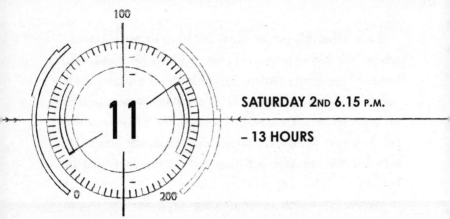

Twilight. Adam rides through Blackwater's Inner Circle. His grey riding suit is fitted with an inbuilt back brace and basic protection for the vitals. He chose the suit instead of a full exoskeleton with maximum protection. The downside of too much gear is restricted movement, especially with the older suits, and weight. Frank told him to stay light. As light as possible.

Lightness gives him speed and manoeuvrability.

Even his chrome helmet is lightweight. It fits him well, close to the skull, complete with a gold-tinted visor that *shnicks* up into the helmet at the touch of a button. He's wearing it now to remain anonymous. Just another Rider cruising the streets.

Adam finds an old abandoned building, worn down by the wind. There are many to choose from. Giant, multi-storey, concrete estate blocks. They used to be teeming with people, filled with the trappings of their messy lives. But not any more. That was long ago, before those with enough money or connections packed up and left for Sky-Base.

Adam pushes open the door and enters a wretched space, filled with booming echoes and the scurrying sound of rats. He leaves the Longthorn near the entrance, knowing theft is unlikely. But he keeps her in the shadows anyway, away from prying eyes. He doesn't want his bolt-hole advertised.

Adam picks his way through rubble and debris: a plastic doll with one eye, fallen plaster and chunks of cement like boulders. He pinches his nose to mask a smell of mould and rot.

The entire ground floor is gutted and all the windows are boarded up, nailed shut. He creaks up a musty staircase and finds a room where the floorboards haven't been busted through. He uncovers his mouth and inhales. The same smell of damp and smoke, but less rank than the ground floor. It will have to do. He's tired and strung out and he needs a rest.

Adam stands and surveys his new crib. The room's been ransacked, but the windows, what's left of them, aren't boarded. The only piece of furniture is a three-legged chair with stuffing coming from huge rips in the sagging seat covering. On one of the walls is a grate filled with a pile of black logs and grey ash. Adam makes his way over and looks at the remains. Someone built a fire in this room. A sharp smell of smoke claws at the back of his throat. He crouches, holds his palm over the burnt ash.

Some time not long ago. Maybe a day.

He stands quickly and moves to the wall – in the shadows – presses his back to the crumbling structure.

Adam freezes and he listens. It's cold and dark. The emptiness is frightening. No sound, bar the moaning wind.

He waits. Five minutes. Ten minutes. Listens for the telltale sounds of feet. He's accustomed to waiting and being quiet. He goes into a kind of trance – similar to the zone he gets into when riding. He stares into the middle distance and uses his peripheral vision to bring every aspect of the room into sharp focus. His heart thumps and his ears stay alert to every creak.

At last, he nods to himself, satisfied. He sighs and pushes himself away from the wall.

This is where he bunks, right in the middle of the squalor, on the dusty floorboards, on his newly issued bedroll. Adam is cold and his skin is covered in layers of grit. He pulls his heatkeeper to his chin, shuffles to get comfortable and then he lies there, wide awake, listening to the moaning wind and the twittering of roaches burrowing through the ash.

He thinks of the oak tree. And the bones in the ground.

He thinks of Kane and he thinks of Levi and he thinks of Frank.

Sleep eludes him.

It's going to be a long night. Filled with endless head-noise and stones flying. The last night before the Race. The night before his new life.

His belly is full of butterflies and not much else, and his eyes are wide in the dark. He stares up at sepia water stains charting the ceiling like ancient maps. His breath comes in clouds.

He tries not to think of anything. Tries to keep his head clear.

He hears a scuttling sound over the floorboards and he's up in a flash, on his elbows, peering through the dark. A hairless rat. Corner of his eye. Big and pink and ugly as sin. It freezes under the broken window, lit by shards of moonlight. It watches him, twitching. Then it scurries away, hugging the wall. It turns at right angles in the corner of the room and it's out of the door and gone.

Adam shivers, draws the heatkeeper round him and sinks his head back.

Then he sees them. Two eyes, white and bright, staring down at him through a crack in the floorboards above.

'HEY!' he screams, leaping to his feet. He throws off his heatkeeper and runs to the door. The floorboards slam above him. A door bangs and the stairs drum with feet.

Adam throws the door closed and its hinges rip right out of the wall, tearing up chunks of the rotting door frame. The door falls inwards with a *whoosh* and it smashes down with a loud, echoing *BANG!* A cloud of dust and splinters balloons up and Adam coughs and staggers back. His heart hammers and his ears buzz.

Think, Adam!

The entire door is gone. Adam has nothing between him and the stairs now.

The drumming feet are loud and he blinks in the half-dark, eyes frantic. Something lands with a *thump* outside in the corridor. He picks up the three-legged chair and holds it before him, waiting. He holds it by the legs first and then changes his mind and switches to the seat back, like a cat-tamer.

Feet, outside the door, scraping through the debris.

'WHO ARE YOU?' Adam calls, hearing a falter in his voice.

Nothing. Complete silence. There's only darkness and shadow. Adam can hear himself breathe.

Then a high-pitched voice from the dark corridor. 'Who are *you*?'

Adam backs into the shadows. 'I'm not answering if you don't show yourself.'

Feet shuffle and a figure emerges from the gloom. A small boy, shrouded in dark, eyes shining. In his hand, the unmistakable shape of a knife.

'Get your own damn place,' the boy spits.

He's no more than thirteen. Shaved head, like every Rider before the Race. Freckles. Pale skin. Blue eyes that glitter as he whips the knife from one hand to the other. A skill perfected, no doubt, to instil fear in his enemy. It works too.

'You can handle that knife,' Adam says, eyeing him.

'Ain't done me wrong yet,' the boy says, making an obvious show of looking mean.

Adam puts the chair down. He dusts the seat back with his hand.

'Well. I know you won't use it. On account of the Laws.'

The boy says nothing, still clutching the knife. His fingernails are chewed to the quick.

'You're aware of the Laws, right?' Adam says.

'Yeah, I know 'em. But I don't go in for rules much.'

'Nope. Reckon you don't.'

The boy looks at him, uncertain for a moment, conflicted, and then he gives a slight shake of his head and pockets the knife.

Adam smiles. 'Name's Adam. Be pleased if you'd let me sleep here before the Race. Got no other place. Not any more.'

The boy stands his ground. 'Nathaniel Skye. Call me Nate.'

'Nate. Sorry about the door.'

The boy shrugs and his big moon-eyes stare at Adam.

Outside a gust of wind throws the branches of a tree against a ground-floor boarded window and Nate turns, as though expecting a new enemy to come barging into the room.

Adam looks at the Plug under Nate's left ear. 'You're riding tomorrow.'

Nate stares back at him. 'That's right.'

'How many summers have you seen?'

'Twelve.'

'*Twelve!* You're nothin but a grommet.'

Nate shrugs.

'They won't let you take the knife,' Adam says.

Nate's hand moves to his pocket. 'Pa gave it to me. Before he died. He was a Rider too, back in the day. He said I might need it. Might need to sink it to the hilt.'

'That's crazy.'

'Callin Pa crazy?'

'No. What I mean is, if the Colonel finds out . . . you'll get Unplugged!'

Nate shakes his head.

Adam looks at him. 'You know what that means, right?'

'Sure. Madness. Maybe even death.'

'And that don't bother you?'

No answer.

'And what about them other Riders? If they see the knife . . . well, they won't like it.'

'Pa said never mind the Riders. There's other things out there much worse'n Riders. Things you never wanna meet. It's for them you keep the knife.'

'What kinds of things?'

'Bandits, wolves . . . all kinds. Maybe even Nakoda.'

Adam's heard of them. He doesn't know anyone who hasn't. When he was little, Frank kept him awake with wild stories about devils and demons . . . and Nakoda, eaters of human flesh. But Frank had never seen them either. Not once.

'They say the Nakoda are worse'n bandits,' Nate says. 'If the desert don't kill you, they say the Nakoda will.'

Adam looks at him. 'They're cannibals, I heard.'

'That's a fact. Nakoda warriors'll eat your heart. They'll rip it from your chest.'

Adam shakes his head and tips his chin at the grate. 'You lit that fire?'

'Maybe.'

'Well. What say we light another and keep the cold out?'

*

Adam and Nate share the dusty room. They lie awake and listen to each other breathe and cough in the close, smoke-filled air. They stare at the glowing embers and stifle the ache of abandonment. Adam thinks of the nights he and Frank stayed up talking, until the fire turned to glowing embers and then to ash.

Adam looks at Nate and feels a conflicting sense of responsibility. He shifts on his hard bed and panics about not sleeping and being too tired for the Race and the more he worries, the more difficult it becomes to fall asleep. He knows he has to be strong tomorrow, able to handle whatever the day throws at him.

Adam lifts a hand to the back of his skull and plays his fingers over the cold, exposed metal.

'How'd you get the money,' he asks Nate. 'For the entry?'

Nate doesn't look at him. They both lie on their backs, staring at the ceiling. 'When Pa died, he left everything he had to my older sister and me.'

'Sister?'

'She lives in Providence. That's where I'm from. I hate the place. I'm never going back.'

'What about your sister?'

'You don't know my sister. She doesn't need help from me. I'm gonna race. I'm gonna win. And I'm gonna get to Sky-Base.'

Adam rolls on to his shoulder. 'You're not afraid?'

'I'm afraid of nothin,' Nate hisses.

Adam doesn't ask any more questions about Nate's kin. He knows not to ask questions when the answers aren't worth finding out. Nate's just a boy. He should be home with his ma and his pa. He should be safely tucked into bed. He should be dreaming. But he isn't. He's *here*.

'Why?' Nate whispers.

'Why what?'

'Why'd you wanna know if I'm afraid?'

'No reason. Just asking, is all.'

Silence. Breathing. The moaning wind.

'You ever ride in one of 'em?' Nate asks.

'Nope.'

'Figure it'll be hell?'

Adam shrugs. 'It'll be fine, I guess.'

Once again, he feels the weight of his lie fill the room.

'Wanna know a secret?' Nate asks. 'It's about the knife.'

'Yeah? What about it?'

'I'm not worried about 'em seein it. It's ceramic. Nothin will pick it up.'

Adam nods. 'I like your style, Nate.'

Nate smiles, teeth white in the dark. Then the smile disappears. 'Pa told me . . . he said don't make friends with them other Riders.'

'Yeah? Why'd he tell you that?'

'Because they ain't gonna be around long.'

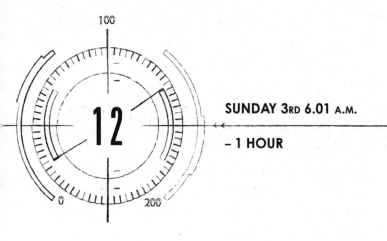

Drums throb and the morning sun slants down on the grim procession. The Riders come two abreast through the dry canyon track, lit gold by the hanging dust, bedecked in flaring sun goggles and visored helmets. Beautiful and terrible in all their gear.

Some, like Adam, are dressed in light body armour only, with no more than kneepads and elbow pads, maybe a backplate to help eliminate the spinal column twisting when they crunch into the ground. Others parade in full exoskeleton suits, with webbing stitched into hard pads covering vitals – shin, thigh, knee, back, chest, shoulder. Some Riders have their bykes fitted with sharp spikes and all manner of barbed, medieval contraptions.

Adam knows – despite the way they look – the Riders' stomachs will be in their boots.

Like his.

He contemplates the days ahead. The tired legs. The aching bones.

The stones. The crashes. The kills.

He sees a kid staring left and right. Sweat streams from him. He looks terrified, set to bolt. Like he's made the biggest mistake of his life. He can still leave, if he wants. It's not too late. They haven't been scanned, so the Race contract isn't binding. Not yet.

But the kid doesn't break the line. Adam looks away.

Up above, the Watchers float. Adam counts twelve airships and estimates about one hundred to two hundred Watchers per ship. All told, maybe two thousand Watchers.

They come from Sky-Base to leer at the action. To get their kicks. To watch kids die in the sun. They place bets impassively, picking Riders they deem worthy.

Referees – who are hand-selected by the Colonel from Blackwater townsfolk – roam through the ranks of Riders with their digital tablets, making notes and calling up odds to the Watchers.

GRUBs patrol the start line, stiff-legged, in visored helmets and black metal casings. Nobody is dumb enough to take on the GRUBs. You can't fight a fusion shooter gripped in a hand of steel. And besides, if you fight the GRUBs, you fight the Colonel.

Adam glances up at silhouetted figures on the canyon ridges. Townsfolk, watching. Maybe Sadie's up there somewhere, looking down on him and all the Riders and the bykes she helped build. He bangs his helmet with a fist to shake her from his head.

Adam isn't sure where he is in the pack. Somewhere near the front. Closer to the middle perhaps. There are too many Riders to be certain. He remembers looking down at the cluster of Riders in summers gone, up at the top of the canyon with Pa and Frank. Frank was animated, pointing out the Riders he knew. He was full of bounce back then. Pa didn't used to say much. He just stared down with his jaw tense.

It's hot inside the canyon, even now, a little after dawn. The Riders keep their heads low and say nothing, bowed to silence by the heat. They listen to the drums roll and the shouts rise.

Adam glances across at the Rider on the Sunblazer byke alongside him. Nate, with his fingernails bitten to the quick. An orphan kid living a life of fugitive solitude. Like so many others. Like animals, left to scrounge and forage. At Nate's belt, he spies the knife handle. Nate sees his glance and gives him a sheepish grin. He points up the line.

A horse-mounted figure stands on the sawn-off redwood tree stump. The rising heat waves play tricks on Adam, elongating and bending the figure.

Colonel Mordecai Aesop Blood.

He sits astride a grey pony – the only one in Blackwater. Adam watches it toss its head. It goes by the name of Bone. Supposedly, the Colonel bought it from horse traders in the Badland, but no one really knows where it's from. It stamps about atop the massive tree stump, standing erect, nostrils flaring, turning its head. Sensing the Riders. The Colonel, by contrast, is expressionless in his silver-mirrored sunglasses.

There are stories about the Colonel. How he shot a kid who refused to shake his hand before a Race. How he sells kids to the Slavers. How he kicked his own brother out of Blackwater, banished him to the Badland.

Adam can't be sure if any of it is true. He knows only what everyone does. The Colonel is all-powerful. He rides a horse called Bone. He carries a fabled pistol. And you do not, under any circumstances, defy the Colonel . . . or you will quickly become dead.

He feels a sudden impulse to turn and flee. To ride away and never stop riding. He clenches his fists and pushes fearful thoughts away.

Frank is all he had. And Frank is gone.

'Used to be in the army, back in the day,' Nate hisses. He leans over in his seat, keeping his blue eyes on the Colonel as he speaks. 'It's how he got the title. Recruited by Sky-Base when they had that trouble over in Providence. That core mine strike.'

Adam shrugs, pretending not to care.

Colonel Blood leans on the pommel of his saddle and he looks at the assembled Riders, who come to a clattering standstill in front of him. He squints up the canyon walls, glares at the referees and the blank-faced GRUBs, and nods in deference to the Watchers, up in their airships. The cries die down and the Riders look up at the Colonel and wait. The horse, Bone, skitters and shakes its neck.

'He was a big deal in the army,' Nate whispers, as if this were some new revelation for Adam, some dark secret of the world. 'Turns out he was good at killing.'

The drums come to a rumbling stop, until the only sound is the snapping of the flags.

The Colonel's voice, when he speaks, is dry and rasping. The curving canyon wall behind him provides a natural amphitheatre, throwing out his voice, sending it up the canyon, travelling to all the Riders. Setting a chill in their blood.

'Riders,' he says, eyeing them all and holding one arm aloft. 'You are about to embark on a journey. A rite of passage. These canyon walls have seen many before you come and go. They've seen the strong and they've seen the weak. They've seen them stand tall. And they've seen them fall.' Here he pauses and Adam finds himself wanting to laugh. From hysteria more than anything else, but also because of the melodramatic manner of the man, his turn of phrase, the style of speech, calculated to instil simultaneous fear and adrenalin.

But you don't laugh at the Colonel. You listen to him and you do whatever he bids.

It's at moments like these when Adam feels most at odds with the world.

'There's room for one – and only *one* – to win this Race,' the Colonel continues. 'To win a ticket to glory. Sky-Base is watching. Sky-Base is waiting.' He looks at the faces tilted up to him. 'Not all of you will emerge from this ride alive. Hell, most of you won't, truth be told. But *all* of you will learn something about yourselves in the heat. The Badland will ask you questions. It will take courage to find answers. You will learn what you're made of. You will learn if you carry fire in your heart . . . and if you don't. And there's no lesson better. You won't live more than you live in the Race. You won't ever be more alive. *This* is your moment. Seize it or fade to dust!'

The flags snap and a few muted cheers go up. Adam thinks of Frank and the cacophony of sound in the canyon blurs into one sheet of noise. His heart beats hard in his chest.

'Good luck,' the Colonel calls. He strokes his cheek. 'And may you live to see the sky.'

Now comes a gaunt man with waxy cheeks and a pale complexion. He wears round sunglasses and a dark suit. In his left hand, he carries a digital tablet. The Race Debriefer.

The Colonel remains on his pedestal and gives a small nod to the Debriefer, who stands on a flat rock to his side, tablet in hand, stroking his thin lips. The Debriefer consults his tablet. In a monotone voice, he drawls out the Laws. Laws each and every Rider knows by rote.

'You are no doubt aware, but I would remind you, that there are three Laws: No knives. No shooters. And nobody quits. Break any one of these Laws and you will be Unplugged. If you elect to quit you will be Unplugged. Make no mistake. The choice is yours, and yours alone.'

Unplugged. It's the right term to use. No diminishing of the truth. Adam knows they can call it anything they like: Unplugged . . . Ended . . . Killed. It's all the same.

'Nothing is invisible to us. Nothing is hidden. We see *every*thing.'

He pauses, waits for the warning to sink in. His accent is refined, as though high-born.

'Slingshots and gripwires are admissible, even advised. Your goal is simple: to survive long enough to win. This will not be easy. As a point of fact, the Race has been designed to be anything *but* easy. It will be a test of your ability. Only the very best will win.'

A murmur ripples through the crowd. The Debriefer stands expressionless.

'The Race is set up with four base camps along the track. These offer serviceable tents, beds, food and O2 saloons where you can jack yourself into the wall for a hit. Plan your route and stop where necessary. Use the camps or don't – it's your choice. Choose wisely.'

He raises a hand to the airships.

'We thank our father on the Ark of Sky-Base, Lord Kolben Vodden, for having the wisdom to conceive the Vodden Circuit and for giving Riders this opportunity to live free, this *gift*. And we thank his hand on Earth, Colonel Mordecai Aesop Blood, for sanctioning the start and the end of the Blackwater Trail on *his* land.' Here he bows before the Colonel and the Colonel gives a slight nod.

The Debriefer looks at the Riders again.

'Ride, brothers and sisters. Ride until your bykes carry no more power. Ride until they are drained. Ride as far into the night as you can. If you win, the rewards are manifold. A ticket to Sky-Base for the sole winner. One thousand dollars cash and two hundred base points for the first three to cross. May you live to see the sky!' the

Debriefer shouts, followed by a raucous cheer from the townsfolk.

He looks at his tablet and barks out a sequence of names in his stentorian voice.

The names are called in no discernible order. One by one, Riders come forward, leaving their bykes behind. They step up on to the sawn-off tree stump, reach up to shake the Colonel's hand, then step back down, to get scanned and collect their Race pack.

Race packs are spartan. Essential survival gear only. Ration biscuits – a pack of thirty. A map – marking out the route. A compass. Rope. Tyre patches. A pump and levers. Gaffer tape. Bolts and washers. A canteen. A camel pack containing five pints of filtered lake water. A med kit with hydro-pills, bandages, a cauterizing iron and jabs of morphine.

Adam's name comes early. Only six Riders step up before him:

TYRAK DANIEL
SILAS VENIM
BLAKE IRONSIDE
ZETA PRIME
HUNTER KIBOW
AARON BLACK
ADAM STONE ...

When Adam hears his name called, he swings off his byke in a daze. He walks forward amid cheers and shouts from the crowd. They don't know him. They don't have any idea who he is and how he rides, but they'll be assessing him, making guesses, reaching conclusions. They won't think much of him. Nobody ever does. Nobody except those who know.

Dollars are changing hands as he reaches out his own.

'ONE DAY!' someone shouts.

'LONG ODDS!' another bawls. 'DEAD BEFORE THE SUN SETS.'

The Colonel's hand is cold and bony. His mirrored glasses drill holes in Adam.

'Stone,' he says. His voice is dry as a desert zephyr. This single uttered word carries an undercurrent of meaning, as if an entire conversation passes between them. A conversation about kin, about *him*. Son of a suicider. Brother of a dead cripple. It's not a word. It's an accusation.

Taking off his helmet, Adam turns to offer him the back of his skull, burning with humiliation and rage. He hears the pop and fizz of the scanner gun. His data drains to the Race server.

His birth date, his kin record, his medical snapshot – *everything* about him – is now contained on the Race server, which, legend has it, sits up on Sky-Base. Adam thinks about the flood of data, whole lives chopped up into bytes of code. He wonders how they make sense of it and whether they'll be able to see inside him with any greater clarity than he can. Either way his fate is sealed.

That's it. Done. It's ride or die now.

No turning back.

The names keep being called, down the list:

VIN BLUE
EZRA DARK
ELLIS CRAB
JET CRANE
MAISHA COLT
NATHANIEL SKYE ...

Nate drops his Sunblazer and moves up the line. He cuts a small figure walking up the row of Riders. A scrawny kid with no hope in hell. The Colonel's shadow swamps Nate. For a moment, he seems to disappear and then he re-emerges, blinking and looking startled, as if what he saw in that shadow held some harbinger of doom.

Adam grits his teeth and wishes he'd never met Nate. He's a liability. A weakness. And Adam can't afford weakness. He makes a promise to himself to lose Nate right off the starting line. But he feels a pang of guilt as Nate comes trotting up the line, winking at him, trying to muster a cool show.

It doesn't wash. He's afraid. Like everyone else.

Adam wonders about Kane and if he missed him. He hasn't seen him. Hasn't heard his name called. Plus some kids are so covered up it's impossible to tell who they are.

And the names keep coming. Some Adam knows; others arc half familiar. Most unknown.

BETH WOLF
KNUT SON
ASH KILLER
BEN CROWFOOT
RENFRO KNOX
THAKRAR KUSH
SOLO HENTAI ...

He stops hearing them. He shuts his eyes and drifts away. Floats up the canyon wall. Hits a hot thermal and *whoosh*, he's up high, above it all. The canyon forks beneath him like a crack in the surface of a vast clay plate. The sun is a blazing white disc and heat rises in liquid waves.

Then he's back in his seat. He sees the terrified kid now standing before the Colonel. Adam watches with mild interest, half expecting revolt, but not with much conviction.

The Colonel scans him. The kid's eyes blow wide. Then he runs.

Adam stands up on his byke and sees the kid breaking away. A commotion of raised voices follows. Shouts from the crowd. The boy is running hard, taking a haphazard route through the Riders, scrambling up a cliff bank.

What's he doin?

'I WANT OUT!' the kid yells. 'I ... I made a mistake. Please ... it's not for me. Please.'

Adam shakes his head. He understands his fear. He feels it himself. But there's nowhere to go. It's too late. The only way a scanned Rider leaves the Race is by crossing the finish line.

A GRUB descends, swift as the devil. It snatches the kid's arm in a metal fist. Then it drags him, kicking and screaming, up the line. The Riders look the other way as they pass. Adam watches in horror.

The GRUB hauls the boy to the feet of the Colonel and forces him to his knees. The kid is wailing uncontrollably now, begging them to release him.

The Colonel looks down at him. His silver glasses reflect the wreck before him. He steps back, as if the boy carries some disgusting fungal disease that might jump from his skin. The Colonel holds out his arm and makes a muffled request for something.

Adam squirms. He knows the nature of the request.

A second GRUB fetches an object that looks like an archaic drill and hands it to the Colonel. He takes it. He doesn't say anything. He doesn't issue a warning to the Riders. No long speech, no dramatic pause to add weight and tension to the moment. He simply holds the object in the palm of his hand and clicks a button.

A gout of dark blood spurts from below the boy's left ear. His body falls slack.

The Colonel hands the hideous thing back to the GRUB and waves his hand. The two GRUBs drag the limp and twitching body from sight.

It happens so fast Adam doesn't have time to feel the full force of shock. He sits on his byke, stunned into silence.

*

More names. Down the list. Read out with indifference, as if the kid never existed. As if his life were no more important or significant than the life of an insect crushed under a boot.

WADE RIP
RAFE APPLESEED
ADAH CAVE
RED STETSON
LEVI BLOOD ...

Levi Blood. The name sends a shudder through Adam. He feels cold sweat run down his spine. His knuckles are white on his handlebars.

He hears boots crunching on the shale. He closes his eyes and he breathes. Every other sound is shut out and all he hears is his own breathing – in and out, in and out – and those boots coming up behind him.

He feels a shadow move past him. Feels the heat of a body brushing close. He keeps his eyes shut and listens to the boots – the scraping sound they make in the sand and the stone.

He can smell him. The unwashed sweat of him.

Adam shakes his head and feels a wave of nausea. He grips the handlebars to stay upright. And he remembers his promise to Frank.

I'll find him. The one who killed you. I'll take blood for the blood he spilled.

Adam is concentrating so hard he almost misses the next name called.

His eyes flick open and he swivels in his seat.

Sadie?

He cranes his neck over the Riders and ... here she is. Tall and graceful. She moves up the line with her cool, easy sway. She looks grim as she comes past him. She doesn't see him.

What's she doin riding the Blackwater?

Her swagger is inhibited by a full complement of high-tech gear. A moulded flak jacket that looks articulated and vented. Body armour, to keep her cool and protected, no doubt with a built-in back brace. Black leather riding boots with steel toes. Protective pads strapped to her shins, elbow pads with extended sleeves to cover her triceps and forearms. But she wears no helmet. Her shaved head is covered. Her goggles sit on top of her red bandanna, which flickers in the breeze.

She's up ahead of the column already, shaking the Colonel's hand. This time the Colonel leans forward and touches her brow and whispers something to her and, while the crowds roar their approval, Adam sees her flinch and step back.

He can't tear his eyes from her. He watches her take her Race pack and come back down the line, pulling the straps on to her shoulders, securing her goggles on her face.

Adam swivels round to watch Sadie retake her seat.

Then a new thought enters his head.

Hell. First Nate, now Sadie.

His odds of riding alone and not caring about anyone are shattered. He knows he'll never be able to stop thinking about Sadie or Nate. He'll worry, start to finish. If he gets that far.

Adam counts Riders to think about something else. Eighty-one, including himself. Eighty-one souls ready to die for the promise of something better.

After each one of them comes forward to get scanned and pick up their packs, they crowd together and they twitch and fidget and rock on their saddles. Now the Colonel hauls the pistol from his belt. It flashes silver in the sun and he cocks back the hammer with a thumb.

Adam's heart leaps in his chest. He takes a deep lungful of air and counts down the seconds in his head. It's hot and close and the canyon fills with dust. No one makes a sound.

Adam resets the timer on his dashboard to zero.

Colonel Blood points his gun to a thin strip of sky . . .

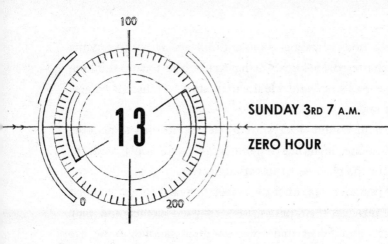

The pistol report is loud as a clap of thunder. It echoes off the canyon walls and loud cries rise up. The Riders, in a seething mass, slam their gears and go.

Adam throws the Longthorn hard right to evade the coming tide. The Riders, simmering with pent up adrenalin, come churning from the start line. They crackle like locusts in their articulated armour. Engines roar and dirt flies. Riders kick and lash out at each other, fighting for the lead.

Adam feels the heat of bodies left and right. Riders, quick on his tail. So close he can hear their ragged breathing.

Stones fly and grit stings him. He snaps his visor down and keeps going. Hips and shoulders back, elbows out, knees bent. His weight driving forward. A position that allows him to attack.

Adam doesn't wait to become a victim. He stays out of trouble, goes wide fast, stays where the bykes are thin, away from the pack. He pushes his fear deep inside and he weaves into another Rider's slipstream – a Dog by the look of him – and he stays there, head down and hell-bent.

The Rider ahead is sinuous and skilled. He leans, twists and rips through the Trail and Adam, in his wake, takes the same line, conserving energy.

The Riders carve through the dry riverbed, over loose stones and gritty sand; they snake in a scarf of dust along its contour, sweep up its banks – the dry, hard ridges – up on to the old watermark, and swerve down again.

Adam's heart pounds in his chest.

The canyon track streaks out in front of him. He glides over the sandy track. All his fears fall away, and the hell of yesterday becomes a vague memory. This is where he's meant to be. Where he was born to be. Here on his byke with nothing but sun and muscle and blood to power him through.

Then the Rider ahead comes crashing off his byke two lengths in front. Adam, with a quick burst of speed, evades barrelling into him and shoots up the bank. He sees another slam into the fallen Rider with a high-pitched wail and this second Rider somersaults over his handlebars and crashes headlong into a tangle of tyres, spokes and limbs. Another swerves, gets thrown, but his boot is trapped and the byke remains upright and she drags the Rider some twenty yards, twisting his leg, smashing his body.

Adam rockets past the chaos, heart thumping, sickened by the sight. But he keeps going.

Stay cool. Keep steady.

The world is a blur, obscured behind a veil of dust. Adam flies along the track, keeping his head down. He feels he's in a void. Apart from it all. Not here.

The byke's suspension bounces under him and he concentrates on the mechanics. Sadie did a bang-up job. The Longthorn has never ridden so smoothly. She rides like new. Better than new. The brakes work with a quick, one-fingered pull and the tyres are fat and thick with treads. The gears slot with slick precision.

The byke feels alive under him. A living, breathing thing, twitching and ticking with energy, like a snorting, pure-bred racehorse from days long before.

But the byke is not enough. Adam knows he'll need extreme powers of concentration and skill to keep strapped to the seat, to negotiate the rigours of the Race.

He pushes himself low against the hot body of his byke. He settles into the rhythm of the ride. Shapes his breathing to the small rises and falls of the track. They're a team – him and the Longthorn – tethered by an invisible link that ties the byke to his consciousness. Rider and byke. One being. Alone against the world.

Adam feels a pang of despair.

What kind of person has a byke for a best friend?

He thinks of Sadie, searches for her in the maelstrom of bykes, but he can't find her. Looks for Nate, but he's lost him too. All the Riders look the same, caked in dust as they are. There isn't any hope of finding Kane either. *Kane.* Could *he* be a friend?

Hell, no! Not ever.

He can't let anyone close. Frank told him not to. Told him to watch those closest to him.

They're the ones end up hurting you the most.

He swerves a ditch and guns the motor past a Rider stranded in a swamp of loose sand. The Rider has been separated from her byke and she dodges the coming pack, like a human pinball.

On they ride. The sun is low and the colour of blood.

The canyon flutes north-east towards the Blue Mountains, into the high desert, for roughly eighty klicks and the dust descends on the Riders, like fog. They ghost their way through.

The Riders disgorge from the cramped and narrow canyon into a deep valley. Huge purple mountains dwarf them and the valley is cast in long shadow by the craggy, scratchy contour of the range. The Riders disperse and plunge their bykes relentlessly forward, storming into the violet shadows and the hanging dust, heedless of whatever lies beyond.

Adam surges up to the crest of a rise to gain perspective. Down the slope, somewhere down in the dirt-enshrouded valley, lies the first obstacle course. He stays up on the hillside, waiting for the dust to settle, away from the pack. He knows there'll be a bottleneck at the entrance.

The Blackwater Trail might be called a race, but it's a misleading word. Frank taught him that. Adam knows to take it easy on the first day. There will be times when speed is necessary, even essential. But there will also be times when speed is a hazard.

You gotta pace yourself.

He hasn't travelled more than a few yards up the hill when behind him comes the throb engine of a byke. Adam rises off his saddle and turns quickly.

A Rider materializes from the gloom, caked head to foot in dust, half obscured in the haze.

'HOLD BACK!' Adam shouts, muffled into his helmet.

The spectral figure swerves and jerks away, but the movement is too sudden. His front wheel jars in the sand. The byke shudders and roars its disapproval and the Rider, arms windmilling, is flung from his seat. Adam is about to surge away when the fallen Rider's byke crashes past him and comes to a thrashing stop. A Sunblazer. Adam swings his head back.

The skinny Rider – dazed but unhurt – stands and watches him.

Adam turns his byke and rides towards him, slow and steady. He comes to a standstill and shicks up his visor.

'You always ride like that?' he asks.

The shadowy Rider looks at him and pulls off his helmet. His eyes are big and blue.

Adam shakes his head. 'How goes it, Nate?'

Nate shrugs. 'Doin OK . . . till just then.'

Adam leans back in his saddle and casts about to see if there is any immediate threat to their position. Nothing. No *feeling* of anyone else approaching. They're alone. For the moment anyway. The other Riders must be carving their way to the obstacle course somewhere in the dust below.

Adam jerks his thumb towards the course. 'No point getting mixed up in all that. Not yet.'

'Booby-trapped, no doubt,' Nate says, helmet in the crook of his arm.

They listen to the muted shouts of the Riders far below.

Adam nods. 'No doubt.'

He knows the way it works. Each course is rigged so a percentage of Riders fall. There are five of these man-made obstacle courses, or trials, with only the first and the last being obligatory. The rest are optional and placed at natural short cuts. But choosing – or *not* choosing – can force a Rider into dangerous territory. The Valley of a Thousand Dead Sons, known for packs of ravenous wolves. The high desert plains where flesh-eaters are said to roam – Nakoda.

Adam looks at Nate. 'Why'd you follow me?'

'Figure you're safe.'

'Nobody's safe.'

'That was rough back there,' Nate says after a pause. 'Seen six Riders go down. One of 'em ain't never gettin up again.'

Adam turns his wheel and puts a boot up on the byke's crossbar. He looks over in the direction of the valley.

Did Sadie make it?

Of course she made it. No question.

Nate follows his gaze. Both stare down at the valley, but there isn't much point. Neither can see a thing in the clouds of dust.

Nate retrieves his byke. He makes a cursory check of the mechanics and he frowns. Then he takes up his seat.

'Damn byke shoulda reacted sooner,' he says. 'Must be busted.'

Adam watches him and offers no opinion.

'Damn byke,' Nate repeats. He looks at Adam. 'Helluva start. See that GRUB take that Rider off the line? I hate GRUBs. They're abominations.'

'Big word for a little guy.'

'Pa said that's what they are.'

'They're just machines.'

'Oh yeah? Your byke, she just a machine?'

'Bykes are different.'

'If you say so.'

'I do.' He pauses. 'Why are you racing, Nate?'

Nate squeezes and releases his brake. 'Same as everybody,' he says, squinting at the hills. 'Got nothin else. Don't wanna die in the mines.'

'How many points you got?'

'None.'

'Yeah. Me neither.'

The boys look at each other, then flick their eyes away and stare at the dust valley.

'Weren't easy following,' Nate says. 'You can ride.'

Adam removes his boot from the Longthorn's crossbar. He pulls off his helmet, rests it on the seat in front of him. 'All I know, I guess.'

'Reckon you're the best?'

Adam thinks of a shadow flashing past him. A lithe form ahead. He sees himself going hard after him, swerving and skidding and leaping small rises that come at him fast. But Kane is too quick. He fades to a shadow ghost in the rising dust. Then disappears altogether.

'Yeah,' Adam says, touching his fingers to the back of his skull. He feels a dull presence at the root of the plug. 'Sure. I'm the best.'

They watch a swirling eddy of dust curl away to reveal a patch of blue sky. In the valley, shafts of slanting sunlight reveal the obstacle course. It has been carved into the heart of the valley. On each side of the course, glinting in the sun, are ten-yard-high razor-wire fences that run right up the hill to the mountain cliffs. There is no way round this first man-made trial. It's the course or nothing.

Adam hauls out a map from his Race pack and flattens it out over his handlebars.

The Trail is marked by a dotted red line and maps a circular route, beginning and ending in Blackwater Canyon. It sets out in a north-easterly direction for a hundred klicks, then directly east for a further two hundred. After the Sawtooth range, it jags south, heading for the open plains, then east again and finally north towards El Diablo. Two thousand, five hundred klicks of pure Badland. Diamonds mark the four camps along the route and an X for each of the five obstacle courses.

It's here – where the stakes are highest – that the Watchers gather in droves.

Adam looks up at the crest of a hill and sees them. A line of unmistakable white sails. Sun flares, dancing off telescope lenses.

Sail trykes eat up the sand. They ride faster than any dirt byke and they're sturdy enough to carry seats over the two front wheels. Each sail tryke carries a pilot and two passenger Watchers. They travel the Trail with the Riders, keeping out of the way, taking notes, observing, feeding information back to the referees in Blackwater and up to the airships in the haze.

A sail tryke might be fast, but it can't navigate the jumps and twists of the obstacle course. They'll stay out of the action and they'll never get into the fray, never lift a finger to help.

Adam looks away from them and searches the first course for Sadie on her Stormchaser, but he can't find her in the hanging dust and the chaos of bykes.

The course is dangerous – narrow and rutted – every ten lengths marred by a steep jump. The turns, sharp and vicious, are clogged with Riders jostling for position. Alone, in front of the hungry pack, a Rider on a white Stinger byke leaps and soars.

He rides with effortless mastery, at a pace that can't be matched by those in his wake. He drives hard at a jump and sails clear, high into the air, up and up, as though an invisible line jerks him skyward. He flies right up and over the following jump, disappears in dust on the far side, only to re-emerge seconds later, speeding low and fast – a stone flung to the next turn.

'You see that?' Nate gasps. 'That kid out front. That's Levi Blood. He's the one to beat.'

'He's nothin,' Adam says, despising the edge in his voice.

He hears the distant *crack* of a slingshot. Sees another Rider fall.

Adam rolls the map and stuffs it into his Race pack. He stores both in the byke's frame compartment, between his thighs. Then he kick-starts his motor.

Nate looks at him. 'Thought you aimed to wait?'

Adam pulls on his helmet. 'Changed my mind.'

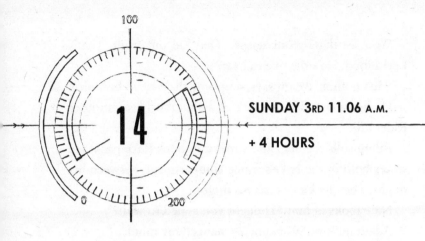

He knows he should take it slow at first, conserve his energy, save his strength for the end. Stay alive. That's all that matters in the first few days. But now he has to go like the wind. Now he has to run the gauntlet. Getting through the first obstacle course will require all his skills. He'll need to be hyper-aware, ready for anything, any trap, any sign of tampering or sabotage.

The Debriefer made it clear:

The Race has been designed to be anything but easy. It will be a test of your ability.

Down the slope they go – him and Nate – two Riders at the back of the pack.

Nate's Sunblazer makes a grinding noise that doesn't sound good. Adam is forced to rein in the Longthorn to keep from bursting away. And it bugs him. Staying alive is difficult enough without having to worry about a skinny kid with blue eyes and a knife in his belt.

He knows the smart choice. Ditch him. Ride out of sight and leave him to his fate. But he can't do that. Besides, he's impressed with Nate. To get through the mess of the start means the kid knows a thing or two about riding. That counts for something. Yet Adam can't suppress a wish that he were riding with someone else. Someone he never expected to be running the Blackwater. Someone as beautiful as the blush of a red Medusa tree in the dust.

Sadie Blood.

Adam and Nate come careering into the course and find devastation. They rip past a figure, caught and twisted in the trackside wire; his torn clothes flutter and swirl in the wind. Another Rider they find wrapped round her byke, bloodied and broken, her head slung sideways.

She doesn't move. She doesn't make a sound.

Adam clenches his jaw and rides.

You have to commit, Adam. You see that jump coming, you put your head down. You go. You don't stop. Not for nothin. You gotta keep trying. Never give up. Not ever.

The first jump is fifteen yards high. Adam guns down the slope, shoots up to the lip and *whoosh* . . . he's airborne. At the apex of the leap, his heart flies to his throat. This is the moment he comes most alive. After the violence of a descent into a jump – after that epic rush when he sweeps up to the lip and gives gravity the finger – the grace of floating free. He is one with the byke and the byke is one with the air.

This is why he rides – for *this* moment – the solitude of a jump. An inbetween state, where the unknown lies on the other side, where anything is possible and nothing can touch him. Time divides into what came before and what lies after. The moment lasts. And then it folds.

He's down the other side. Rubber hits gravel. Loose stones come rattling down after him and the byke clatters under his body. He sweeps into a turn that throws him high up a wall and spits him into a tight run rippled with quick jumps. The narrow channels and turns are terrifying and mesmeric.

Adam slots into a groove. The Longthorn rides with style, absorbing each shock with her lightweight frame and Sadie's fine-tuned suspension. She rides like a dream.

He's not alone on the track. He feels, rather than hears, Nate behind him.

Nate slipstreams him and they go hard and fast. As fast as they can with Nate's lagging Sunblazer. Adam has eyes only for the track. It comes at him relentlessly.

Turn after turn.

Jump after jump.

No sign of traps. Not yet.

Adam rounds a sharp bend and he descends into a steep and furrowed part of the course. His senses are on fire. Every nerve in his body crackles. Every muscle is taut.

He's in a narrow, V-shaped area, so narrow at the base it allows for the width of two side-by-side bykes only. Either side of him tower walls of earth.

No mistakes possible. No margin for error.

Here comes – by far – the steepest jump yet. A monster of a wall.

Adam accelerates hard. He knows it will require massive speed. He steels himself, flattens against the byke frame and guns the throttle. The byke swoops down the track and glides up to the top . . .

Boom! He's high up in the air again – climbing to an incredible height. He lets go a whoop of pure delight into his helmet. For a moment, just a split second, he forgets who he is and what he's doing. He floats away with the dust.

Adam pulls off his helmet and sits quietly on his byke. A restfulness flows through him. A sense of accomplishment, even smug satisfaction. He looks at the completed obstacle course and smiles. The high jumps and the crazy turns – all defeated.

He pats the side of the Longthorn. 'We did good.'

'Hell, didn't we!' a voice hoots next to him, breathing hard.

He turns. Nate grins at him and slaps his helmet. 'Did you see that? We licked it!' He removes his helmet, throws it in the air and catches it. 'Hoo-haa!'

Adam feels a small stab of resentment. 'Blind luck if you ask me.'

But Nate won't be brought down. His eyes dance. 'You're a damn fine Rider, Adam. You got yourself Voddenite balls.'

Adam looks at the kid with the freckles and the blue moon-eyes.

Nothin gets to this guy.

He looks away and he shakes his head. But he can't help smiling. And soon the two boys find themselves sitting on their bykes in a hell-desert, laughing like crazy.

They saddle up again and ride through the day. They take turns on point, watching for traps and Riders. They ride through wide country, nothing but rock and desert scrub. They ride across a flint-strewn plain with wispy grass. Then tall cypress trees, shaped like rockets, impossibly green in the rock dirt. They see Riders scattered up ahead, each one churning a virgin line. A multitude of plumes drift to the sky.

They stay behind the pack. Biding their time. Riding with sun goggles, stowing their helmets in favour of less restrictive headgear. Nate's Sunblazer makes a clanking noise that neither boy can figure or fix and they pretend the sound is nothing more than a trick of the desert.

Their conversation turns to Sky-Base.

'Heard they got swimming pools,' Nate says, leaning back in his saddle, as far as the seat will allow. 'Blue pools, warm as bathwater. They have it all.'

Adam watches a mini tornado swirl across the earth. 'Yeah. I heard they got story screens – 3-D holographic. You walk up into the story. Talk with the characters. Spit in their faces.'

Nate shakes his head. 'I like the sound of that. Yessir. No working the mines or racing death tracks. Just sitting up there, watching all those story screens.'

'You and me both.'

'Got some weird customs too, though. Coming down here, watching us die.'

'Yeah, well. Nobody's perfect.'

It's dusk when it happens. When his guard drops and he allows their small success to get the better of him. Adam decides to open the throttle. They let their bykes stretch and growl on a vast bake of hard sand. They make up lost ground. Haul in other Riders and overtake them. Lose them in their dust. They blaze onwards, side by side, pushing Nate's ailing byke to the limit.

Adam storms ahead and sees a jump coming. He calls Nate to tail him.

It's nothing to speak of – a routine lip formed by summers of soil erosion and ceaseless wind – a jump made by the gods. Adam gets a creeping feeling suddenly, racing into the lip. But he ignores it. A wedge like this, carved out of wind and rock, is a gift. He *has* to jump.

He leaps. He flies. And Nate blasts after.

It's only coming down the other side that he sees the glint of gut-wire. But it's too late. He's committed to the drop.

The gut-wire is strung taut across the track, at waist height. His instinct, as soon as he sees it blinking in the sun, is to duck low, to go under, but something, some inner force, warns him. Ducking under a waist-high wire may present the soft flesh of his neck. All eventualities flash before him.

Flipped backwards, sent crashing into Nate.

Sliced and garrotted.

Decapitated on day one.

His mind probes the gory possibilities. All in seconds. Split seconds.

He knows evasion is useless and so he takes the only decision worth taking. In mid-sweep down the slope, with the athletic agility of a circus performer, he somehow conspires to swing his feet up on to the narrow saddle, and then he lets go the handlebars – and he jumps, all in one fluid movement, without hesitation.

He flies up and forward in a pantomime of a perfected trick. Only this is no trick and there are no circus nets to save him.

Time slows. The air is jelly.

Adam feels a vibrating presence of someone. A feeling of being watched. He hears a voice, as real as if the person were right there.

Frank's echo.

Roll, Adam. Pull in your shoulder and roll when you hit the dirt.

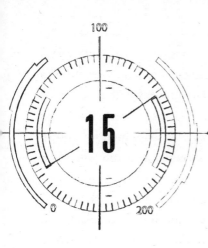

Weightless. That feeling mid-jump. The feeling underwater, when he slips through the cool darkness, suspended in a black void. He's in the air again, riding a hot thermal. Far below, on the arid sands, a trail of Riders kicks up plumes of dust. Insects, from above – an army of ants.

Frank stands over him. He towers upwards into the sun.

'Your angle was all wrong,' he says. 'You lost focus. Gimme your hand.'

Adam blinks in the sunlight. He knows he's dreaming, or *remembering* . . . or both. He knows it isn't real, but he reaches for his brother's hand anyway. His eyes swim. Blood streams from his grazed knees and elbows, from his nose and his lip.

He hears Frank's voice. 'On your feet. If you fall, you get right back on your byke.'

Adam mumbles something and his brother grabs him by the shoulders and shakes him.

'You understand what I'm telling you? You can't relax. If you relax, you die.' Frank keeps his hands on Adam's shoulders. His grip is steel. 'The ground will come up at you. It comes up like a cur and it snaps its teeth. But here's the deal: when it comes, there's only one thing for you to do. Roll, Adam. Pull in your shoulder and roll when you hit the dirt.'

He opens his eyes and sees a blurred pair of blackened jeans ending in a pair of ravaged leather boots. The world is turned upside down and the boots are at the top of his vision against a sky of dirt and the legs trail downwards to a shapeless body and a blue abyss below. The sun lies up beyond his chin. Blood drips from his mouth into his eye and the world turns as he swings. Every bone in him aches. Every muscle burns. His head throbs and his feet are numb.

Uneasy and uncertain, he waits for the world to be right itself. But no such thing comes to pass.

He strains his neck, looks up at skeleton branches and listens to the creak of rope. He groans and turns his head. His eyes and mind try to adjust to a flipped world.

Nate!

Stripped to his underwear, Nate is being held up by a man in a dishevelled coat, while another hunched figure lashes a rope to his ankles. They throw him loose and Nate makes an audible grunt when his back hits the ground. Then he's whipped upside down and hauled feet first into the air, the rope acting as a pulley over the bony limb of a dead tree.

Nate swings from his ankles. His arms, above his head, point towards the ground, flailing like a marionette. His eyes are shut. His face is bloody. His pale body bright with sweat.

Fear seizes Adam. Fear and guilt and anger, all at once.

I was too confident. Too relaxed!

Should've listened to Frank's echo. Should've listened to my gut.

He knows he should have expected the wire. He should have seen it coming. He could have avoided it – he *could* have – if he had been more careful, more aware. But he didn't see it coming. He wasn't thinking. And now . . .

Adam struggles in his bonds. He's still dressed in his riding suit, but his arms are crossed, tied at the wrists, fastened at the small of his back. The pain is excruciating.

He blinks and studies the boots in his vision. A second pair swings into view. Then a third. Shadows fall on the ground. Adam sees the clean domes of three heads.

He knows to whom these shadows belong.

Bandits.

His head fills with blood and his heart fills with dread.

They live deep in the backcountry, up in the Sawtooth Hills, with their scattered goat herds. Adam has heard stories. About their miserable, violent lives. How they have nothing to lose. Nothing to fear. And, when Riders pass, how they descend for the take.

They take more than things. They take dignity. They rip it away.

Bandits usually stay clear of Colonel property, for fear of reprisal attacks, but the Blackwater Trail tempts them from the shadows and Sky-Base turns a blind eye.

There are three of them, standing insolent and slit-eyed before their dangling captives. They chew betel nut and stare at their prey. The sound of their breathing is obscene. They say nothing and they watch.

Adam listens hard for the drone of airship rotors. He hears none. No sound of bykes either.

He swings and feels his head begin to bloat. He blinks the blood away, but it continues to drip, and drip, and drip.

'Please,' he manages to croak. His voice is a dry, foreign thing.

He hears one of them expectorate. A wad of red spittle flies and hits the dirt in a small and grotesque explosion of sand. Adam considers the bloodlike splodge and feels the fight seep out of him. He has nothing left.

Dead before the sun sets.

He loses track of time. He swings and swings, in a weird state of semi-consciousness. Now he is asleep. Now he is awake. Now he drifts, somewhere in the middle. There are moments in this dream state when he's lucid and he sees things with clarity.

He knows he must act soon.

Nate swings into sight and panic grips Adam. He struggles, but it's futile. His wrists are fastened so tight behind his back there is no way to dislodge a hand from the rope.

Back and forth he swings in the wind.

No hope in hell.

Adam looks to the upside-down hills and he's certain he sees the flare of a telescope lens. Watchers. Doing what they do best. Watching.

'Nate,' Adam whispers.

Nate groans. He coughs, blinks open his eyes and sees Adam. 'Can't feel my legs,' he says in a rasping voice.

'Me neither.'

'No ... I mean ...' His voice rises in panic. 'I CAN'T FEEL 'EM! They ... they're a bunch a savages ...' Nate begins an incoherent babbling. Snot streams from his nose.

'Shh, Nate. We're OK. It's gonna be fine.'

'I *AIN'T* OK!' he screams, his face turning purple.

'Listen, I know we're in bad shape, but I'll figure a way. They haven't spoken yet and –'

'They *never* speak. YOU SACK OF DIRTY BASTARDS! YOU SAVAGES ...' Nate's words are lost in a slurred frenzy. He sobs and coughs and spits blood.

Adam waits until the only sound is Nate's whimper and the creak of rope.

'Your pa ever tell you how to handle bandits?'

Nate makes a snorting sound – more a cough than a snort. 'Nobody handles a bandit.'

Adam grinds his teeth in frustration.

Nate swings desperately. 'Where the hell are they?'

'Tending to their fire, I think.'

'Are we gonna die?' Nate's voice fades to a whisper.

Adam doesn't answer.

*

The men come on foot to them. The ominous sound of their breathing sends a bolt of fear shooting through Adam. He struggles in his knots of rope and he yells out at them in a hoarse voice.

'I'VE GOT MONEY!' he lies.

They say nothing.

Adam swings and blinks and tries to focus. A bandit stands right in front of Nate with something half concealed in his hand. Nate's knife.

'NOT LIKE THIS!' Adam bawls. '*PLEASE!*'

A mournful sound comes from Nate – a choking, sobbing sound.

'Let him go,' Adam begs, in a quieter voice.

The bandit has a thin, starved face. A scar for a mouth. Taut lips. Cold, hard eyes. Small. Close together. He glances at Adam, swivels back to Nate.

'Adam,' Nate blubbers. His voice is a feeble, broken thing. Light as air. Made of dust.

'It's OK, Nate. We're not gonna die. We're talkin to 'em. They understand.'

The bandits say nothing and their silence is terrifying.

Adam creaks on his rope and sweat falls from him. 'Please. He's just a kid.'

Silence.

'Why? *Why*'re you doin this?'

But he knows the answer, even as he asks.

Because they can. Because life is brutal. Because somewhere along the line one of their brothers was probably killed and this is their retribution, meted out against defenceless Riders.

'I don't believe this is what you want. There's gotta be another way . . . listen to me, I'm beggin you.'

But his pleas go unanswered. Then his worst fear comes true.

The bandit thrusts his fist forward, into Nate. A sharp, upward blow.

Nate grunts, jerks back and swings. Adam screws his eyes shut and holds his breath. He waits for the Blackness to come. Waits for it to slide over him. But there are no certainties. No patterns. One thing doesn't follow the other. He stays awake.

He's about to cry out, one final time, when a dull knocking sound carries to him. A clean sound – like a bat hitting a hard ball. Adam flicks his eyes open. A bandit grunts and, with a loud crash, pitches face first into the dirt. Then a second later a muffled *crack* echoes through the hills. In quick succession, both remaining bandits fall. Each fall is preceded by the same knocking sound, then a grunt, and they come crashing down. From the hills two more distinct staccato sounds.

Crack! Crack!

And silence.

Adam finally falls into Blackness.

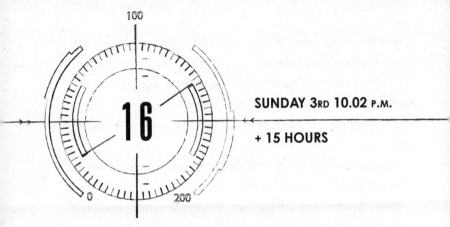

The first thing he hears is the snapping of a fire. The next, a low murmuring of wind and the sound of something flapping. The cold is in his bones and he aches head to foot.

He opens his eyes and sees blurred shapes against a blue-black twilight. He breathes and his breath plumes in the chill. He raises himself on to his elbows and his head pounds and throbs. A wind whips the silver heatkeeper wrapped round him.

Before him sits a figure, hunched at a fire, stoking red embers with a stick.

Adam coughs and struggles up into a sitting position. 'Frank?' The figure turns to him and a pair of yellow eyes burn through the gloom. '*You!*'

Kane looks at him. 'That's right. *Me.*'

Sparks whirl upwards and the flames saw back and forth.

Adam feels a familiar uneasiness. He glances at a shape lying motionless a few yards from the fire, covered to the head in a heatkeeper. A pair of small feet with pitch-black socks pokes out of the bottom. A pale, freckled cheek lies exposed at the top end.

Adam stands and limps to the unmoving shape of Nate. He looks down on him, hands crossed at the chest, pinning the heatkeeper to his shoulders.

'Nate?'

Nate groans and rolls over. He doesn't speak.

'How bad is he?' Adam says, feeling a wave of guilt and relief. He's alive at least.

'It's not good.'

'What do we do?'

'*We?*'

Adam regards the fire. He feels Kane's eyes on him.

'We leave him,' Kane says.

Adam shakes his head. 'We're not leaving him.'

'So how you do you reckon we take him and his byke?'

Adam massages his wrists. They ache to the bone. Even in the half-dark he can see the spiralling rope indentations and the livid blue bruises.

He looks at Kane, in the shadows. 'What happened?'

'Use your imagination.'

'Are they . . .'

'Dead?' He nods. 'Most of 'em. One got away.'

Adam looks at him. 'What were you doin back with the stragglers?'

Kane's eyes blaze from the dark shadows, as though the fire is burning inside him rather than reflected there. 'Biding my time. Gotta know when to make your move. Lucky for you, I guess.'

'I guess.'

Adam looks at his watch. But it's not there.

'Relax,' Kane says. 'Nobody's riding this late. I reckon they're doin a headcount at Camp One and figuring us dead.'

Adam hobbles to the fire and loses himself in the trickery of the flames. He holds out his hands to warm them and looks at the red weals on his wrists. He feels tight and twisted, as if his entire body has been wrung out like a dishcloth.

He stoops for a burnt stick and stirs the embers. 'It was you who cut us down.'

Kane says nothing. Adam looks at him. The features of his face are buried in complete shadow. All he can see is the gleam of yellow eyes and a flash of teeth.

'They steal anything?' he asks. 'Besides my watch?'

'You mean like your byke?' Kane points to three bykes parked on their stands, side by side, throwing strange shadows with the sawing flames.

Adam's Longthorn. Kane's Drifter. Nate's Sunblazer.

'My Race pack?'

'Not much left.' Kane points at a crumpled trio of bags. 'But they were lean to start with. Got nothin but the basics in mine. That and two bottles of pop.'

'Two bottles of pop?'

'Yep.'

Adam shakes his head. 'It don't figure.'

'Nope,' Kane says. 'Nothin much does.'

Adam hurls the stick into the fire and straightens up. 'I don't get it.'

'Get what?'

'You say your name's Kane, but who has just one name? You come and go like smoke. It's like you don't exist. But here you are.'

Kane takes a swig from his canteen and squints at him. 'Here I am.'

Adam stands there, fighting an urge to scream. He's afraid of Kane – of his eyes that see everything – but he can't help admiring him too, even liking him. This admission irritates and frustrates Adam. It's as if Kane were playing him. And he doesn't like being played.

He glares at Kane. 'You say you're from other side the desert, but nobody's ever been to the other side. Not any that came back alive.'

'Riders don't come back from Sky-Base if they win. Doesn't mean it don't exist.'

'Where *were* you? When it mattered?'

'Reckon it mattered when you were swinging upside down.'

Adam balls his fists. 'Where were you *yesterday*?'

'You've got an interesting way of thanking a person.'

'I need to know. Why'd you leave?'

Kane sighs. 'Why does anyone do anything?'

'What kind of an answer is that?'

Kane shrugs and pokes the fire. 'Went to see a man about a horse then.'

Adam shakes his head. 'They *killed* him. Did you know that?'

Kane doesn't speak.

Adam stares at him. 'You *hear* me? They killed *Frank*!'

Kane's eyes flick from the fire to Adam and back again. For a second, the line of his mouth seems to tighten. Just for a second. Then his thousand-yard stare returns.

'I'm sorry,' he says. 'I am. But people die. They get killed all the time.'

Adam stumbles back a step, dizzy and out of breath. 'What kind of person are you?'

Kane looks at him. 'Know what kind of person *you* are?'

'I know enough ... I know right from wrong.'

Kane keeps his eyes fixed on the fire. 'Trust me. You know nothin about yourself till the time comes.'

'What's wrong with you? Why are you like this?'

Kane roots through a pile of dried kindling. The gnarled wood is old and bare and bleached of colour, like a pile of white bones. He picks out a few sticks and feeds the fire.

'S'pose I got bad in me. Bad straight to the bone.'

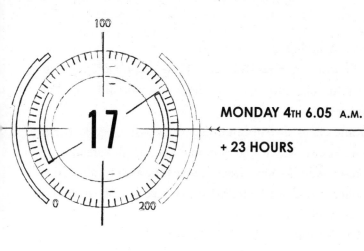

They sleep on their rolled-out mats, taking turns to stoke the fire. When it dies, the darkness is absolute. There are no stars. No moon. No lights to guide them. They wake before dawn, alarmed by some internal clock that understands peril.

'We can fashion a sled from branches,' Adam insists after a breakfast of nutrient biscuit and hydro-pills. 'We can drag him.'

'Won't work,' Kane says, watching streaks of pink and orange light up the sky above hills black as pitch.

'Why not?'

'What about his byke?'

'We can haul 'em both.'

'You forget what this is?'

'I know what it is, but I'll bet we're not the only ones in trouble.'

'Trouble? I'm in no trouble.'

Adam looks at Kane. 'I never did thank you. Not properly.'

'No. You didn't.'

'I'm not sure how you did it. How you took 'em down like that, like they were nothin. But you did and I'm thankful.'

Kane claws dirt-smeared fingers over his shaved head. He makes his way to the motionless shape of Nate.

Adam watches him. Then he scans the area for the limbs of fallen trees. 'We better get moving if we gonna build a sled to haul him.'

'Don't trouble yourself,' Kane says.

Adam feels something twist in his stomach.

'Remember when I said people die?' Kane says, without a change of tone in his voice.

Adam flicks his gaze to the small, dust-covered figure on the ground. Unmoving, like a rock, a part of the desert.

Don't say it. Don't you say it.

'Well, they do,' Kane says. 'They up and die. Just like that.'

They bury Nate's thin body in a shallow grave, dug with byke parts. They work fast. They don't pause and they don't speak and sweat pours from them. Now they stand, looking down at the overturned soil. Adam wonders if they dug deep enough to guard against rooting night animals.

'He didn't deserve it.'

'He's free now,' Kane says. 'Death's his reward.'

Adam shakes his head and stares at the horizon. A line of silhouette sails steeple into the sky. Above them float the airships, moving away, silent and watchful. He pulls a dry energy biscuit from his supply pack, looks at it and throws it into the scrub.

'Why do they have to make it so cruel?'

'Hell. Only reason they don't leave us for good is because they need the Voddenite and us Left-Behind to work the drills till we die. Rest of us are here for entertainment. Pure and simple. We're dogs. Fighting on a chain.'

Adam watches the trykes. Glances up at the silent airships. 'I think they're afraid. Afraid of what we'll do. Look at the bandits: they're savages. Sky-Base would never let 'em up.'

Kane kicks dirt over Nate's grave. Adam watches him and does the same.

'And those Dog Soldiers? Heard they steal babies. Sell 'em to the bandits. Or sacrifice them. Sky-Base wouldn't let them up either.'

'Yep. Dogs are berserk. That's a fact.'

Adam stands with his arms pinned to his sides. Sky-Base is all that's ever sustained him. The place of his dreams. But a seed of doubt plants itself in his brain and he feels it sending out crawling roots. He looks at the mound of earth that holds Nate's body. Dead before his thirteenth summer.

'Where do you think we go?' he says to change the subject. 'When we die?'

'Does it matter?'

'To me it does.'

Kane looks at him. 'S'pose we come back.'

'We come *back*?'

'That's right. We come back and avenge all those who wronged us.'

'And after? After we avenge 'em?'

'Then it ends.'

They stand like this for a long time. Until their thin shadows begin to shrivel across the mound of earth and shrink back into their boots.

'It's my fault he's dead,' Adam says.

Kane shakes his head. 'Hell it is. Kid chose to race. He knew the risk.'

'What choice did he have? It's the Race or the mine.'

Kane squints at the sun. 'We gotta move.'

Adam turns to him. 'You planning on riding with me?'

'Reckon so. Why?'

Adam juts his chin at the grave. 'I've just buried two in two days.'

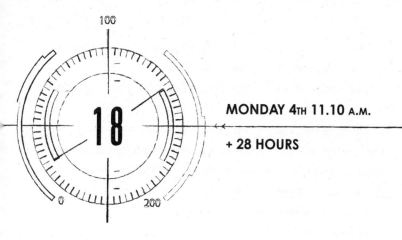

MONDAY 4TH 11.10 A.M.

+ 28 HOURS

The two Riders on their metal horses tremble in the heat. They ride east, through the scorched earth, under the watch of the Sawtooth foothills, out on to the desert plain. Their bykes kick up dust and it trails them, slow and red in the blazing sun. Far away, in the blue distance, lies the dusky shadow of El Diablo. It seems nearby one minute and the next unreachable. A mirage. A trick of the heat. On a flat-out track Adam knows he would arrive at its lava slopes in one day, no more.

But the Blackwater Trail is no flat-out track. It's a mean and twisted loop.

It will be long days under the bare sun before he gets to El Diablo and slingshots round the old volcano, back west towards Blackwater. If he gets there at all.

They settle into an easy rhythm, keeping the pace even and strong. They follow stone Race markers painted white and they don't speak as they ride. Adam feels the heat on his face and the bite of grit. He spreads out his arms and closes his eyes, riding blind and hands-free.

They ride out of sight of the trykes, until they are alone.

Kane's words haunt him. *They up and die. Just like that.*

He feels the loss of Nate like a festering wound. A pain that won't let go. The way Frank's death never relents. Adam chokes back tears. Frank was all the kin he had and the world took him. And now the world has taken Nate. The way the world takes everyone.

Dammit, Nate. You and that stupid knife.

Adam looks at Kane – who rides five or six lengths in front. He sees Kane's sling, whipped back by the wind. But no sign of a knife handle. He tries to think if he saw it in the grave, if they buried Nate with his knife, but he can't think straight.

He throttles hard, flips the gears and stands up off the seat. He powers down a well-tracked road, leaving Kane behind, lost in a screen of dust.

I need air. Need space to breathe.

They come to a broad, sandy valley where granite and sandstone mesas rise sheer-sided and flat-topped. Here the desert shimmers in the heat and stark, silhouette trees float in the haze. Tyre tracks course through the sand, disappearing into the milky distance.

The sky is an opaque pearl colour and the noon sun, stuck at its zenith, blazes cruel and hot.

They pass several wrecked bykes. Four of them. A Backtrail, a Sandblaster, a Rainchaser that won't be

chasing much of anything any more and, last, a lone
Scorcher. The bykes are Riderless, yet to be reclaimed. All
except the last. The Scorcher has a Rider still clinging to
her frame.

They come to a stop.

The Rider doesn't move.

A girl. Her helmet is gone. Her neck is twisted. A stream
of dried blood comes from the corner of her mouth, open
in the rictus of a death leer, as if expressing disgust at
something she's seen. Adam dismounts and places himself
behind the Rider. He crouches low, in her line of sight.

Whatever was there is long gone.

Adam places two fingers to the girl's wrist. No pulse.
The skin is warm.

'It sickens me,' he says, rising.

'It is what it is,' Kane says, still seated on his Drifter.

Adam turns to him. 'You feel nothin?'

Kane shrugs. 'S'pose you want *her* buried too?'

Adam shakes his head. 'I'm done laying people in the
dirt.'

They stand on a rise and survey Camp One, helmets under
their arms, mopping the sweat on their brows. They came
upon the camp quite suddenly – over a rise and into a
sandy valley.

It's deserted. All that remain are flagpoles and their bits
of coloured cloth, flapping in the weak breeze, and the
carnage of byke gear and empty enviro-tents – built to
withstand extreme temperatures. The ground is littered

with trash, a network of criss-crossing tyre tracks and the ash of several fires.

Adam and Kane drift through the camp, looking for signs of life. But all they find is a silent pack of unarmed service GRUBs – first generation – moving through the camp, collapsing tents and clearing garbage. And, looming above them, a digital hoarding. A Race notice.

'They have these at every camp,' Kane says. 'Race stats.'

The sign doesn't make good reading.

CAMP ONE. BLACKWATER TRAIL. MONDAY 4TH RACE STATS. 81 RIDERS RECORDED AT THE STARTING LINE. CURRENT STATUS: 10 DEAD. 5 MISSING, PRESUMED DEAD. CURRENT ODDS FAVOURITE, LEVI BLOOD AT 3:1.

'That'd be us,' Kane says, grinning. 'Missing. Presumed dead.'

But, as they sit looking at the sign, they see the numbers change. The 5 shimmers and flicks to a LED-lit 3.

Adam blinks and rubs his eyes. 'What the . . .'

Kane grins. 'Sign reads our Plugs.'

Adam shakes his head. 'How far behind you reckon we are?' He squints into the distance, holding up a hand to shield his eyes. The stone markers seem to map a course into infinity.

Kane looks down at the tyre tracks. 'Couple hours. No more.'

Adam shifts in his seat and swivels to look behind them, as though seeking some reassurance there. There's nothing in the desolate landscape. Nothing but death. He turns and looks ahead.

An hour's ride down the track they come to the second obstacle course. They slide to a stop and watch. No sign of Riders. The course is constructed between two rising mesas. From an elevated vantage point, they can see it cuts through a narrow pass leading uphill to the High Plains.

An alternative route, one that avoids the obstacle course, leads down to the valley floor. The Lowlands.

'High Plains will be faster,' Adam says, consulting the map.

Kane looks over his shoulder. 'No question.'

Adam squints into the sun. Beyond the entrance, the course makes a sharp dog-leg and the rest of it remains hidden to them. A chute into the heart of darkness. He sees movement.

A salvage crew, going to work picking up Riderless bykes for reconstitution.

'Retrievers,' he says. 'Not a good sign.'

Adam watches the Retrievers load carts behind their sail trykes. He knows they will haul the bykes back to Blackwater and, from there, either sell them for scrap or use Bykemongers like Sadie to reconstitute them. They work in the dark shadow of three waiting airships.

Kane spits and wipes his mouth. 'Think it's true what they say? Sky-Base gives bykes back to your kin?'

Adam shifts in his seat. His saliva is thick. The air feels sorrowful.

He remembers the day well: the Longthorn being returned – unloaded and left at the well. But no Frank. Until he showed up a week later. Minus a leg.

'Yeah, they return 'em. But damaged.'

Adam looks south, to a road that leads down to the valley and the course.

Kane shakes his head. 'Not this one.'

Adam nods. His instincts are buzzing. In silent agreement, they kick in their motors and take the low road.

The haunting call of a carrion bird comes to them and they look up and see a black-winged buzzard, turning slowly on rising thermals. The buzzard's blue shadow ripples over the sand and disappears. Then a familiar glint, thin as a needle. A tower of white jet stream climbs the sky and a faint engine drone carries to them across endless klicks of empty space.

A rocket, blasting its way up off the planet. Up into the unknown.

Kane leans to the side and spits. He wipes his mouth with the back of his hand. They avoided the obstacle course three hours back and both boys are tired.

'Beautiful,' Adam says. 'Seen one close?'

'Once. When I was a kid.'

'How do they work, you know?'

'Something to do with Voddenite, like everything nowadays.' Kane squints at the rocket, knocking back his canteen to take a slurp.

Adam hauls out his own water bottle and shakes it. He's down to the last dregs. He looks at Kane and he can see –

164

by the tilt of his canteen and the weak sloshing sound – he's in the same predicament. Adam knows it will be all hydro-pills from this point forward, but once their supply is depleted ... Death comes quick in the desert without a supply of hydro. Hydro-pills quiet the craving for actual water. A poor substitute for the real thing, but they allow Riders to survive days longer, sometimes weeks.

'We need water,' Adam says, taking a small sip.

'Still got them two bottles of pop.'

'But we need *water*.'

Adam stares into the distance. He sees something move, down on the plain. A wavering smudge. It floats above the surface of the earth and bends in the liquid waves. Appears. Vanishes. Reappears. Then dissolves again.

'See that?'

Kane slakes his thirst, wipes his mouth, replaces the stopper and reaches behind his shoulder to drop the canteen in his Race pack. He keeps staring ahead. 'I see it.'

'A Rider?'

'Has to be.'

They strike out on to the low plain. Their motors purr and their speed is constant and measured. A curl of dust hangs over them and they ride with their helmets stored and their goggles drawn over their red eyes and their air-filter masks covering their dry mouths.

Two outlandish figures, tooling through the dust.

They ride in slow pursuit of the single Rider – up ahead – swimming in the heat haze. The figure floats and drifts in and out of sight. They ride all day after the Rider. All day under the sun. The heat becomes unbearable and they clutch their canteens and take careful sips. They ride until the mesas are black shadows cut out of a blue dusk. Stars come out, cold and bright.

They dismount from their bykes and gather wood for a fire. Across the sands, in the velvet dark, they see a lone, guttering light. A primitive howl carries to them, across the dunes.

'Hear that?' Adam asks.

'I hear it.'

They listen to more howls – plaintive and wild – and they don't speak further.

They eat meat for the first time. A sand rat the size of a small dog that Kane struck dead with one quick slingshot – the raw *crack* of the sling hanging on the cold air. Kane guts the critter with Nate's knife, removed cool and casual from his back pocket. Adam watches him and says nothing.

I knew it. I knew he had it.

Kane skewers the rodent with a sharpened stick – one end to the other – and they roast the evil-looking carcass over swirling flames. Adam smells the meat, hears the popping of the fat and the wood crackling, and his stomach growls.

'It's protein.' Kane hands him a thin sliver of meat in greasy hands. It's charred black and looks as unappetizing as it was alive. Adam takes it all the same.

They chew with slow, grinding jaws, watching the flames, and the other fire of the lone Rider, across the black plain, flickering like a star in the darkness.

Adam wakes at dawn to the sound of Kane relieving himself in the ashes of the fire. The jet of his urine is almost fluorescent yellow. The sky above them is bright orange, a brilliant dome of colour, and the desert comes to life with a surreal glow.

Adam looks out over the plain. Nothing. No movement. 'Where'd the Rider go?'

Kane finishes pissing on the fire, zips up his black riding suit. He squints into the dust and shrugs. 'Out there. Somewhere.'

After a lean breakfast of rat meat leftovers, they ride. The Rider they pursued the day before has vanished. They don't see him throughout the morning. They keep their pace fast and strong. The heat builds and builds until, by midday, the desert is a furnace.

Kane pulls up. He looks at Adam. He squints at the sun. 'Too hot to ride.'

'Can't stop,' Adam says, slowing down. 'Gotta keep moving.'

Kane shakes his head. 'Keep moving and die right now. Gotta know when to stop, when to move. It's a game. And it's a long one.'

They collect sticks to erect their heatkeepers as tarps for the shade and they sit on boulders alongside the track.

Kane removes two bottles of pop from his Race pack. He leans them in turn against the rock and slams down the heel of his palm on their tops, sending their caps spiralling.

'Haven't had one in summers,' Adam says when Kane hands him a sun-warmed glass bottle with its distinctive ridges and hourglass shape. He watches bubbles rise in the dark liquid.

'It's like they're mocking us,' he says.

Kane tilts his head back for a long pull. 'How you figure?'

'Giving us things that aren't available any more. A taste of the way life was.'

'And might be again,' Kane says, pointing to the sky. He burps and takes another slow swig.

They drink in silence, savouring the warm sweetness, each of them in their own private world. When the bottles are drained to the bottom, Kane carries them to a flat stone twenty paces away and places them upright, two inches apart. The two glass bottles stand and reflect the sunlight.

Kane returns, slingshot in hand. He loads a stone in silence. Then he plants his legs apart, turns the knot of the cord round his left ring finger and grips the release cord between his thumb and the second knuckle of his forefinger. He pauses and looks at the bottles.

Neither boy says a word.

Kane swings. Three lazy circles above his head. One . . . two . . . three . . .

Then more. Getting faster and faster. Seven or eight revolutions per second.

One last vicious swing and Kane releases. The sling's braided cord makes a loud *CRACK*! And the stone missile shoots out.

The first pop bottle doesn't just crack and fall, it explodes in a shower of glass. In a blur, Kane loads another stone.

'Hell!' Adam exclaims. 'That bottle didn't just break, it doesn't exist any more.'

Kane squints at him. 'Seen you carry, but never use your sling. You'll hit the bottle, I reckon . . . if you shoot the way you ride.'

Adam shakes his head.

'Might've got you out of trouble,' Kane says. 'If you'd known how to use it before.'

Adam hears the creak of rope, sees Nate hanging upside down in the tree and a pair of shabby boots and dirt-stained jeans before him. 'I know how to use a sling.'

'Thing about a sling,' Kane says, ignoring him, 'you gotta trust it, like you trust a brother.' He gazes down at the cord in his hands and gives a rueful smile.

Adam stoops to collect a stone from deep in his own stone bag. He chooses a walnut-sized pebble, round, grey and smooth. The bag is almost empty.

Kane nods. 'River stone's always best. That's a good one. I'd say one-inch thick. About a half-ounce. Perfect.'

Adam tests the weight of the stone in his hand, worries it around in his palm until the stone is warm against his skin. He places it in the sling pouch and his fingers play with the knot.

'Hold a sling like you hold a woman,' Kane says. 'Loose. And strong at the same time.'

Adam looks at him. Kane shakes his head. 'You ain't done that either, have you?'

'I know what I'm doin.'

Kane grins. His wolf eyes shine.

Adam hauls out his sling and swings it in loops, first above his head and then to the side of his body. He allows his arm to ease into the momentum, to feel the tug of gravity. He waits . . . he waits . . . and waits. Propellers his arm faster and faster, then . . .

CRACK!

The snap of the sling booms loud and the stone flies.

A miss. Nowhere close. If the glass bottle were an enemy, Adam would be in serious trouble. He clamps his jaw shut and fetches another stone from the pouch.

'Sling won't work with anger,' Kane says. 'A sling needs tenderness.'

'How do you figure a slingshot needs tenderness?' Adam snaps.

'You gotta relax. Same as riding. See the flight. The stone's path all the way. See it hit the target. See it all in your head first. Trust the sling. Trust it to do what your brain is telling it. What it *knows* how to do. Breathe easy now. See it done.'

Adam nods. This actually makes sense to him. He stares at the remaining bottle, charting the course to it in his head, the arc of a travelling stone. He calms himself. Fixes on his breathing.

In . . . Out . . . In . . . Out . . .

He begins swinging again. He closes his eyes and gets into the rhythm of the swinging. Gets into *the zone*. Now he opens his eyes again, concentrates hard, eyes trained on the target, all around him a wall of silence. No movement. He keeps swinging. Still slow. Then faster.

Much faster now. A blur, and . . . *CRACK*!

Explosion. A mist of glass. The top half of the bottle smashed. The bottom section still standing on the rock.

'Nice.' Kane walks to retrieve the stone missiles. When he returns, he hands the stones back to Adam and grins. 'Feels good, huh?'

Adam nods and takes them both. He slips one into his pocket, pouches the other and practises swinging again, enjoying the weight of the stone in the cradle, the resistance of the hemp and Voddenite cord, the tug of gravity, the fluid movement of his arm. He could get used to this after all.

'ADAM STONE!' a voice yells.

He jerks his head up, releases the sling and the entire thing flies from his hand – slingshot and stone together.

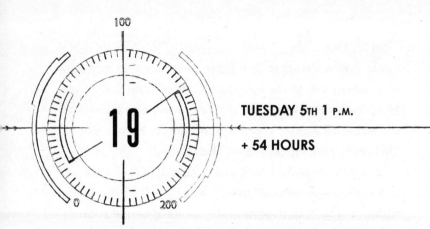

'*Sadie Blood?*'

She sits on a rise astride a jet-black Stormchaser that looks mean as hell. A Stormchaser is a byke built to do just that – hunt down storms. Sadie, like her byke, is layered in a powdery dust. Her goggles perch on top of her head and her hazel eyes have a glaze to them. Her jaw is tight.

'Sadie Blood,' Adam repeats. 'That was *you* out there?' He stands with his hands dangling at his sides, staring at her.

Kane takes a step towards her. 'Hell are you doin here?'

Sadie blinks and licks her lips. She looks exhausted. 'I saw you pitch camp behind me. Figured I'd double back. See who you are.' She glances at Adam. 'Just to be safe.'

Sadie darts a look behind her, over her shoulder.

Adam senses palpable fear in her. Something primal. 'What's wrong?'

She swivels back to him. 'Have you seen them?'

'Seen who?'

'They followed me. They're out there. Haven't you heard them?'

'Heard *who*?'

'Not who. *Wolves.*'

Nobody speaks.

'A person can outride a wolf,' Kane says finally.

Sadie flashes him a look. 'Not these ones.' She turns to Adam. 'Thought you ride alone.'

'Well, I was . . . but, see, I –'

'It doesn't matter,' she says. 'We have to go. We have to go now!'

They burst on to the plain with a white sun at its peak in the giant sky. They pass rock piles, clumps of bare trees and looming mesas that cast no shadow. The heat is colossal.

'THE VALLEY OF A THOUSAND DEAD SONS!' Sadie yells as they ride.

The wind screams in their ears and their bykes rattle beneath them. Adam is acutely aware of one distinct noise – a terrifying yapping and howling behind them. He swivels in his saddle. And sees them.

The wolves come in a loping, ragged run. He can see the glint of their eyes and the white flash of teeth. He tries to count them. *Eight? Ten? Maybe even a dozen.*

A huge animal leads the pack. It jags across the sand with black lips bared, snout rippled, and muscles taut on its shoulders – a mean thing, of skin and bone . . . and teeth.

'RIDE!' Adam yells, seized with terror. 'RIDE LIKE HELL!'

And that's what they do, the three of them: they ride like hell with the animals coming after.

Adam feels the burn in his muscles as he powers his Longthorn through the ever more parched terrain. Sadie's Stormchaser is a slick machine. She clicks and purrs as she navigates the cracks and rocks. Kane's Drifter goes hard and strong, as ever.

Adam looks over his shoulder and he sees the wolves dropping back. Dropping back, but not giving up – the lead wolf yaps to urge them on. Adam turns and rides for his life.

They go hard for a long time. He has no idea how long. All he knows is that he reaches a point of exhaustion. He sucks a ragged breath from his air-filter mask and looks behind. No sign of the wolves. But they're out there, beyond the sand rises; he can hear the yips and howls.

'We can't keep this pace up,' he shouts.

Kane arches his neck to look behind. He pulls his brakes and skids. Adam does the same.

'They never let up,' Sadie wheezes, when she too comes to a stop. She licks her lips. '*Never.*'

'Wolves don't do that,' Adam says, casting about, looking for a way out. 'They don't track people, do they?'

'They're hungry, is all,' Kane says. His expression is neutral.

Sadie breathes hard. 'Still sure about outriding them?'

Howls rise up. Loud and close.

Kane doesn't answer. 'Seen a cabin,' he says, pointing to the east. 'Bound to be deserted out here. If we can make it there, we can hold 'em off. Long as it takes.'

Adam follows his gaze and, sure enough, diminished in the distance, a small brown speck. Nothing at first glance. But it isn't nothing.

'Might be bandits.'

'Bandits don't live in cabins.'

'You know that for certain?' Sadie asks.

There's no time for response. As if conjured up, they come bursting over a rise. All of them together. Eyes lit up, swarming forward. A pack of devils.

Adam feels a spike of fear. He kicks in his motor and blazes. Seconds later he turns in the saddle. Sees Sadie lagging behind. A wolf close at her heels.

'HEY!' he bawls and jags towards them.

He drives hard at the wolf. Throws the Longthorn into a last-second jackknife turn. The byke screams. A spray of sand and rock. The wolf snarls, arches and leaps back. Adam jerks away. But he's lost ground. Now *he's* the one lagging.

'Get to the cabin,' he shouts to Kane and Sadie ahead. 'I'll lead 'em away.'

Sadie turns in her seat and stares at him.

He doesn't wait for an answer. He wheels his byke round and goes back the way they came. With a quick glance behind, he sees Sadie and Kane throwing up dust, hurtling to the hut. Howls rise up and turn his blood to ice. The wolves come after him. Adam swivels forward and flies.

Stupid. What've I done? Leaving Sadie with him.

He shakes his head to silence the roar.

Keep it together. You gotta keep it together.

He didn't have time to think. That's all. It was instinctual. He knows he has to trust his gut and his gut tells him Kane will keep Sadie safe.

Or will he? Trust no one, Frank said.

He turns in his saddle. Feels a fresh wave of panic.

Where the hell are they?

He can't see the wolves.

He needs a plan, but nothing comes to him. Only fear. A twisting knot in his stomach. He rides hard, freewheels, stands up off his seat. Then he sees them.

They come spearheaded by the big one – the leader. It sees Adam, glares at him with furious eyes. It throws a wild look behind and yips to urge on the others. There are seven of them. Not twelve.

Even in his terror, he is struck by their beauty. The sleekness and the silence of their run, their bony limbs moving with such symmetry. Each wolf a thing of no wasted flesh. Every fibre bent to the task, ruled by the moon and assembled by a common desire. Blood.

The lead wolf snaps its jaws and a thin stream of saliva spins from its white teeth. It gives him a look of unconcealed ferocity. There is no pity in this beast.

Adam jacks hard right and flies up a slope. He ramps a rise, sails into the air and lands with a jolt. His back wheel spins out, but he manages to pull the Longthorn in and steadies himself.

He knows if they get hold of him there'll be nothing left. They'll strip his flesh to the bone in minutes. They took out an entire coop of Frank's hens one night. Left nothing but blood-matted feathers stuck to the wires. They took one of Old Man Dagg's last remaining pigs. All he found were their tracks, pools of congealed blood and a single hoof – half chewed and discarded.

Gotta focus. Can't fall.

He blasts out on to the plain, sending dust spiralling into the air, carving a new path through the sand. He tears through a ditch and flies up the other side. He scrambles round a cairn of rock and heads for a grove of acacia rising out of swaying plain grass, zigzagging as he goes.

Thorns! Acacia have thorns long as fingers, sharp as daggers.

Adam turns, looks back, sees them coming. Still coming. He cuts a path through the sudden swathe of long grass, burnt brown by the sun, rising to his waist. He can't see the shape of the ground beneath him and he rides blind.

Seven invisible shapes burrow swift through the grass behind him in a violent rustle. Snaking out and swooping in like giant burrowing worms.

The grass peters out and he flies down on to a flat, sandy stretch. There is nothing in front of him – nothing but sand and sun and waves of heat. The air is thick and humid now and the sky dark with billowing storm clouds. A weird light makes the sand ochre against the bruised and brooding sky.

Adam rides in a weaving pattern, feeling himself slow, feeling the byke lose speed.

A flash of coruscating light.

A booming clap of thunder.

It begins to rain. Fat drops, slamming into the sand. The skies unleash a torrent. The rainwater reinvigorates him and he goes with fresh legs. But not for long.

The sand churns into mud so thick it flies up and hits him in the chest. Mud that clogs and sticks and sucks at his byke. His front wheel fixes dead with a suddenness that shocks him and he jerks forward, over the handlebars, flailing through the rain-soaked air.

All in seconds.

He's on his hands and knees, staring down at the mud, the rain streaming from his sodden clothes. He looks up and he sees the Longthorn, upside down, with a spinning wheel showering sparks of rainwater. It's ten yards away. Adam hears a low growl. He freezes, heart hammering in his chest, then turns. He is surrounded.

The wolves pad back and forth. The rain pours and runs slick over their patchy fur. They encroach on him as a violent storm would a battered island. In waves. First one, then another. They snipe forward, snapping and spitting, frothing at the mouth. Time loses meaning. Seconds are minutes. Minutes hours.

Adam wheels to face each assault, adrenalin pumping through his body. He stays on his hands and knees. Like a dog.

'GET AWAY!' he shouts. 'GET BACK!'

He crawls and he snarls and he throws handfuls of mud that fall short.

'YOU BASTARDS! YOU DAMN *BASTARDS*!'

Then he barks at them. A crazed dog bark.

'*RHRAFF! RHRAFF RHRAFF RHRAFF!*'

The sound bursts from him without warning. It springs from somewhere inside, some deep well of pain, and it explodes out in a strange high pitch.

For a brief moment, the wolves stand and stare. Their ears prick up and they eyeball him, as though seeing some new prey here. Then they shake off the doubt and tread the mud channels, growling. The lead wolf comes forward, shoulder bones spiked up, back slunk low. It reaches out with splayed front paws, testing the ground.

Adam fishes in his back pocket. He hauls out a stone in his dripping, muddy hand and collects his sling from his belt, every inch of him shaking with fear. He rises slowly off his hands and sits back on his boot heels, keeping his eyes on the wolf. With fumbling fingers, he places the stone in the slingshot cradle and wraps the knotted end of cord round the forefinger of his right hand. In his left he conceals the stone in the sling cradle.

The wolf advances, snarling and baring its teeth.

Adam begins to swing and the animal stops – not ten yards from him – one short leap away. Adam thinks of Kane and how he smashed the pop bottle. He concentrates all his attention on the small rectangle of space between the wolf's eyes. The wolf prances and yips.

Adam swings, and swings, and swings . . . and *CRACK!* He releases.

The stone wobbles into the maelstrom, curving away. It hits nothing. The wolf springs back and forth, agitated, yipping and barking. Adam loads another stone.

Two more. Two more stones . . . And then? What then?

The sky lights up and all the wolves are caught in sharp focus, bright and drenched and full of teeth. Adam glances at his byke – out of reach. Then gloom again. A clap of thunder rips through the sky and echoes all around.

He loads the second stone. Aims, swings and fires.

CRACK!

Once again, the stone loops wide and out of sight.

The wolves pace and spring with pricked-up ears. Another white flash, another thunderclap, and the rain hammers down.

One stone. One left. Gotta make it count.

His shaking hand brings the last stone to the cradle. He fumbles and the stone falls into the mud. He falls forward, searching for it, frantic, scrambling. The wolves edge closer. Here comes the lead wolf. A creature of the plain. A terrible beast. Beautiful. Savage. Wild.

Adam finds the stone, on his stomach in the mud. He flips on to his back and kicks backwards, slipping and scrabbling, watching the wolf coming at him. A few yards now. One clean strike.

But there are seven . . . and I've got only one stone.

He is guided by a single thought. If he kills the leader, the rest will scatter.

He swings the sling like a propeller above his head. Three, four, five times. The wolf stops, looks at him, sniffs the air with flared nostrils. It quivers with anticipation. Black lips pulled back, teeth gleaming white. Eyes blazing.

Adam fixes his attention on the stone, willing it to find the target, projecting the flight path in his mind. All the way from the sling to the wolf. Covering a distance of four, maybe five yards in under a tenth of a second.

The world flashes white with lightning and Adam releases.

CRACK!

Thunder booms and the ground shudders. In the fierce light, he sees the stone go wide. Adam shuts his eyes and waits. A strange calm has settled on him. Then another burst of light, behind his eyelids. He opens his eyes and here is the wolf, all teeth and bone and wildness.

He pushes himself back and his hand closes round a jagged rock. The wolf growls and Adam squeezes the rock in his fist . . .

And the Blackness comes.

It comes fast. It runs through him. Dots of light appear. The curl of pain in the back of his skull. The blur at the edges of his vision. He can't stop it. He can't shove it back.

No! Please, no!

He is powerless to stem the tide. A wave of darkness rolls over him. He feels it cut him down at the knees. He feels the crushing weight on his shoulders. Then nothing. The wolf warps and recedes into black.

A bad feeling pulls him from the dark. A spurt of fear. Adam flicks open his eyes in a panic. It's teeth he expects. But what he sees instead is the shape of the lead wolf, laid out on the ground.

Dead.

The rest of the wolves are gone.

Adam uncoils, drags himself up from the mud. He stands bowed in the deluge, shivering.

There's something trapped in the wolf's teeth and blood leaks from it. The side of the wolf's head is bashed to a red pulp. Bits of stone are stuck in the ragged skin. Adam sways in the rain and sees the bloodied rock lying in the mud.

He tries to swallow and tastes iron in his thick saliva. He feels dizzy and his head throbs. Painful cramps twist in his stomach. Every part of him aches. He wipes the water from his face with his hand and blood drips into his eye. He staggers through the mud to his byke, feeling stunned.

He reaches for the byke handlebars and that's when he sees. His left hand is a mess of blood and gore. And worse. Something is missing. Something that ought to be there. That has always been there.

His thumb.

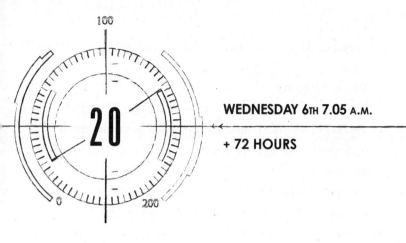

He wakes with a start. Sits upright, blinking, trying to get his bearings. He's on a hard bed. It smells of mould. He coughs and glances round a gloomy room. Curtainless windows, smeared with dirt, give a dim light. A candle, guttering on the table, illuminates plank flooring and stone walls. Exposed wooden beams criss-cross the roof. The room stinks of wax and dead things.

'You were having a nightmare,' someone says behind his shoulder. Adam spins round.

Sadie. Holding a tin mug in her hand. 'You were crying and shaking.'

He blinks and stares, as though he's come up from Blackwater Lake and seen a herd of antelope taking water.

'Relax. It's *me*.'

'What happened?' he croaks. 'Where . . . where am I?'

'In the cabin,' Sadie says. 'The one we saw.' She sits on a rough wooden stool next to his bed. One leg crossed at the ankle over her knee, the way a man sits. She looks cool and unflustered. In control again – the way she was before the wolves.

'How'd I get here?'

She shakes her head and extends the mug. 'It's water.'

He takes it in his trembling right hand. 'Some nightmare.' He brings the mug to his lips with both hands. 'I dreamt I lost . . .'

He stops short. The bandage covers his entire left hand. It's clipped tight with a pin and it feels numb. Adam freezes, turns the bandaged hand. Sees a brown stain in the cotton wrap.

'I used my med kit,' Sadie says. 'Treated the tissue with a cauterizing iron and disinfectant spray. But you'll need sutures.' There's no shock in her voice.

Adam feels a twist of panic in his gut. He says nothing. Just stares at the bandage and takes a careful sip.

Sadie watches him. 'You OK? You're right-handed, aren't you?'

He looks at her over the rim of the mug. 'It doesn't hurt. Why doesn't it hurt?'

'It won't. Not for a while. Gave you a morphine jab. It'll hurt like hell later.'

'Got needle and thread for the sutures?'

She shakes her head.

He looks at his bandaged hand. The brown stain marks the place where his thumb should be. Where his thumb won't ever be again. He takes another long sip. The water is cool and sweet and feels like honey running down his throat.

'Take it easy. You'll get sick. You've lost a lot of blood.'

He drains the mug anyway and places it on the floor. 'Who lives here?'

Sadie plucks off her red bandanna. Slides it from her head. 'I don't know. No one, I guess.'

He stares at her. She's drop-dead beautiful. Hair or no hair. Some people are lucky that way. Their heads are beautifully shaped. Others have lumps and dents. Hers is perfect.

He looks away to keep from staring too hard. 'I can't remember what happened. I think . . . I think I must've blacked out and –'

'You rode here. Your byke's outside. I woke up in the other room and found you on the floor, and your hand . . . I can't exactly remember getting here myself. It's all a blur.'

He rolls the stiffness from his neck and pictures the wolf: the yellow eyes, the snarls, the teeth. He sees it slinking through the rain. Then the flash of lightning and sheets of rain. Thunder pounding like cannon shot. The rock in his fist and the wolf dead at his feet.

A vague memory of climbing, bone-tired, on to his byke. Drifting through the dunes. Riding one-handed, clutching his left hand to his chest, reeling with shock and pain. Finding the cabin, lit up in a flute of sunlight from a gap in the clouds. A Jacob's ladder to the sky.

Falling at the door.

Sadie looks at him. 'What you did out there . . . leading the wolves away like that. It was stupid. But it was brave.'

Her expression is difficult to read. Somewhere between respect and reproach. It's not the sort of expression someone can easily fake if they're just *trying* to be sincere. It feels real. But there's an edge of wariness in her look too. She's keeping her distance.

Adam shrugs, as if her acknowledgement doesn't mean much to him, but inside he swells with pride. Sadie Blood thinks *he's* brave.

'Where's Kane?' he says, changing the subject, immediately annoyed with himself for bringing *him* back into the conversation.

'He left.'

'Where'd he go?'

'He was gone when I woke.'

Adam shakes his head. 'He's a ghost. He appears and disappears. Like the damn rain.'

Sadie stares out of the window, as though expecting to see him there. 'Who *is* he?'

Adam feels a stab of jealousy in his heart. 'Hell should I know?'

'It doesn't matter. We have to go.' She turns to him. 'Can you ride?'

He stares at his bandaged hand and doesn't answer.

'You can't quit,' she says. 'They'll Unplug you.'

'They'd never find me. I'd disappear.'

'Don't be an idiot. They'd do it remotely. They wouldn't need to find you. You saw what the Colonel did. Just pushed a button and –'

'The Plug deactivates. Everyone knows that. After the Race is over. Frank told me. He –'

A loud bang interrupts them and they turn and see the door flung wide open. A swirl of grit flies into the room. A silhouette figure stands in the doorway, a bright sky behind him.

'What are you doin?' a voice barks.

Sadie leaps from her chair. Adam fumbles for his sling.

'Better kill me quick,' the voice says.

The glare outside is fierce and Adam visors his eyes with a hand and squints into the light. He feels an ache where his thumb should be. His eyes adjust to the brightness.

'Kane,' he says. 'Hell you been?'

Kane moves into the room, dipping his head under the door frame. 'Scouting.' He lifts a foot-long, rusted knife from a dust-strewn counter. Runs a finger along the edge. 'So. Planning on leaving without me?'

He grins and throws the knife from one hand to the other.

'They took his thumb,' Sadie says, still standing.

Kane nods and looks away. 'Wolves are liable to do that.'

'Is everything a joke to you?'

Adam sees Kane smile in the mottled window reflection. 'Why are you riding the Blackwater?' he says, turning to Sadie. 'Don't you have a Bykemonger Station to look after?'

Sadie shakes her head. 'Colonel took it back the same day Levi came around.'

'I'm sorry,' Adam says. 'I should've –'

'He's an animal. You saw what he did at the start. And Levi is just like him ... maybe worse.' Her voice falters. She clamps her jaw shut and stares out of the door.

Kane flings the knife across the room into empty space. It embeds itself in the wooden wall of the hut with a startling *thud*, shuddering there. 'Enough. Time to ride.'

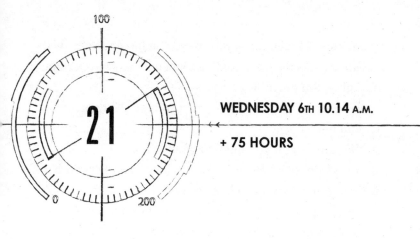

The desert bakes. Layered in a film of dust, they labour across the sand. The barren landscape blurs and swims in the heat. Adam squints into the sun, shielding the glare with his bandaged hand. He feels exhausted. Light-headed. The effort required to ride is overwhelming. Sweat runs from his temples. Each stone under his byke delivers a jarring ache along his spine.

He leans forward. A sharp pain rips through his hand. His thoughts are haphazard. The ground tilts. He looks at the bedraggled bandage and pulls it tight with his teeth.

The wound is a problem. He's not worried about infection – the cauterizing would have stopped bacteria taking root – it's his balance. His natural rhythm is upset. The rhythm he's always taken for granted.

It's gone.

He feels unsteady on his byke. Out of control. With no opposing thumb for grip, his hand keeps slipping. Nothing is the same. He glances at the others and he can see by their sidelong looks that he's holding them up. They haven't said anything. But he knows.

Sadie drops back and rides next to him. 'All right?'

'I'm fine.'

'We can stop, if you like. We're –'

'I said I'm fine.' He accelerates and pushes beyond her, feeling foolish, riding close behind Kane, who doesn't acknowledge his presence. He feels his face flush hot.

Gotta find a way. There's no growing a new thumb.

He concentrates. Pushes down the panic in his chest. Searches for the old zone feeling. He grips with his right hand, his good hand. With his injured left, he pushes the heel of his palm against the handlebar. He almost shrieks. The pain is fierce and quick as whiplash. He clenches his jaw and feels tears spring to his eyes.

Where are you, Frank? I need you.

They come to rest in the shade of a screwbean mesquite. Kane stretches. He leaps up, hangs on a branch and performs ten quick chin-ups, his body rigid, his back arched. Sadie rolls her neck and watches him. Adam drops to the ground and sits with his legs crossed, not speaking.

'What do you think?' Sadie says, unfolding her Race map. She flattens it out on the ground, flicking away stones and tan-coloured, twisted seeds.

Kane swings down from the tree. He crouches and consults the route with her. Adam watches them.

Sadie plants her forefinger down on the map, pinning it to the ground. 'I reckon we're about here. On the edge of the Valley of a Thousand Dead Sons.'

Kane leans across her to study the map. Adam drags himself closer.

Sadie moves a slender finger along the route. Her skin is dark and her fingernails pale. She indicates an area near Camp Three. 'Race leaders will be here.'

Kane nods. 'So we'll take the third obstacle course. That removes the fourth from play.'

Sadie points to a spot where the contour lines come swirling together. 'But taking the third course means we'll be forced through this area.'

Adam looks at the bunched up contour lines. 'That's a ravine.'

Kane tilts his head. 'A steep one. No way down most likely. We'll have to jump it.'

Sadie slides her finger across the ravine and meets the dotted line of the Trail. 'On the other side, we'll connect with the main track to Camp Four. The last camp.'

'Right,' Kane says. 'It's a massive shortcut.'

Uncertainty flickers in Sadie's eyes. 'But . . . no Riders in their right mind will take that route. We'll be alone.'

Kane stands and brushes the dust from his black riding suit. 'You afraid?'

She shakes her head. 'No. There's no other option.'

'They say you go in there, you don't come out. Might as well be a black hole.'

'Why?' Adam asks.

'Because that's Nakoda territory.'

Nakoda. A word seared into Adam's brain as a boy. The worst kind of people anywhere. Witches, sorcerers . . . and cannibals. 'They don't exist,' he says.

Kane grins and saunters over to his Drifter. 'Course they don't.'

Adam stands. Too quickly. He waits for a sudden head rush to fade.

Then he turns to Sadie. 'Sadie, I –'

'Don't worry about the Nakoda. We'll outride them . . . *if* they even exist.'

'It's not that. It's . . . When you found us . . . you were alone. Why? After you gave *me* a hard time for riding alone.'

She folds the map, stands and looks at the horizon. She fixes the red bandanna on the perfect dome of her shorn skull. 'I wasn't. I was riding with two kids from the shop. It's just me now.'

Adam understands the implication. 'I'm sorry. About everything. Your shop. I can't believe the Colonel took it back. After all the work you put in. What you did for my byke . . .'

He leaves the sentence adrift and watches Sadie fight with the straps of her pack, tugging at them in frustration.

Adam kicks at the dirt. 'Why didn't the Colonel . . . your *pa* . . . ever use his money and power to get up to Sky-Base?'

Sadie turns and glares at him, pulls the straps tight. 'He was offered a place. For him *and* his kin . . . D'you know what he said? He said he'd rather stay. Stay and run Blackwater the way they wanted. He condemned us all to short lives. That's the kind of man he is. Kin is nothin.'

'Yeah, like my pa.'

'No. Nothin like your pa. Your pa ever force your brother away?'

Adam knows about Sadie's oldest brother. Joe Blood. They say the Colonel treated him so mean he up and left one day. Just walked out. Into the desert. Didn't even take a byke. He never returned.

'Pa might as well have taken Frank away. He'd still be here if Pa hadn't killed himself.'

Sadie shakes her head. 'You don't get it, do you? Your pa loved you. He worked the mine for you. He cared about you. My pa? He's a murderer. Only thing he cares about is himself.'

The riding is no easier. Adam sweats and struggles with his grip. His missing thumb is beginning to look like more than just a liability. It's beginning to look like a disaster.

He fights the Longthorn. And the byke fights back. It's as if the byke is annoyed with him. And on top of that Frank's echo has abandoned him. He's alone. Even Sadie and Kane seem to have separated from him, riding side by side up ahead. Adam curses under his breath. Fatigue and bitterness take hold. He shuts his eyes.

How much longer can I last?

That's when he feels an unsettling prickle along his skin. A shift in the air density. Then the sudden, unmistakable presence of someone with him on the byke. A voice enters his consciousness. It shudders up through the machine. Not Frank. Someone else.

I'm with you, Adam.

The nearness of the echo is profound. Adam can almost feel breathing on his neck.

He flicks open his eyes. 'No! You don't have the right to be here. You left us.'

The voice moves through the machine. It vibrates in his head.

I didn't leave. I'm right here.

Adam pushes down the heel of his left palm. Ignores the flash of pain. Holds his breath in anger. *Why are you afraid? Stop fighting. Go to that place you know. Breathe.*

He shakes his head and grits his teeth, but takes a deep breath anyway. He feels the pull of the hot wind. Listens to his heartbeat. Drifts away.

Warm skin. A shout of joy. Spring desert flowers. The smell of cedar. A red kite in a pale sky. It dips and snaps. Loops manically. They follow the kite through a field. His hand in Pa's hand. Frank running ahead.

The day and all its sensations flood back to Adam. That's when he feels the byke again. All the infinite vibrations of the Longthorn. A byke passed from his pa to his brother to him. Carrying with her all their memories and feelings, like strands of DNA. He feels their power and their strength. He feels their frailty.

And he falls into a new rhythm with the byke. He goes to a place of light where the byke syncs with him. A secret collusion. A different dimension. He opens the throttle and goes like the wind.

He's in *the zone*.

*

Airships. Floating over the desert. It can mean only one thing: the third obstacle course. Here they see a scattering of Riders, ploughing into the entrance. Watchers up above like vultures at a kill. They have arrived at the nub of their decision, an hour's ride after Sadie hauled out the map

The course is lethal. Adam can see that at first glance. A series of tight turns and radical dirt jumps, leading into a narrow, perilous section, built on towering stilts, high up in the air. A thin, snaking wooden bridge, wide enough for one byke only, with no barriers either side.

The fall? Fatal.

As if to prove his thinking right, he sees a Rider, alone, high up. They watch him navigate the narrow wall with skill. A good pace. Not fast. Not slow. Then painfully slow, grinding almost to a standstill.

He applies his front and back wheel brakes to control the byke, hopping from one narrow angle to another. Then disaster. He misjudges. The byke wobbles.

The Rider struggles to compose himself.

He falls.

There. Gone. All in seconds.

The fall is soundless. Rider and byke together, through the air. No scream. No shout. Nothing. Absolute silence. Just an object, plummeting through space.

Then a puff of dust. A faint thud. Another life taken.

'The hell with this!' Adam yells.

He charges towards the entrance, gunning the Longthorn's motor hard. Sadie and Kane burn after him, their bykes swift and slick in his wake. First Sadie. Then Kane.

The first jump they hit through the chute entrance is a giant, fin-shaped wall. It curves up at an angle, almost reaching ninety degrees. Adam leaps into space and lands with a punch of his shock absorbers. Perfect. They rip through a deep channel and fly into the next jump, a showpiece booter – about forty yards long, with a fifteen-yard-tall lip and a twenty-yard-tall landing slope.

Adam shunts down the slope – floats in the air – looks below, mid-jump.

The forty-yard space between jump lip and landing slope is embedded with wooden spikes. A Rider impaled below. Adam looks back over his shoulder.

Sadie is up and over. Then Kane. He boosts up and wrenches the Drifter backwards, executing a radical backflip. Insane. No fear. He lands with a slight wobble, pulls the byke straight and keeps going.

Adam looks forward. Head down, going hard. The course is fast. They blaze through at massive speed. Adam's bandaged hand jars and the pain is fierce. But he feels stronger, more connected to the byke. The Longthorn has learned to compensate. She pulls harder to the left now, guiding his injured hand. Almost taking over. Controlling his body in the sharp left turns.

They twist into the raised platform section. The pace slows. They snake along the narrow wooden path. Adam sweats and keeps focused. The drop either side is terrifying.

He slows to a crawl, applies the brakes. Hops from one section to another. Every sense tuned to the moment. He turns a corner and sees Sadie, behind him. Her front wheel teeters an inch from the edge. She slips.

'SADIE!' he shouts into his helmet.

She brakes. Comes to a complete standstill. Then she pulls her byke back on track. Adam watches her edge across the wooden bridge section. The planks of the bridge lurch and sway. Each movement of her byke causes a ripple along the length of the platform.

Adam cruises through the last few bends. The path widens. He's out!

Sadie comes sailing through. Kane is a length behind. Then he's out the other side.

They drop back down into a steep dirt chute. The byke roars under Adam. He hits top speed coming into the final jump. He swoops into the lip and launches high into the air, manoeuvring the byke under him. He sees it, a subtle glint in the sun. A line running straight across the landing slope. Waist high.

This time he's ready. This time he's focused. This time he thinks about the Rider behind him. And the one behind her.

'WATCH OUT FOR THE WIRE!' he bawls, his voice snatched away.

Adam closes his eyes. He lands with a jolt and he looks back.

Inches. That's how close he came. If he'd hit the jump any slower, it would have taken him. No question. Sadie flies over the wire and disappears in a scarf of dust. She makes it. And so does Kane.

The three Riders burst out of the far side of the obstacle course, whooping and hollering in the dust. They slide to a stop and look at each other, eyes filled with light.

'Hell!' Adam shouts. 'Nate would've got a kick out of that!'

'Who's Nate?' Sadie asks, breathing hard.

He looks at her, feeling a surge of relief and adrenalin pumping through his body. And something else. Camaraderie. A slow bloom of belonging.

'Just some kid,' he says. 'Some kid I liked.'

They blaze north, into a shimmering heat that bends trees. They ride through a white haze and come to a plain strewn with desert flowers by the millions – cantaloupe-coloured, mustard and fuchsia – blooming despite the heat, somehow surviving.

Adam floats. The desert is quiet. The kind of stunned quiet he knows at the height of a jump, that in-between state.

They ride up beyond the flowers on to a high, arid plateau with scattered rocks, strewn like grey teeth. The wind moans. It hauls up dirt and flings it at them. In the distance, they see a wall of copper-coloured sand. And the light turns amber then brass-coloured.

Warning lights flash red on their instrument panels. Bad weather. A rotten egg smell carries to them.

'Sulphur storm!' Adam shouts. He pulls out the map to get his bearings and a sudden gust snatches it from him. All three watch it dance away, like a paper aeroplane. No one says a word.

They flounder forward, into the wind, and are swallowed in dust.

Now the wind settles and dies altogether. The air is close and hot. They drift through the sulphur dust, leaving swirling vapour trails of yellow smoke. Adam concentrates hard. His focus is absolute.

Dust hangs in the air, thick as fog. The sun is an obscured halo and sounds become distorted, as though they're making their way across a body of water. There's a weird expectancy in the silence.

The desert waits. Adam's instincts kick in and he waits with the desert.

The ground climbs under him. His instincts crackle and spit. A bad feeling crawls in his neck. The same bad feeling he got just before shooting over that jump with Nate. The jump that hid the gut-wire. This time Adam listens.

He jerks the Longthorn to a sliding, wheel-spinning stop. Two shadows, next to him, do the same. The dust billows.

'What's the matter?' Sadie yells.

Adam stretches forward, over the handlebars, and points.

They squint through the settling dust and they see it. A yawning chasm. Their bykes not five yards from a drop that disappears into darkness.

Adam dismounts, boots a stone over the edge and leans forward to watch it fall. It vanishes without a sound. They wait and they hear nothing.

'The ravine,' he says.

'How did you know?' Sadie asks him.

Adam shrugs. 'I just knew.'

He follows the edge and sees a strip of land, like a peninsula, jutting out from the edge, extending over the void. The ground of the peninsula rises steeply to a lip – a natural jump.

'Might be big enough to launch us over.'

'We can't even see the other side,' Sadie says.

'We can make it,' Kane says, squinting into the dust. 'We'll go together.'

They turn and ride back sixty yards. Then they bring their bykes around and wait, trying to pierce the gloom.

'Don't think,' Kane says. 'Just ride. GO!'

They put their heads down and ride low-slung and taut. Hard. Fast. Determined. All three together. They come quickly to the strip of land. Adam blinks and sweats. The far side is a blur. He powers upwards, vaguely aware of the lip coming.

He feels the jump. Senses the gulf beneath him. He looks down. The fall is sickening. His stomach lurches. He thinks about Sadie. Wills her up and over.

He sails. Then down he comes. Fast as a flung stone from a Voddenite sling. The byke smashes into the earth. Brutal force. Front wheel first. Air punches from his lungs.

He pulls the handlebars and shifts his weight, but the byke goes under him. He flies. Waits for the impact. Pain hits like a lightning shock. And the world turns to black.

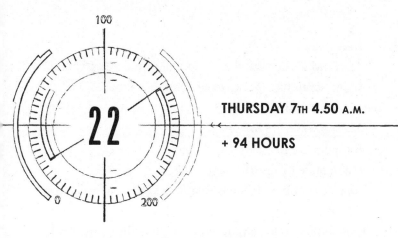

He sits bolt upright. A searing pain tears through his hand and his ankle. Something sharp strikes the back of the head and he spins round. A branch, protruding from some kind of structure, rope-lashed and covered in tarpaulin. Lit by candlelight. The air smells perfumed – oil or incense. It's hot and close. His heart hammers and his mouth is dry. He licks his lips and breathes, light and fast.

Then he senses movement.

In the vague light, at an open flap-door, stand three figures. There's an other-worldly strangeness about them. The air seems to shift in the tent.

The foremost figure extends a hand.

'GET BACK!' Adam yells in a hoarse voice. 'I'm warning you. Stay back or I'll . . . I'll –'

'You'll what?' The figure with the offered hand steps from the shadows. Most of his face is hidden in darkness. But eyes are visible, gleaming yellow in a band of flickering candlelight.

'Kane.'

'That's what they call me. Took your time coming round.'

Adam scrambles back, feeling for his sling. 'Who are these people with you?'

'These people are *my* people.'

'But who are they?'

'Nakoda. Who else?'

Total fear knifes through Adam. 'SADIE!' he yells, top of his voice.

Kane holds up his hands. 'Take it easy. She's safe. I told you. They're my people.'

The figures bend their heads and vanish through the low door, without a sound.

Adam stares after them. '*Your* people?'

'That's right,' Kane says.

'Then you're a cannibal.'

Kane grins. 'Yep. That's it. A cannibal. Should've carved you up long ago.' He pulls out Nate's knife. Then he steps forward and the polished ceramic gleams. Adam shrinks back, but the yurt branches tip his head forward.

Kane laughs and pockets the knife. 'Watch yourself.'

Adam launches to his feet. A sharp pain lances his ankle and he howls and reaches down to feel the swelling. His fingers probe a sticky green substance.

'Poultice,' Kane says. 'Chopped-up leaves mulched with spit. For the pain and bruising. You came down pretty hard. Damn lucky it's only the ankle.'

Kane hands him a calabash of water. Adam wants to bat it away, but his thirst is a wild animal. He stumbles upright and reaches for the calabash. He drinks and he drinks, until Kane rips it from his hands.

Adam wipes his mouth with the back of his hand and looks at Kane, who doesn't seem to be carrying any injury at all. Then looks at his left hand. Fresh bandages cover the wound. He raises the hand and sniffs the bandage. It smells of grass and woodsmoke. There is no pain.

'Nakoda have got powerful meds,' Kane says, watching him. 'They stitched it up.'

Adam looks at him.

'You should see that jump,' Kane says. 'You remember?'

Adam shakes his head.

But he *does* remember. Fragments. Powering into the jump at full tilt, low on the byke. Compressing his body deep into the lip. Pushing his byke upwards and backwards, exploding into the air at the final moment. His body high and extended on take-off. Weight. Then weightlessness. Beneath him only darkness. Then smashing into the ground. And nothing more.

Kane tosses Adam his riding suit and Adam dresses with his back to him. Together they duck through the tent flap door and emerge blinking into a spectral haze. The air is still thick with dust and eerie in the predawn gloom. Blurred figures drift in the half-light.

Moving through a camp of about a dozen yurts are a people Adam has never seen. The men have naked torsos and their bodies are lean and toned, painted with an ochre mud. Their heads are covered – some in feathers, others in wide-brimmed hats. Their arms are ringed above the elbow with golden bangles. Slung on their shoulders are long pipes made from a dark wood. The women are clothed in robes, and also wear elaborate headgear – feathers and hats. They look just as fierce as the men. They too carry the yard-long pipes on their backs.

Adam blinks and stares. 'What are those things they're carrying?'

'Blowpipes. Dead quiet. Shoot over two hundred yards. Lethal at sixty.'

Adam shakes his head. 'Hell. Wonder what Nate would've made of all this.'

'Hi,' a voice says behind him.

He swivels round fast. Finds Sadie smiling at him. She has a bandage wrapped round her head with a dark bloodstain on her temple.

He reaches out instinctively. 'You OK?'

She pulls back a fraction. 'I'll be fine.'

Kane glances at Sadie. Looks at Adam. 'Get the shaman to look at your hand again.' He points north-east into the dust. 'We should ride at sunrise. Through the pass yonder.'

He moves among the Nakoda. They greet him as he passes, holding up a hand, palm forward, ghostlike in the gloom. Kane returns each greeting. He makes his way to a group of young men, no more than shadows, putting up a yurt on the outskirts of the encampment.

Adam watches him and shakes his head again. 'This is madness.'

'They're nomads,' Sadie says.

'They're *savages*!'

'I thought so too, but . . . they have this ability to heal . . .' She presses her fingers to the bandage on her head then juts her chin at his hand. 'How does it feel?'

'Sadie, you're nuts! Haven't you heard the stories?'

'I know. I flipped out too. Went berserk. Yelled at them. Kane had to hold me down. And then *she* came, the Nakoda woman. Kane calls her the shaman. You look at her and –'

'They eat human flesh!'

'I'm just as scared as you. I *am*. But, I don't know . . . something tells me we can trust them. They're not dangerous. They're just . . . different. Maybe all those stories were lies.' There's an edge in her voice. As if she's trying to convince herself as much as reassure him. Her eyes are filled with wonder, but also fear.

Adam says nothing. He watches the Nakoda. The men carry stacks of rope-lashed branches, clay pots, wooden bowls of berries and roots. The women sit on square wicker mats, whittling the long blowpipes on their knees. Fashioning needle-thin darts from the hard stems of desert wintergrass.

Something catches Adam's eye. Moving from one yurt to another, a woman shepherds a small group of hatless children, hurrying them along. The children are like all children – laughing, screeching and fighting as they go. But they are different too. Adam stares. He's certain he isn't dreaming.

Each child's head is covered in swirls of hair. Long hair. Just like the Watchers.

Before he has a chance to say anything, they have vanished into a hut and a woman arrives and positions herself in front of him. As though by magic.

Jade-green eyes. A face smeared with ochre. High cheekbones. She wears a man's wide-brimmed sun hat frayed at the black rim, hiding her hair. She is old. Older than Old Man Dagg by some margin. She extends a hand. On her finger, a black smudge of ash. She points to Adam's mouth and opens hers. Her teeth are stained red.

Adam freezes.

'She wants you to open your mouth,' Sadie says.

'I don't think so.'

'The ash is medicine, Adam. It's good for the hand.'

'You need,' the woman murmurs.

Before Adam can do anything, she clamps her hand on his wrist and pulls him forward. He feels heat rush through him. He opens his mouth, without meaning to, and she brushes her finger on his tongue. Then she's gone and he's left standing, mouth open, tasting bitter ash on his tongue.

He grimaces, spits and spins round. But she's nowhere in sight. 'Who was that?'

'*Her*,' Sadie says. 'The shaman. Kane says she can read the future.'

Adam shakes his head. He watches Kane helping the young men and he can't help feeling irritable. 'Kane says he's one of 'em. Says they're *his* people. But he doesn't look like 'em. Not at all.'

'The shaman told me a story about him.'

Adam looks at her. 'What story?'

'She said they found him. In a river. Half drowned. She said they took him in.'

'Half drowned? Not likely. I've seen him swim.'

'That's not all. The river where they found him runs through Providence.'

'What were they doin near Providence if *this* is their land?'

'Like I said, they're nomads. They move between territories.' She shakes her head. 'Anyway, you remember the story. A fire swept through the town –'

'Yeah. I know. People died. Their Warlord blamed the slaves.'

'He didn't just blame the slaves. He *killed* them. He took them – men, women, children – took them down to the river. He chained them and he drowned them. *All* of them.'

'I remember. In Providence River. A river that runs with gators.'

Sadie looks at Adam. Her voice lowers. 'They say it was a bloodbath. The gators took Kane. They sunk their teeth into him and they dragged him down.'

Adam says nothing. He remembers the scars on Kane's body.

'Nobody knows how, but *somehow* he escaped,' she continues. 'Only him. The Nakoda found him downstream, days later. They found him torn to shreds. Half dead, they say . . . Only the medicine woman says he wasn't *half* dead, he was *all the way* dead.'

Adam swallows hard. 'What? That makes no sense.'

'The Nakoda have magic,' Sadie says. 'Maybe they brought him back. If you believe all that stuff.'

'*Back?*'

'Back from the dead.'

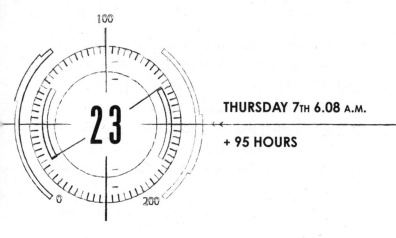

Adam looks at the medicine woman. She wears the same wide-brimmed sun hat. A bead necklace on her neck, tight to the throat. Her eyes, in the shade of her hat, are green and piercing. Her high cheekbones are still smeared with ochre mud and her teeth are stained red with betel-nut juice.

They are sitting in her yurt, examining his left hand. It looks freakish, unwound from the bandage. Like some insect with half its legs torn off. It looks lopsided. What it doesn't look like . . . is his hand. Not the way it was. Not ever again.

Dark stitches thread the red skin at the first knuckle of the absent thumb. Adam stares at the wound in stunned silence.

'I see a Rider,' the woman says, treating the tender skin, smearing on a green paste with light touches. A pungent, grassy smell fills the yurt. She doesn't look at him when she speaks.

'What Rider?' Adam asks, flinching, not from pain, but the expectation of pain.

'He rides through the desert, chasin demons. His ride is a silver one and his heart is black. In the shadow of the devil hill, he will come to see himself.'

'What else do you see?' Adam asks.

'Here for blood. Three dark Riders. In single file. One byke white. One red. One black. The one on the white byke throw his face down. Three meet three. Then comes hell.'

The woman floats her fingers over his hand, hesitates, then lifts a clean bandage and begins to wrap the wound carefully.

'The sun is high. Shadows fat and short. Three Riders remain. They go a new way. Across a black plain to the end of ends.'

She splits the bandage and ties the two tails. Then settles back on to her seat.

Adam turns the bandaged hand, surprised by the lack of pain.

The woman leans forward and punches a finger into the air. 'I have seen what you have done and what you will do. But beware. You run towards what you seek to escape.'

Adam glances up and sees the silhouette of Kane standing in the doorway, watching.

'What does that mean?'

She looks at him and her eyes seem distant. Then she grins and throws her hands into the air, as though absolving herself of all meaning. 'Bad wind comin,' is all she says.

He wants to ask her more, but he can see in her eyes the conversation is over.

They are back on the road, taking a track worn smooth by the Nakoda. The dust fog still hangs and they can see no more than ten yards. They ride through a strange landscape, where green, fat-leaved plants rise up into the air. Tall succulents, drawing water from the earth. They stand like sentinel spirits in the haze, guiding the Riders on their way.

They enter a grove of trees where the ground feels soft and spongy. Adam looks down, sees a tangle of vines and roots. An invasion of moss, thick enough not to be ripped by their churning wheels. A spore cloud floats up. A chittering of insects and birds.

He rides close to Kane.

'This place,' Adam says. 'It's . . .'

'Different?'

'Not what I thought. The people . . . even the plants . . . It's all –'

'Forget the shaman,' Kane says. 'She fixes to put your mind in a twist for the sheer game.'

'It's not her. It's . . . something else. Something I saw.'

Kane turns his head, looks at Adam as he rides.

Adam glances at the weird ground under his byke, at the green succulents with their dagger-like leaves. He looks back at Kane. 'They had *long hair*. Just like the Watchers.'

Kane turns away. 'So what?'

'*So what*? Don't you see? They live off the land, but they've got meds no one else has. My hand . . . I don't feel a thing. And that shaman woman, she's older than anyone I've ever met.'

'Maybe so. It changes nothin.'

'It changes *everything*.'

Kane turns his head, straightening. 'What's on your mind? Something else is eating you.'

Adam feels a prickle of goose bumps down his arm. He blinks in the red glare of Kane's sun goggles. 'I know,' he says. 'I know how you got them cuts and wounds.'

Kane looks at him. His eyes darken. 'We've got a Race to win.' Then he pulls his throttle and churns away.

They come to the edge of an escarpment. The ground is rocky again. They skid to a stop and feel the wind lift. A north-easter blows here – the Banshee – and they watch the dust unfurl, revealing a salt pan shimmering in the heat. Across the pan they see a crew of Riders, their silver dust plumes scattered by the wind. Beyond them stands a towering structure, warping in the heat.

'Looks like an abandoned launch pad,' Sadie says. 'Badland is full of them.'

Adam nods. 'S'pose they wouldn't let us get close to a working one. Too dangerous.'

'For them or for us?' Kane says.

Sadie looks at him, then at Adam. 'You ready?'

'Guess we'll find out,' Adam says, glancing at his hand. But Nakoda medicine is strong. The pain is no more than a dull ache. He remembers hearing somewhere that if a person loses a leg, or a hand, or even just a finger, they still feel it, long after it's gone. Something about nerve endings. It makes sense to Adam. He can still feel his thumb, if he thinks about it.

With a crazed and primitive howl, Kane kicks down his gears and tears away from them, hurtling down the dirt slope. Adam and Sadie give chase. Their wheels blur and dirt churns. They dice with each other, riding head down and hell for leather.

The trail opens out on to a flat stretch of ground. They ride hard over it, sending up three plumes of dust behind them, like vapour trails from rockets. Then they come to a skidding stop.

In the dust ahead, the pack of Riders warps and floats.

'Bad guys or good guys?' Adam asks.

Kane gazes at them, unperturbed. 'No difference.'

There are four Riders, close together. Their alabaster skin shines in the sun.

'Deads,' Adam says.

Kane nods. 'Don't look at 'em. Don't acknowledge 'em. Ride past and say nothin.'

He throttles and flies straight towards them . . . and past them. Close. He doesn't look at them as he passes. They turn and stare. But they do nothing to stop him.

Adam waits. He can hear Sadie breathing next to him. Kane keeps going into the haze.

Adam and Sadie slide past the Deads. Slowly. They give them a wide berth. Adam keeps his head fixed on Kane's byke, up ahead in the dust. He senses the Tribe near. Feels the weight of their eyes. Then something in him – some dumb curiosity – causes him to turn. He looks at them. The Deads stare back.

Gold goggles. Plum-coloured lips. Skull and crossbones tattoos. Pale skin, despite the sun. They don't make a sound. All they do is stare. Four of them. Battered and bloodied. Blackwater Trail has exacted a heavy toll. They do not look in the mood for a fight. They look exhausted.

Adam wonders how he and Sadie must seem to them. As broken, no doubt. He gives them a slight nod. He doesn't know why. It just happens. Maybe he feels a fraternity. A brotherhood. It's a mistake.

One of them veers out from the group and begins to haul them in. Steadily at first, just a slight adjustment to his line, then with more speed and at a more direct angle. He makes a low-throated sound, like a dog calling out to its mate.

Sadie looks now. She glances at Adam. Looks back.

All four Riders jerk their throttles and gun at them. Frantic, Adam looks ahead. But Kane is gone in the dust.

He knows they can't outride them. The gang's angle is too steep coming in at them. Escape is impossible.

Adam and Sadie reach the same conclusion in the same instant. He senses that. Sadie is first to react. She floors the Stormchaser and pulls her handlebars hard left, jacking the byke into a massive turn. Her momentum carries her and she leaps, almost cartwheels, from the byke. She lands on her feet and guides her machine to a churning stop in front of her. The byke is between Sadie and the Riders. In the same instant, she removes her sling.

Adam nails his back brake and skids sideways. He leans forward over the front wheel, swings the rear wheel round and releases the brake. The back wheel catches and he bombs out of the turn, spraying shrapnel dirt. He flies off his byke and hits the ground next to Sadie, breathing hard, hands still holding the byke, fingers pressed to the brakes. Less graceful maybe. Just as effective.

The Longthorn and the Stormchaser stand between them and the Riders. A last-ditch wall of defence, like the broadside of a miniature warship. The Riders bear down on them regardless.

CRACK!

Sadie sends a stone loose and it takes the lead Rider in the chest with an audible *thud*. He veers off course and ditches, flying from the byke. Adam watches him rise and retake his byke.

Armoured suits.

Adam barely has his own sling loaded when Sadie releases a second, third and fourth stone in rapid succession.

A quick-fire salvo of accurate shots. Each hits a Rider. But the stones ricochet off the Deads. Only the first Rider falls.

They fire back, riding at them, sniping forward like the wolves and looping back, loading stones as they ride and firing shot after shot after shot. The stones hit the bykes with loud smacks and Adam and Sadie duck their heads and lean their shoulders to the hot metal.

'You sure about this?' Adam whispers. 'Gotta be safer on the bykes.'

Sadie shakes her head. Loads a stone. 'On three,' she hisses.

'*Three*? Why's it always on three?'

'One . . .'

'OK, look, let me just load this thing. I –'

'Two . . .'

Sadie spins and crouches. Adam loads his sling with shaking hands. 'OK, OK, I'm ready. I got it. I'll take the –'

'THREE!' Sadie roars and she's up and over the bykes in a single leap.

Adam whips round. A memory flashes before him. Hunkering down behind his couch, frozen with fear – his back pressed to the fabric – listening to an awful crunch of footsteps through broken glass.

He grits his teeth and leaps to his feet. Then he follows Sadie over the bykes, yelling obscenities and, blurred over his right shoulder, the sling goes to work, singing in the air.

His stone flies out and sails three yards right of his intended target. Sadie is already ten yards ahead, running hard, flinging stones. Adam looks down, loads another stone. Looks up.

Sadie has come to an abrupt stop. Her sling is pouched in her hand. Ahead of her, the Deads – all four of them – are still as statues on their bykes. They look at Adam and Sadie – almost through them – or beyond them. Then one of them clutches at his neck. He makes a gurgling sound and topples backwards from his byke. His comrades see this and they turn and they flee. Hard. Fast. No looking back.

Adam comes to Sadie's side. She stares away from him, back towards the escarpment ridge. 'It wasn't me that got him.'

Adam follows her gaze. And he sees them. Three motionless figures. Up high on the ridge.

Even at this distance – some hundred yards – Adam can see who they are, and he can easily see the long, dark shapes of their weapons.

Blowpipes.

He squints back at the fallen Rider and sees a needle-thin dart impaled in his neck.

'Thought you said they weren't dangerous,' he says, looking at Sadie.

Beyond her, he sees Kane, slicing towards them through the gloom and dust. Adam removes the stone from the pouch of his sling and replaces it in his stone bag. When he turns back to the ridge, the figures are gone.

They drive out on to the plain at speed, to put the Riders well behind them. Adam rides hard and he wonders about the strange and ghostly Nakoda. The way they appear and disappear. Just like Kane.

Up ahead the old launch pad rises from the dust. A mirage at first. Floating above the ground, disappearing and reappearing in the haze. Until it resolves into a solid object, fixed to the land.

They ride up alongside the beast. A steel structure, about ninety yards high. At the base, it's all concrete wall and razor wire. There's no rocket in sight. But why would there be? The launch pad is disused and left to ruin and rust. The wind picks up a piece of sheet metal, near the top, and it makes an eerie moaning sound. Adam looks up and sees a buzzard take flight, shitting as it goes.

They ride on. Beyond the launch pad, another shape floats in the dust.

The last Race camp.

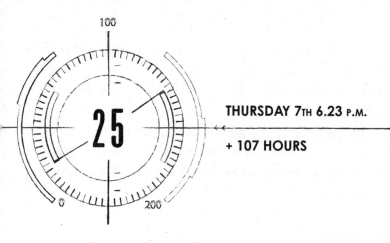

This camp is different from the first one. For one thing, it's not deserted. Adam can see small figures moving to and fro, and the shadow play of bykes distorted in the evening light. And, for another, it's built like a fortress. Enclosed by a high, spiked fence – to keep the Nakoda out, no doubt – with a makeshift watchtower looming over the entrance gate. Adam sees the glint of glass from the sentry post at the top of the tower. Eyes are on them

They ride to the camp in silence.

The squealing gate is swung. A GRUB stands before them. A fusion shooter – oiled and bright – clipped to its thigh. The GRUB's head turns left and right. It looks at them.

'Bad weather coming,' it says in its metallic voice. 'Survival chances in the storm: nil. You will stay here until it abates.'

'Maybe. Maybe not,' Kane says.

The GRUB looks at him. No expression. 'You will stay here. Race leaders are encamped. The Race will restart when the storm passes. No advantage will be awarded to early arrivals.'

'Bad luck for them, I guess,' Sadie says.

The GRUB points to the far side of the camp. 'You are assigned tents twelve, thirteen and fourteen. Wash in the reservoir tank. It is cold.'

The GRUB makes a jolting, clicking noise. Then it stands motionless.

'That's it?' Adam spits. 'Has it shut down?'

'What did you expect?' Kane says. 'A grand tour?'

'C'mon,' Sadie urges and she kicks down and rides past the GRUB, close, to show her disdain. The GRUB doesn't react. It doesn't move at all.

The camp is a miasma of smoke raised by cooking fires, strewn between fireproof enviro-tents. Knots of dishevelled, exhausted-looking Riders huddle close to the flames, like beggars in the gloom. Each looks up and stares at them through warping waves of heat. Nobody speaks to them as they drift through the haze.

Adam can't help feeling ill at ease in the stillness. His instincts are buzzing. He knows that quiet sometimes only comes before the storm.

Then – in the heart of the camp – surrounded by flags that flap and snap in the breeze, they find a digital race sign. Like the sign in Camp One. Only here, the numbers tell a new story.

CAMP FOUR. BLACKWATER TRAIL. THURSDAY 7TH RACE STATS. 81 RIDERS RECORDED AT THE STARTING LINE. CURRENT STATUS: 19 DEAD. 14 MISSING, PRESUMED DEAD. CURRENT ODDS FAVOURITE, LEVI BLOOD AT 2:1. WARNING: CATEGORY 8 STORM INCOMING. ESTIMATED DURATION: 24 HOURS. ADVISORY ALERT: STAY IN CAMP.

On a hill at the north end of the camp, against the wall, is the reservoir. A tank of water held fast by a round container of dented iron. A rusted pipe rises out of the ground and bends into the reservoir, feeding it from some unseen underground source.

Kane begins to strip. Sadie and Adam watch him.

'You can see it's cold,' Adam says, testing his weight on the bruised ankle. It's tender, but already much stronger.

'It'll be freezing,' Sadie says.

Kane, in his underwear, steps up a wooden staircase to the rim of the reservoir. He looks into the dark water and then he turns and gazes down at them, hands on his hips. Once again, Adam is struck by the mean-looking scars and his defiant yellow eyes. There isn't anyone in the world like him. He senses Sadie's shock next to him.

'Only one way to get clean,' Kane says, grinning.

Adam feels Sadie's gaze resting on Kane's toned and wounded body. His broad shoulders and lean stomach. The scars that run the length of him.

'Well, do it if you're gonna do it.'

Kane salutes. A touch of his finger to his forehead. Whether this is directed at Sadie or both of them is not clear to Adam. With startling agility, Kane throws up his arms and leaps skyward, diving backwards into the water – a perfect arc. A wild splash and he's gone.

Adam and Sadie feel water rain down on them as sharp and stinging as ice needles and they shout and stumble back.

Sadie laughs. 'C'mon. I'll race you in.'

In seconds, they strip down to their underwear and, blue and goose-bumped in the cold, they climb the stairs. Here they stand, hugging themselves, semi-naked, watching Kane shout and splash. Adam sneaks a look at Sadie. Her skin is dimpled in the cold. Her plain white underwear is tight. He can see the taut bumps of her nipples, dark beneath the white.

Sadie turns to him and grins.

Adam stands, holding his crotch, opening and closing his mouth, unable to speak.

Sadie lets out a crazed yowl and dives.

Wet through and cold to the bone, they stamp through the mud, clutching their bundled clothes. They haul them on with teeth chattering, grab hold of their heatkeepers, wrap themselves and run, blundering through the dusk, to their tents. They pass a gusting fire and stop to warm themselves.

Behind them the moon is huge and crimson in the darkening sky. If a storm is coming then the moon knows nothing of it. It looks restful and at peace in the sky.

They're not alone at the fire. Four huddled figures crouch near the flames. They don't greet them, nor do they turn them away. A silence hangs over the group. All they hear is the roar and the crackle of the fire and all they feel is the comfort of the heat.

Kane and Adam rest on their haunches. Sadie remains standing.

One of the figures in front of them speaks. A shadowy kid, wrapped up in his heatkeeper, his face orange and floating in the firelight. His eyes flick from Adam to Kane and linger on Sadie.

'You fellas goin to the saloon?'

'The saloon?' Adam says.

'That's what I said.'

'Sure,' Kane grunts, next to Adam. 'We're goin.'

Adam glances at Kane. He's a shadow in the dark.

'They got O2,' the huddled figure says. He doesn't look at Kane or at Adam. His eyes are on Sadie. 'They got betel nut and khat. Jhet Fuel too. Keep you goin to the end, that stuff. And the O2'll make you feel like new. Better'n new. Even sexed up.'

Silence. The fire crackles.

'Hell, it'll make you randier'n a pig!' another kid snorts, his eyes in shadow. He laughs until something catches in his throat and he coughs and hacks and spits.

'Ain't that a fact,' the first kid says, nodding, leering at Sadie.

Adam hears Kane's heatkeeper rustle. Sadie remains standing.

'Damn straight. And prime Jhet Fuel will ease all pains,' the kid says. 'Everyone knows it.'

'It's poison,' Sadie says.

The huddled figure shows no visible reaction. 'Gives you energy. What you need on a cold night four days into the Blackwater with a badass storm comin. That and somethin else.' He grins. His teeth are bright in the dark. His eyes roam up Sadie's body.

Sadie doesn't move. Her face gleams from the swim.

'But it makes you slow,' she says. 'Slow and stupid . . . You must've had a lot.'

The kid blinks. He glances at his buddies. Licks his lips. Looks back at her. Adam can see that he doesn't know what to do. The kid misjudged Sadie Blood.

'Or maybe you think you're not slow,' she says. 'Maybe you think you're fast. Is that it? Just how fast do you reckon you are?'

The kid's hand moves to his belt, slow and tentative.

Kane rises off his haunches. 'Mind yourself, friend.' His voice is cold and low.

Sadies flashes him a look. 'Back off, Kane.'

Kane looks at her. Sits back down.

'What Tribe are you lot?' the kid says, hand frozen in the air.

'We're not a Tribe.'

'Sure look like one.'

Sadie glares at him. 'What Tribe are *you*?'

'Hawk Nation. Rafe over there, he's a Crow.' The kid drops his hand and wraps himself tight, fists at his throat, elbows pressed to his stomach.

No one says a word until Kane speaks. 'So,' he says, real casual. 'Where's that saloon?'

'Yonder,' the kid says, jutting his chin.

The saloon bar is lit from within. It emits a yellow light from a door flung wide to the night. Figures move like ghosts inside.

'I got a bad feelin about this,' Adam says.

Kane smirks. 'Long O2 dose will do you good. You know it.'

'But *you* aren't here for O2, are you?' Sadie says, looking at Kane.

Adam remembers Kane stumbling down the stairs at Sadie's Bykemonger shop, the stink of Jhet Fuel heavy on his breath. He feels another stab of jealousy.

What was Kane doing there anyway?

A commotion of raised voices comes from the far side of the saloon. They make their way towards the noise.

In a pool of light cast by a blazing torch, a circle of figures stand, waving their fists. From within the circle comes a familiar sound. Grunts and shouts and the dull thumps of fists hitting flesh.

'A fight,' Sadie says.

'No ordinary fight,' Kane says, pointing to a referee, who holds a finger to his ear and mumbles something into a hidden mouthpiece. 'What we have here is a cash game.'

He moves into the circle of figures with bright eyes, like a vampire drawn to virgin blood. Adam and Sadie follow.

They press themselves into the throng, muscle a way to the front. Here they see two boys, stripped to the waist.

The boys hold up bloodied fists and pace around each other. Both are well built. One has his broad back to them and his body gleams with sweat. The other stumbles and drops his fists. The muscular kid in front of them rocks forward and plants a violent uppercut that sends his opponent flying to the ground. The sound of him hitting the earth – a loud *SMACK*! – is stark above the cheers. He doesn't move. The referee flies into the circle and raises the victor's arm. When he turns the fighter to acknowledge the crowd, Adam sees the bruiser's face.

A face he knows well.

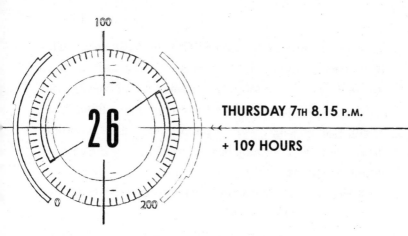

Sadie grips Adam's elbow, digs her fingers into him. 'It's Red,' she hisses.

Adam feels a hot flush of electric current run up his arm, through his shoulder. All he can think about – all his brain can cope with – is the feeling of Sadie touching him. Her skin on his skin.

Adam concentrates on facts to bring him back to reality. He makes a cursory scan of the faces in the crowd. No Wyatt. No Levi.

Where the hell is he?

He turns to look at the parading duo – the boxer and the referee. Red stands proud and upright. Huge. His chest the size of an oil drum. He is notorious for his strength. Kids have been coming to Blackwater to challenge him as far back as Adam can remember. And, as far back as Adam can remember, Red has never lost. Not once.

'Who'll step up?' the referee yells. 'Who'll step up and face the beast? Any one of you got the stomach?' He glances at Sadie in the crowd. 'Got the *balls* for it?' The man paces, holding Red's arm aloft. 'Will nobody test themselves?' He waits. No answer comes from the assembled throng. He plays the crowd, eyes sliding over them, resting longer than necessary on Sadie. 'Every kid has a limit. Won't be long before he snaps, right?' He glares at them. 'Nobody?'

'I will,' a voice says and a hush falls on the crowd.

Kane steps into the light.

His presence is greeted with loud cheers. The crowd smells blood and they grow restless. They jostle and throb and carry Adam away from Sadie. He spins round to grab her, but she is also thrust away. She disappears behind shoulders and arms.

Kane stands quietly in the midst of all this, loose-limbed and narrow-eyed. Opposite him towers Red, the man-mountain.

'I know you,' Red says, when the referee manages to quell the crowd.

'Maybe. Maybe not,' Kane says.

'Don't matter either way.' Red flexes his pecs to the admiration of those gathered. 'I'll be wiping the floor with your head, whether I seen you before or not.'

Adam scans the crowd again and freezes.

A face. Lit up in the gloom. Far side of the fight. Dark eyes, staring at him. A crooked smile.

Levi.

Adam looks at him, horrified, unable to move, pinned in by the crowd. Levi returns his gaze. The light falling on his face makes him look ghoulish and unreal. But he is every bit real. His eyes are full of bristling confidence and self-awareness. They taunt and mock.

Adam stands there. And suddenly he's under the old oak tree, staring down at the bloodied wreck of his brother. Cold hatred takes hold.

He lurches forward. But, as he does, someone barges in front of him. Adam shoves and searches frantically. But Levi is lost from sight. As if he were never there at all. Adam seethes and paces. Levi is gone.

The voices of the fighters drift back to Adam.

'Pretty certain of yourself,' Kane is saying.

'Got no reason not to be,' Red answers.

'Everyone gets beaten in the end,' Kane says. 'Just a matter of time.'

Red shakes his head. 'No one alive can lay me down.'

Kane smiles and strips off the top of his riding suit. Now he stands peeled, naked to the waist. A collective gasp rises. His torso looks more tracked and cratered than usual in the deep shadows cast by the torchlight.

'Looks like someone got to you before me,' Red says.

Kane looks at him. 'I've seen a thing or two.'

This new revelation, of Kane's battered body, has the crowd on edge, bristling with energy. They whisper and surge. Adam searches for Levi and Sadie, but sees neither.

The two fighters begin to circle each other.

'What's your name, friend?' Kane asks.

'Red. If it's any of your business.'

'Red?'

'Red.'

'On account of *what*?'

'On account of it being my name.'

Kane grins.

Red rolls his neck, pulls each elbow in turn to his chest, an elaborate show of stretching. 'I aim to fix that grin for you.'

'That a fact?'

'It sure is.' Red squats, bounces on his hamstrings. Leaps up. Squats again. Leaps.

Kane doesn't move.

Red paces, eyes on Kane, cracking his knuckles, snarling up phlegm, spitting.

'FIGHT ALREADY!' a voice yells from the crowd and they begin to goad the fighters, hurling abuse at Kane, taunting him.

'He your friend?' a sour-breathed kid says next to Adam. In the weird light, Adam can see two missing front teeth. Dog Soldier.

Adam tries to move away, but the kid moves with him and leans into him.

'Tell him to walk away, brother. Walk away before Red here makes him crawl away. He ain't got the size. He's got nothin. Red'll turn the dirt red.'

'Red *is* dirt,' Adam says, surprised at himself. 'I got a dollar says my friend takes him.'

Friend.

The word comes bursting out. It surprises Adam. He didn't expect it. But he said it.

The two fighters circle, fists up, eyes locked on to each other. Red's fists are slabs of meat; his knuckles dent inwards. Kane moves with grace, light on his feet.

Without warning, Red explodes forward and swings. Kane ducks the blow and, lightning-quick, slides to the side. Red wheels and launches after him. Another wild swing. Another miss.

Each assault thrown down by Red is countered by an athletic step out of the way from Kane. Red swears and comes after him and Kane, yet to break sweat, moves as a wolf would move – fast and lithe. Untouchable.

Red's face burns the same colour as his name. Each evasion from Kane produces in Red a reaction of increasing rage. He thrashes and stumbles after Kane like a bull.

Kane is too fast. Too slick. The crowd watches, wide-eyed and silent.

Kane torments Red, dodging and weaving, making a mockery of his attacks. And the strain begins to tell on Red. He lunges and Kane, quick as a wolf, slips out of the way. It's as though he disappears and reappears, out of reach. He seems not to be watching Red at all. He even looks away from him, towards the crowd, or rather beyond them, to some unseen encouragement.

Red's eyes are wild. He swings and he grunts and he misses. Then he rushes Kane. A mistake.

Kane turns, sidesteps, plants a kick in the seat of Red's pants, sends him flailing to the dust. Red pauses for breath, on his hands and knees. He leaps up, roars and barrels forward.

Kane dances away, this time delivering a kick to Red's knee from the side, and Red goes buckling down with a howl, clutching his leg, his face contorted in agony.

It's not over. Red staggers to his feet, bends forward, rubs his knee. Then he straightens and comes at Kane, limping and snarling.

Kane grins. He keeps his fists up, shielding his face, the way good bare-knuckle fighters do. Red swings. Kane angles out of the way. Red swings again, a huge uppercut, and misses. The crowd roars. The fighters pace. Red sweats and his chest heaves. Kane has him beat. Anyone can see that.

Then it changes. Kane looks at Red, glances at Adam and he drops his guard. A fraction. Lowers his fists so his face is exposed. Red sees it and flies at him, swinging wild haymakers. The first enthusiastic swing misses, over Kane's head, but the second connects. A shocking blow. It sends Kane stumbling back into the crowd.

They collect him, like a human wave, and throw him back into the circle with loud shouts. Red swings and connects again. Kane stumbles back and slams to the ground. Now a figure comes flying from the crowd.

Sadie!

She leaps up on to Red's back and digs her nails into him. Red roars and turns about, reaching over his shoulder, trying to dislodge her.

'SADIE!' Adam's voice is drowned by the noise. He sees a rush of people come to take her. A kid throws a punch and Adam launches forward. He barrels into the kid, takes him at the waist with a dropped shoulder. A thumping tackle. They go sprawling across the floorboards. When he looks up, the kid is being hustled from the ring by the referee.

Sadie is hauled from Red's back and dragged, kicking, into the crowd. Adam feels hands on his shoulders and he is plucked up and shoved into the throng. He staggers round and watches Kane rise.

Kane stumbles in a circle round Red, until he stands with his back to Adam. Red lashes out. A left jab to Kane's chin. Connecting hard. A right, low, to the solar plexus. Kane doubles forward. A blow to Kane's cheek sends him flying into Adam.

Adam catches him under the arms. 'What are you doin? You had him beat!'

Kane turns, grins, blood smeared on his teeth. 'You got dollars, you put 'em all on me.'

Then he ducks a swinging fist and staggers forward, back into the circle.

Adam thinks about the story Sadie told him. He begins to understand. There isn't anything ordinary about Kane. A slave boy thrown, chained, to river gators. Left to die. Kane has nothing to lose. Maybe Kane *needs* the pain. Needs pain to feel anything at all.

'He's dead,' the Dog kid with the sour breath says next to him.

Maybe Kane is dead. Maybe he's a ghost after all.

Adam shakes his head. 'You're wrong. He's not finished.'

Red attacks again. This time, Kane dodges right and takes Red with a hard jab to the jaw. Red staggers and blinks. He rounds on Kane. Swings. Misses. Kane snipes left and jabs. One . . . two . . . three. Clean punches that stun Red.

His arms drop to his sides. Kane walks up to him and takes him by the shoulders, a benign gesture, as if they were about to embrace, and then he dips his head and slams it forward.

The headbutt is perfect. He catches the bridge of Red's nose with the top of his forehead and Red, spouting blood, goes down like a tree.

Game over.

The referee comes from the crowd to raise Kane's hand. But Kane is gone.

Adam reconnects with Sadie on the edge of the crowd. She stands there, brushing dust from her jacket. She looks furious. Her face is red and her eyes are narrowed, bright and fierce.

'Did you see that?' she snaps at his approach.

'I know. Never seen anyone fight like that.'

'They pulled me off him! The bloody morons.'

Adam reaches out to help her brush away the dust and she pulls back.

'What happened?' she says, glaring at him.

He throws up his hands, a gesture intended to display surprise *and* inevitability. 'Kane won.'

Even as he says it, he feels another prick of jealousy in his heart.

Sadie shakes her head. Her eyes lose a fraction of their hardness. Then she exhales a long, shuddering breath and smiles. *Smiles.* 'I saw what you did. With the tackle. Nice move.'

Adam feels heat climb his neck. 'It was nothin.'

'I know. Thanks anyway.' They look at each other and the moment stretches. Adam feels warmth in his gut. A strange sliding feeling.

'Some fight,' he says.

'Yeah,' she answers. 'Kane's a crazy bastard.'

They find him in a dingy and stale-smelling alcove of the saloon, a glass of amber liquid in his hand. Jhet Fuel. The table is bare in front of him. Outside the wind screeches and howls. A shutter bangs. The saloon shakes and groans. The storm has hit.

'That was something,' Adam says, sliding into the booth opposite him, making a quick scan of the huddled shapes moving through the place. His instincts are buzzing.

Kane rolls the glass in his hand. His cheek is bruised. There's a cut above his right eye.

'You shouldn't have done that,' Sadie says, slipping in next to Adam, still flushed.

Kane says nothing. All he does is stare at his drink, holding the chipped glass up to a dim candle flame.

Sadie watches Kane. 'Levi won't like Red being made a fool of.'

'Well then, he should pick others to ride with.'

'You don't understand what he's capable of. He can –'

'Do as he pleases,' a new voice says.

They turn abruptly. The voice comes in a dry whisper from a figure cast in shadow. It's a voice that sends a chill right through Adam. Right to the bone.

'Well. Look at the brave scrapper,' the voice says.

Out of the corner of his eye, Adam notices others in the bar shift themselves away from their table. They slink into the darkness.

The figure steps into the pool of yellow light and his face materializes from the gloom. Levi Blood's eyes gleam as he turns from Kane, to Adam, to Sadie.

'Sister,' he says, looking at Sadie.

'Levi,' she answers.

A flash of light. A loud *KA-BLAM*! The shock of rolling thunder outside.

Here he stands. The kid who killed Frank. The devil's son. Flesh and blood and bone. Right in front of him.

Adam feels anger churn inside him. And fear too, weaving through the hate. Fear mixed with anger. Anger threaded through with vengeance. His right hand slips beneath the table and goes for his sling. He glances around the saloon. Too many eyes on them to kick-start anything. He sees Wyatt saunter through the gloom, slim and tall. He leans against the bar counter, knee cocked, boot on the railing behind him.

'Mind if I take a seat?' Levi says.

There's nothing hurried about the way he speaks. Everything about him radiates self-assuredness. And something else. Frank would call it evil, but Adam doesn't believe in evil. He believes people make decisions and these

236

choices make them who they are. Make enough bad decisions, you get to be plain bad.

'*I* mind,' Adam says, unable to mask the waver in his voice.

Levi looks at him, at his bandaged fist resting on the table. 'I understand the wolves took your thumb. Riding must be ... rather a *challenge*.'

Under the table Adam's hand traces the corrugations in his braided sling.

Not now. Not yet.

At the bar, Wyatt picks his teeth and watches them.

Kane says nothing. He stares at his glass. The scar on his cheek is livid in the half-light.

Levi grins. He turns to Sadie. 'I'll ask you to come with me.'

Sadie stays put. 'You go where you damn well like. I'm not going with you.'

'You're a Blood, Sadie.'

She looks up at him, both hands flat on the scarred and dented table. Levi slides his eyes from her to Kane, from Kane to Adam.

He sighs. 'You boys know about Bloods?'

Nobody answers.

'Pig-headed, most of them. Bloods have been in Blackwater longer than anyone,' he says. 'When the Bloods first came to Blackwater, they say the lake was filled with fish. You imagine that? Fish!' He grins at them. 'Anyway, do you know what they did? Those Blood forefathers?'

Adam finds himself shaking his head, despite himself.

'They fished them out,' Levi says. 'Fished them all out, until there wasn't a single one left. Not one. And they didn't bother creating colonies either. No plan for sustainability. They left that lake barren as the desert.' He smiles. 'Might be the sole reason we rely on Sky-Base for supplies.'

He pauses. No one speaks.

'You do understand what I'm telling you, right? They got rid of their food source. That old lake is full of death now.' He looks at Adam. 'Isn't that right, Stone?'

Adam grips the table, white-knuckled. Kane contemplates his glass, rolling it in his hand.

'What's your point?' Sadie says. Her voice is tight.

'My point, Sadie, is that Bloods own things. When we want something, we hunt it down. We never quit until we take it. All of it. Good or bad, it doesn't matter. Right or wrong. Consequence, no consequence. We don't answer to anyone.' He looks at Adam. 'We have principles, if you can call them that. We never ride with Stones.' Then he looks at Kane. 'And we certainly don't tolerate scum. Not in Blood country.'

Kane tilts back his head and throws down the fiery-coloured liquid in one gulp. He smacks the glass, empty, back on the table and pulls a grimace as though he's bitten into a wedge of lime. When he speaks, he looks down at the glass, not raising his eyes to Levi. 'We passed through Blood country a long way back,' he mutters.

The wind screams and batters the saloon windows.

'Speak up, Outsider!' Levi says, leaning forward.

Kane looks at him, slow and cool. 'Sadie asked you to leave. She's asking nice. I won't.'

Levi massages his chin. Holds his head raised so he looks down his long nose at them, through lowered eyelids. His mouth contorts to a sneer. 'You and me will have us some words,' he says. He stares at Adam and Sadie. 'Some words are comin all the way around.'

Then he turns, nods at Wyatt and both slide away into the shadows.

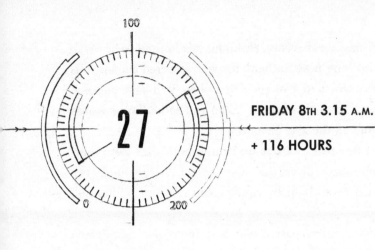

He sails high above the desert, looking down at the corrugated sand, the rock sentinels, boulders riven with deep cracks, ragged and crumbling mountains. To the east, a silver sun rises and cirrus clouds streak across the sky. A green valley snakes up through the mountains. In the middle of the valley runs a river and the colour of the water is blue.

'Adam?'

He glides over the valley and he knows he's not awake. He knows it's a mirage. A dream. Green valleys and blue rivers don't exist.

'Adam, you hear me?'

The valley warps and blurs and the colours fade to uniform whiteness.

'ADAM!'

He opens his eyes and sees Sadie standing over him. He blinks and looks up at her. Her face is lit by candlelight and her eyes burn out of the shadows.

He rips the O2 mask away from his mouth and tries to swallow. His throat is dry. He props himself up on his elbows. He's lying on a bed of cushions. His riding suit hangs at the foot of the bed. His body is lean and covered in a film of sweat.

'You look pretty jacked up,' Sadie says. 'Where were you?'

'Some other place,' he answers, looking around. The curtained room is lit by candles and reeks of bodies and incense.

Adam reaches past Sadie and pulls the moth-eaten curtain back a yard. In the gloom, he sees figures lying on cushioned beds like his own. Clamped over their faces are the O2 masks connected to clear pipes fixed in the wall. The O2 is free here. Courtesy of the Race. A first-generation service GRUB moves through the room, checking the connections.

Adam lets the curtain fall shut. 'Storm still blowing?'

'Wind has died. But it's all sulphur dust out there. No one's going anywhere.'

He sits up and rolls his shoulders. Pins and needles dart in his legs.

Sadie sits down next to him. 'Feeling OK?'

He nods, hearing the springs creak with her added weight. He *does* feel OK. In fact he feels good. No headache and, apart from a burning throat, no significant pain to speak of. Not even from his ankle or the shredded nerves of his left hand.

'Not bad,' he says.

She nods. Her eyes gleam. 'It'll be fine. I know it will.'

Without understanding why, Adam doesn't share this sentiment. Perhaps it's the dream, lingering in his memory. It always unsettles him to dream this way. No point to it.

Sadie takes his left hand in hers and turns it. She touches the place where his thumb should be. He lets her manipulate his hand and says nothing.

'What do you think?' she says. 'About us?'

Adam hears a buzzing in his ears. The look in Sadie's eyes is something he has never seen before. Not fierce, the way they always are, something else. Something like hunger.

'About . . . *us*?'

'What happens to us? When the Race is done.'

'I guess . . . I mean, I never . . .' He struggles to find something else to say, *anything*.

Then Sadie pins him back down and kisses him. Hard. On the mouth.

She pushes against his shoulders, levers herself upright, locks her arms at the elbows and looks down at him, studies his face. He lies there, trying to make sense of all the sensations running through him. Shock. Surprise. Lust.

Sadie bites her bottom lip. She leans forward. Her tongue is hot inside his mouth. He cups a breast, without thinking, his pulse quickening. He feels her body heat and smells her skin. She smells of dust and grass, of woodsmoke and sun-warmed stones. A need contracts in Adam's gut.

He *aches* for her.

Sadie breaks away, breathless, and he stares up at her. She draws down on him again, her breath blasting warm jets on his face. Her eyes are so close he can chart red capillaries and follow iris fibres, like unspooled threads of coloured cotton. He looks at her skin, dirt trapped in the fine lines, pebbled sweat under her eyes.

Her fingers dig into his shoulder muscles. The pain is beautiful. Fevered thoughts swirl in his head.

This is it. Me and Sadie Blood. It's real.

His hands come alive. They grab at her riding suit – pulling, tearing, ripping. His calloused fingers tremor against her skin. The sight of her naked freezes his hand. His eyes fix on the hollow curve at her throat, a tiny artery jumping beneath drum-taut skin. He follows the birdlike ridge of her collarbone, the hard undulation of her ribs, the flatness of her stomach, the dark mouth of her navel. She lifts his chin and looks at him.

He leans in and pulls on her lips like a drunk on a bottle of Jhet Fuel.

They lie next to each other, their slick bodies covered in a fine film of sweat. A heat still on them. A haze. Adam's internal clock has been blown apart. He has no idea how long they've been lying, side by side, fingers interlocked. He stares at the rafters of the roof. Crossbeams of a heavy wooden timber. Old, dark and knotted. No makeshift hut. The encampment must be used every year. Then he remembers what just happened and feels the heat of the body next to him. Adam lies still and stares up, arms pinned to his sides, thrown by the impossibility of it.

He hears the rustle of cushions, feels Sadie move next to him.

'God . . . Sadie. I . . . This is . . .' His face throbs.

Sadie releases his hand and he feels her roll on to her side. Away from him. She grinds her back hard into him. 'You didn't want to?' she whispers.

He turns in to her. 'No, I . . . I mean, yeah, but I thought . . . you know –'

'I don't know.'

He stares at her ear, mesmerized by the infinite detail of the structure. A perfection of intricate curves and silky skin.

'It's just that I thought . . . you and Kane . . .'

Sadie turns her neck and looks over her shoulder. 'You thought Kane and I?'

'I guess . . . Yeah. I guess maybe I did.'

She smiles and her cheeks dimple. Then she shakes her head. 'You don't get close to a person like Kane.' Sadie rolls and looks Adam in the eye. 'How long have I known you?'

'A long time, I guess.'

'But not properly.'

'Nope.' He grins at her. 'Until now.'

'I could never figure you. Always coming round to the shop, looking at the gear as if you wanted to buy. But, whenever I came near, you'd disappear. You were like a shadow.'

Adam stares into her eyes and says nothing.

'I watched you ride once,' she says. 'It was just some stupid street race. I was getting supplies over at Grover's when I saw them setting it up. Then you came. There was something about you. You weren't like the others, I could see that. They laughed at you, at your torn clothes and your scuffed byke. You just looked at them. And when you rode it was like nothin I'd ever seen. You led most of the way. But you didn't win. Remember why?'

'I remember.'

'You went back. You went back to help that kid who'd fallen and broken his arm.'

'We should go look for Kane,' Adam whispers, fighting a surge of hormones.

Sadie's eyes laugh at him. She bites her lip. 'Kane can wait.'

They find him where they left him – in the table section of the foul-smelling saloon. He sits in the booth with his head slumped on crossed arms. A bottle stands before him, down to a third of its amber contents. A thin line of spittle connects the corner of his mouth to the table.

Sadie kicks a table leg. The bottle rattles, topples, falls with a bang and rolls to the table edge. It drops, smashes on the floor. The sound is startling and the stink is wretched.

Kane stirs and gives a muffled grumble. He drags his head from the cradle of his arms and looks up. His eyes are slits and his mouth a grimace.

'You broke my bottle,' he rasps. He clears his throat and swallows and pushes the table away. He leans back against the booth and look at them, bleary-eyed.

'That stuff will kill you,' Sadie says.

Kane smirks. 'Let it try.'

*

They emerge, all three, from the lit saloon into the black night. The cold grips them and they shiver in their suits. They don't speak as they make their way through the swirling dust to their tents. The rank smell of sulphur is thick on the air.

Kane stumbles as he walks. Sadie, on the other side of him, says nothing.

Adam squints through the dust and takes shallow breaths. His head spins with what happened. Her lips, hot against his. Her body pressed up to him. Every fibre in him, fit to burst. He's lost in the sensation of skin on skin, when three ghost figures materialize from the dust.

Adam feels a hot spurt of fear through his gut.

This isn't good. Not good at all.

A throwing gripwire whips out from the shadows. It whines through the air and entangles Kane's ankles. Locks them together with the momentum of its weights. He falls, face first, in the dirt.

Sadie lets out a strangled cry. Hands wrap themselves round her waist and jerk her up and backwards. In the same instant, a massive blow lands on Adam's shoulders and he flies forward. He goes down. Flat on his stomach. Feels a flash of pain. Something hard, maybe a knee, jammed into the small of his back. A hand slams down on his head and shoves his cheek into the grit.

He blinks and tries to speak and he feels himself whipped up to his feet, as though his weight is insignificant. His arms are twisted and jerked up behind his back. He struggles and kicks, but the grip is violent. His wounded hand is on fire.

A low voice snarls behind him. 'You ain't goin anywhere.' Adam smells stale breath and recognizes the voice. Red. 'You brought this on,' he growls.

Now a spectre emerges from the darkness.

Levi Blood.

Levi looks at Adam with a steady gaze. He glances at Sadie. Then he looks down at Kane, who has crawled up on to his knees.

'Well, well. Look see what fate has bestowed on us.'

He kicks Kane – in the jaw – a crunching blow that drives Kane backwards. Kane grunts and rolls, clutching his face. He moans and draws his knees to his chest.

'LEAVE HIM!' Sadie shouts. She is across from Adam, on the other side of Kane. Behind her stands Wyatt, gripping her tight, his arms across her breasts.

'Shut her the hell up,' Levi barks at Wyatt.

Wyatt clamps a hand to her mouth. Then shrieks in pain. 'Bitch bit me!'

Levi glares at him. 'Call her that one more time and see where it gets you.'

Wyatt yanks her by the neck, but Sadie pulls loose and slaps him. A hard, fat slap across the cheek that rocks him back. The sound is bright and sudden. Wyatt grapples with her, bats her arm away. But Sadie is slippery and quick. She spins and knees him in the balls and Wyatt squeals like Old Man's Dagg's hog. He goes crashing to his knees.

Sadie whips round, hunched and snarling like an animal. She doesn't say anything. She attacks. She launches herself at Levi, leaps up on to his chest, clamps her legs round him, grabs hold of his ears with both her hands and headbutts him.

Down they go, brother and sister. A heap of arms and legs.

Adam feels himself jerked about and flung like a rag doll. He crashes into the ground on his shoulder and rolls. He is up, and back on his feet, in seconds. He whips round and sees Red pull Sadie off Levi. Sadie lashes out and shrieks, smashing Levi in the face with a steel-tipped scissor kick.

'SADIE! Adam yells, leaping up from his knees.

'Stay where you are, Stone.'

Adam spins. Wyatt – shaking, eyes wild with anger – fumbling with his sling. Adam looks at him. Seconds. That's all he has.

'Adam!' Sadie chokes. 'Do something!'

But he can't move. He wants to. He *needs* to. But his feet seem stuck in thrown cement. His eyes dart from side to side. Red rips both Sadie's arms up behind her and he pushes his massive palms together, down flat on the domed curve at the back of her skull.

Wyatt mumbles something inaudible. Something like: *Go ahead*, or *Try me*. His sling is loaded now.

Adam doesn't try him. He doesn't move.

Sadie looks up, struggling. Her eyes are wide and furious. There's something else in them too. Disbelief? Disgust?

Levi wipes a smear of blood from his nose with a greasy smile. He looks at Kane, grappling on all fours. 'It's time to make you ugly, son.'

*

The beating is relentless. Barbaric. Levi rains down blows on Kane. Kicking and punching. His ribs. His head. His stomach.

Adam cries out for them to stop. He begs them. But his shouts are like vapour. He tries not to look, but Wyatt's sling keeps him pinned to the spot. Then he feels it creep up on him. The rising Blackness. Coming for him. The spots of light. A spike of pain in his head.

The last thing he sees is Kane, on his knees, beaten and bloody. Staring with his wild yellow eyes and his blood-smeared teeth. His mouth open wide. Screaming.

Adam's vision warps and blurs. He feels the weight on his shoulders. His knees cave. But, before the Blackness takes him down, he realizes something with frightening certainty.

Kane wasn't screaming. He was laughing.

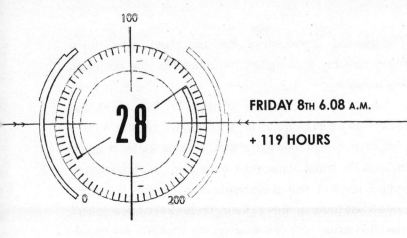

Adam lies on his back. He blinks. Tries to order his thoughts. He can't focus. He knows he blacked out. But for how long? He rolls on to his stomach. Sees Kane sprawled out, unmoving.

He remembers the violence of the beating. The look on Kane's face. The way he goaded them with his eyes. His fearlessness.

Adam sees Levi, chest heaving, shrouded in rain. Squinting down at him. Red and Wyatt stand next to him, looking drenched and tired. Adam blinks. Glances from side to side. Sadie is gone.

Levi smirks. 'Looking for your girlfriend, Stone?' He spits rainwater. 'She won't be riding with you again. Those days have flown.'

Adam staggers to his feet and casts about. 'Where is she? What've you done with her?'

'She's a Blood. She's where she belongs.'

Adam wipes rainwater from his eyes. Looks down at his boots. Follows the channels of red mud to the broken figure on the ground. He can't think straight. His head throbs and he clenches and unclenches his fists. Feels the absence of his thumb.

And that's when he notices the rock in his right hand. He looks at it and blinks.

Levi laughs. 'You don't remember, do you, Blackout Boy? Never seen anything like it. You were possessed. Isn't that right, boys?'

'Sure is, Levi,' the others chorus.

Levi looks up at the sky and the rain sluices down on him. He shakes his head. Wyatt and Red seem uncertain, waiting for his direction. Levi has a deep gash in his forehead, above the eye, and a stream of blood runs down his cheek.

'You don't remember?' he says. 'Picking up that rock?'

Adam stares down at the rock in his fist. It's covered in blood.

Levi grins. 'Never seen someone beat his friend like that.'

Adam looks at Kane. 'What are you saying? I –'

'You were jealous. He was the one my sister liked. I could see it in her eyes. You knew that. Maybe you wanted him out the way. For the girl?'

'I didn't . . . I couldn't –'

'You *did*,' Levi cuts in. 'You picked up that rock and you attacked your friend.'

Adam takes a shuddering breath and squeezes the rock in his fist. 'It's not true,' he says, but he remembers the wolves and the primitive feeling in him. The rock in his hand. The sound of bone crunching.

'Looks like we have ourselves a situation,' Levi says. 'What do you say we do, Red?'

'I say we take that rock and give him the same treatment, Levi.'

'Figured on you saying something like that. But look at him. What do you see?'

'I see a damn coward,' Wyatt barks.

'Well,' Levi says, 'that's why I'm leading this Tribe and you're nothing but a muttonhead. Thing is, he's neither coward nor fool.'

'How you figure, Levi?'

'Well. It isn't rocket science. If this Blackout Boy were a coward or a fool, he wouldn't have got this far in the Race, would he?'

Adam feels the rock in this right hand. It's as heavy as lead.

Levi looks at him, shifts his weight from one leg to the other. 'Something eating you, Stone? Is there vengeance boiling up inside you?'

Adam says nothing.

Levi turns his head to the side and spits. His dark eyes never leave Adam.

'So ... what do we do, Levi?' Red asks.

'We leave him.'

'What?' Wyatt cries, starting forward.

Levi nods. 'We leave him.'

Adam begins to shake. He can't control it. His whole body goes into a violent tremble.

Work for me, hand. Throw the rock, dammit.

His traitorous hand does nothing but shake.

'It's over,' Levi says. 'Anyone can see there's nothing left in him. He's broken.'

'Then why don't we just kill him?' Red asks.

'You don't kill something that's already dead.'

Levi smiles and steps backwards, into the shadows and the rain. On either side of him, Wyatt and Red do the same; their eyes remain fixed on Adam. Then all three turn their back on him – like he doesn't matter, like he's dirt – and they vanish from sight.

A cold, wet wind stirs and a sound comes from Adam's throat. A growl. He tilts back his head and releases a torrent of guttural howls, more animal than human. He lifts Kane and hauls his human cargo through the mud. He stumbles. Falls. Rises again.

People come through the rain. They shout at him over the storm, but he doesn't hear them. All he hears is Sadie's voice.

Adam! Do something!

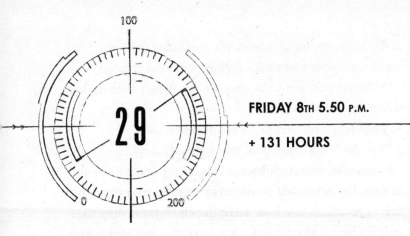

The bad weather keeps Riders another day in the muddied camp, holed up in their drenched tents, waiting and watching. Adam lies in the infirmary with his spirits withered. He looked for her. Scoured the camp, one end to the other. But he couldn't find a trace. Not of her. Not of *them*.

Levi and the Scorpions – what's left of them, Red and Wyatt as far as he can reckon – have hightailed it into the desert. Flouting the rules. Leaving before the rest. Anyone else would land in trouble for that. Anyone but Levi Blood.

Adam sits on his bed and holds his head in his hands. He thinks about the Race.

Six days. Six days of hell. He tries to chart them in his head.

Day one . . . the start, churning through the canyon. Then blasting out on to the plain. The first obstacle course. Huge jumps. Nate next to him, going strong. Then the bandits.

Everything flipped upside down. And Kane comes. They bury Nate in the ground. Leave him behind and go. Day two ... in the desert with Kane, riding hard. Day three ... Sadie appears and then the wolves. After that a blur ... another obstacle course ... the ravine ... the Nakoda.

He shakes his head. He's tired of thinking.

In the bed next to him, surrounded by a wall of white curtain, lies Kane, fed by an array of tubes and pipes and ticking machines that hum and blink and bring disinfectant-smelling medical bots jerking into the room, brandishing weird-looking implements.

Adam has no injury, besides fatigue. The swelling on his ankle is almost gone and the throb of his missing thumb is faint.

A woman stands beside his bed and taps a stylus against a digital tablet device.

'Let me see if I've got this right,' she says. 'You say you were attacked by none other than Levi Blood. Correct?'

Adam turns away from the woman. Nothing will come of this.

He hears the woman sniff and the tapping continues unabated. 'I take your insolent non-response as an affirmative, then. That'd be a *yes* in plain speak.'

'Take it any way you please,' Adam says. He looks at the door. A silent GRUB stands there.

'Let me ask you once again,' the woman says. 'Was this alleged fight perpetrated or instigated by the aforementioned Levi Blood ... son of the Colonel?'

She didn't need to say *son of the Colonel*; the point was already well made. The fight never happened. Adam dreamt the whole thing.

He glances at the white curtain wall and the faint shadow of a figure beyond, and he tries to discern the sound of breathing. But nothing comes.

'Your answer,' the woman says. 'Were you attacked by Levi Blood? Yes or no?'

Adam looks at her. 'No, dammit. *No!* Now leave me alone.'

The candlelight bounces off the woman's dark spectacles and she smiles, revealing brown teeth. 'Storm's lifted,' she says. 'Come morning you will saddle up.' She glances at Kane's bed. 'And you *will* be alone.'

An ether smell, soaked into the bedsheets, keeps Adam from falling asleep and he listens instead to the night sounds. A door closing, down the corridor. Someone coughing, hacking somewhere in the dark. The drone of the machines feeding Kane.

At dawn, he finds himself dozing, half awake, half asleep.

'Sorry, Sadie,' he says aloud to the room. 'I should've done something . . . I could've –'

'Should've. Could've. Would've,' a voice croaks in response.

Adam rises off the pillow. 'Who said that?'

Silence. The murmur of humming machines. Someone snoring. Adam waits. No answer. His eyes adjust to the dim light filtering through the window. The clouds must have dispersed. There's no sound of rain. He stares at the gauzy curtain next to his bed and he swears he can see movement. And there it is, a hand, beckoning him.

'You gotta go,' Kane whispers, laboured and slow. Adam leans right into him, holds his ear to Kane's split and swollen lips. 'And keep goin,' Kane murmurs, his breath on Adam's ear.

Adam watches him breathe. Watches his chest rise and fall. Kane's face is almost unrecognizable. At least one tooth is missing. His nose is broken. One eye is swollen shut. The other open just a fraction, revealing a bloodshot orb, more black than yellow. A lurid stitch cuts across his temple and countless other nicks and bruises mark his face.

He squeezes Kane's hand, then drops it, feeling awkward and at the same time more bonded to him than before. 'Kane . . . did I . . . do something out there?'

Kane looks at him. 'Like what?'

'Levi. He said . . . I attacked you.'

Kane looks at him with his half-open eye. Even now a dim flame burns in him. 'No,' comes the hoarse whisper. He points a finger at Adam. 'You did nothin.'

It isn't meant as an accusation, Adam knows that. But it feels like one.

I didn't hit him with the rock, but I did nothing to stop them hitting him.

'I'm sorry, I –'

'Don't beat yourself up . . .' Kane's mouth twists with pain.

Adam lifts his head and helps him get comfortable. His wounds are horrific in the candlelight. It reminds him of Frank.

You can't break people like Kane or Frank.

You can put 'em down and you can make 'em bleed. But you can't break 'em.

'Reckon Sadie's OK?' Adam says, watching him.

Kane nods. 'She's a survivor.' His voice sounds like the rattle of stones in a tyre.

'I should've done something,' Adam says again.

'What could you do? Wyatt had you covered.'

'I don't know . . . *something*. I tried to, but –'

'You love her.'

Adam looks at Kane and feels himself blush. 'Doesn't everybody? Don't *you*?'

Kane smiles weakly and shakes his head. 'Yep. But not that way.' He squints at Adam, as if trying to convey some idea in his head. 'Thought you had it figured,' he whispers.

'Had *what* figured?'

Kane rolls his head, looks away. Turns back to Adam. He reaches out a hand from under the covers – quick despite his condition. He grips Adam's wrist. 'What are you gonna do?'

'I don't know, I . . .'

Kane shakes his head. 'Say it. What are you gonna do?'

'Find her, I guess,' he mumbles.

'Say it again.'

'I'll hunt 'em down. I'll find her.'

Kane coughs. '*Again!* Like you mean it. Loud.'

'I'LL FIND HER!'

A horn blasts outside. Long and sharp. It stops abruptly, leaving a trembling silence.

'Damn right you will,' Kane says hoarsely.

A roaring cacophony of bykes carries to them through the window. Shouts and raised voices. The floorboards roll and a rattling metal cart careers sideways across the room. A bottle topples and crashes to the floor. It shatters, spilling a red liquid.

Adam looks at Kane. 'It's started.'

'Take the Drifter,' Kane says. 'Fastest byke there ever was. Best way to get her back.'

'The Drifter? Hell, I can't ride the Drifter.'

'Told you before ... she'll let you. Let her guide you. Listen to her. *Feel* her.'

'But the Longthorn, I –'

'I'm not asking. Go! I'll ride the Longthorn after.'

Adam looks at him. 'You're hurt bad, Kane.'

Kane smiles. 'Hell. This ain't nothin.'

'But –'

'One more thing ... Under my byke seat you'll find a small package. Bring it to me.'

Kane's Drifter. It feels like stepping inside someone else's body – what it *must* feel like – sliding inside his skin, inside his mind. Adam tries to manipulate the byke, but he can't. His hands shake and weird tremors run through him. Riders gun past him and leave him cursing in their dust.

He starts the engine and she stalls. He kick-starts her again and she stutters and lurches. Adam sweats and his stomach turns. Another Rider barrels past him. A blast of noise and sand. Adam squints and coughs in the dust.

Hell was I thinking? Drifter will never work for me.

He knows the byke has speed, if he can harness her power. No byke is faster. Not on the Circuit. Not anywhere. If he can hold it together ... if he can just fuse his legs to the Drifter ... *will* her to move ... imagine the byke's frame an extension of his own body.

He starts the motor and she runs. He rides in a jagged, ill-defined way until he senses something. Remote. Vague. A throb in the back of his head.

Adam feels the byke pull and he feels himself drift away. The air is thick as water. The desert begins to warp. Now he's floating, far away.

He's swimming in the deep. Not the lake. Somewhere else. The water is cold. A strong current pulls at him. He's not swimming. He's sinking. Going down fast. His legs are heavy, weighted at the feet. He holds his breath and feels panic rise in his chest. Down he slides through the water, pulled to the depths by dead men on a chain. He hits the bottom and the sand churns. Under the soles of his bare feet, the soft flesh of the dead and the dying.

A shadow snakes by, smooth and silent in the black. He sees teeth, clawed feet and a scaled back. It's huge. A behemoth. It disappears with a powerful flick of its tail, leaving a whirlpool swirl of current. He pulls at the chain, frantic, feeling his lungs burn. He stares up to the moonlike sun beyond the surface. An impossible distance away.

Instinct tells him to turn. And he sees it coming. The monster, sliding in the deep. With its rows and rows of bone-crunching teeth. He shuts his eyes and he waits for the pain.

But what he feels instead is the grind of sand. The dirt beneath his wheels. He feels the coarseness of the ground. He feels rubber grinding rock. And some other feeling . . . an aloneness . . . a wildness. No pity. No remorse. No fear.

And he knows – he *knows* – whose echo he feels, whose uneasy skin he inhabits.

That's when he feels the build-up of energy, a *connection* between him and the byke. He feels the wind, scouring him. The sun, scorching him.

Adam expands his consciousness to become the byke. He transcends his body and merges with the machine. A singular, symbiotic organism – Rider and byke – one entity.

He shifts gear and the Drifter growls and moves. Oh and how they move – loose-limbed and ferocious.

The way a wolf moves.

Adam rides hard. He lost valuable ground struggling with the Drifter, but he begins to make up time. He cuts past Riders. Hauls them in and leaves them trailing in the dust.

He comes to a place of long grass, bleached by the sun and beaten flat by the wind. He cuts a path through it and keeps his eyes dead ahead. There's no sign of life. Alone in his helmet. The byke vibrates.

A bleak wind cuts across his path and he's caught in a shower of stone shrapnel. He leans into the wind. Grit gets between his teeth and crunches between his molars. His eyes stream with tears and his throat burns. He scans the broken terrain.

I let Frank down. Let Nate down . . . Kane, Sadie . . . Let 'em all down.

No more. Not ever again. I'm coming, Sadie.

He squints into the dust. Someone out there, not moving. A figure.

He brings the bike to a stop and flicks up his visor. The figure materializes from the murk, no more than a shadow. Adam has the sling in his hand. He pouches a smooth stone and swings it in a steady circle above his head. The figure stops. Holds up both hands. The sling whines in the air.

'Speak!' Adam calls to him. 'Or die standing.' The threat is swallowed in the choked air.

'Thakrar Kush,' the voice says. 'Byke's been totalled and my gear got stolen.'

'Nobody steals gear.'

'Those bastards took mine.'

Adam stops swinging the stone. He keeps it pouched and hanging at his side, ready to strike if needed. He steels himself for deception.

'Who? Scorpions?'

'The same. They've got no respect.'

Thakrar Kush stands with the hood of his jacket over his head, to protect him from the sand. He coughs intermittently. Adam can't see his eyes.

'They have a girl with 'em?'

He pauses. 'Might've done. Hard to say.'

Adam grips his handlebars. Under normal circumstances he would have disappeared into the sand long before getting close.

Keep your head down. Stay low. Say nothin. That's how you survive.

But these are not normal circumstances. And he is not himself.

'Say . . . you don't have water, do you?' Kush says. 'I'd be grateful. Hydro-pills were snatched with the byke. I figure two hydros will do me till I get back to camp.'

Adam watches him.

'Listen, I'm not a threat,' Kush says. 'You're the one on the byke.'

Adam pops a flap on his breast pocket. He removes a pack of six hydro-pills.

'I'm asking for charity,' Kush says. 'Lead off with that fine Drifter and I'll die here.'

'People die,' Adam says. But he flings the pack at Kush anyway. 'Take 'em.'

Kush drops to his knees and snatches up the pack. He rips it open and pops a blue pill, throwing his head back to swallow it with spit. Then he stands with the pack in his hand, watching Adam. 'You ride alone,' he says.

It's not a question. It's a statement.

Adam has a bad feeling. 'What Tribe are you?'

'Tribe?' Kush stares at Adam with red-rimmed eyes. 'I'm standing here alone.'

Then, in a way so subtle it seems not to happen at all, Kush tilts his head. The vaguest gesture. A slight inclination. Enough to make Adam's stomach twist.

A signal!

Beneath the hood . . . his skin . . . alabaster-white skin . . . plum-coloured lips. Eyes painted . . .

Deads.

Deads are never alone; there are always . . .

ZZZLICK!

Adam flinches. The stone zips past his ear, so close he feels the displaced wind on his cheek.

GO!

Adam doesn't hang around. He opens the throttle, pulls the front wheel of the Drifter back in a huge wheelie and guns it straight for Kush. As he does this, he hears them.

The others. And he sees them in his peripheral vision, closing in at speed from each side. Exploding out of the dust.

Frank's voice leaps into his head.

If you have to fight, fight dirty. No kind of clean fighting left.

In front of him, Kush does a panicky jig, trying to pre-empt Adam's next move.

He gets it wrong.

Kush sidesteps right into his path. Adam doesn't bother swinging the sling. There isn't time. The byke seems to take over. Heading straight for him. But – right at the last second – Adam swerves.

I'm not Kane. I'm not Levi.

Kush gives a strangled cry and disappears under the Drifter's wheels. Adam feels the byke leap and jolt. A sickening crunch. Then the wheels take and he spurts forward. He looks back.

He sees Kush limping. Wounded. But alive.

He keeps well ahead of the Riders for roughly five klicks. There are four of them. All Deads he sees now. They look familiar. Might be the same Deads they encountered on the plain after the Nakoda camp. They come hard after him, bent on some revenge, or just to knock him out of the Race. It doesn't much matter.

The landscape changes. The ground is black and hard. Fissures and cracks open in the earth. There isn't a tree in sight, not a blade of grass. In the distance, a black, conical shape looms. A mountain. A grey billow of smoke from the summit. Not just any mountain. A volcano.

El Diablo!

The Race end is near.

Adam glances over his shoulder, acknowledges the Riders still coming. The Drifter is fast and he's opening a progressive lead, but not enough. By nightfall, when the bykes lose their power, they'll be close enough to make an attack on foot.

Something occurs to him as he rides. Back there, when he rode clean through that kid, he did it without thinking, without panic. And he didn't feel the Blackness. Any other time like that, the Blackness would have risen and that would be him . . . gone. Blacked out.

But he's different now.

He is not afraid.

He *will* find her.

He *will* do what he needs to do.

He *will* become what he needs to become.

A Stone Rider.

Adam squeezes both brakes, releases the front one and leans low, kicking out the back wheel so that he slides out and turns, using the force of his momentum to spin himself upright and whip the byke round to a dead stop, facing in the opposite direction. A one-eighty-degree stop.

The Riders, specks in the distance, keep coming. Clattering over an earth remade from fire.

Adam opens the throttle and the Drifter throbs. A perfect sound. He releases the brakes and the byke jerks forward, throwing him back in the seat. The Drifter eats the ground, rips a fat-wheeled track under him.

All four see him come at them and continue onwards, their pace unchecked.

He sees them grow in size, rising from specks to machines, to Riders.

Chicken it is, then.

Adam removes the sling from his belt with his right hand. With his left, the damaged hand, he pushes down on the handlebar to keep the byke steady. His heart beats a calm rhythm. The braided cord feels good in his hand. It feels like it belongs there. It feels part of him. One fused organism: byke and boy and sling.

He unleashes the first stone in a dreamlike state. The sling crack is loud and startling. A Rider wobbles, falls, tumbles backwards, and the Riderless byke careers away from the pack, then flips and somersaults, tearing up chunks of earth.

One down. Three to go.

Stones whistle overhead, the overturned byke whines, the Deads scream obscenities, but Adam doesn't heed them. He ducks down, flattens his body against the byke's frame . . . and charges.

The Dead in front of him swerves, eyes wide and white, fixed on Adam coming at him low and hard. The Dead leans left and rips the throttle back.

Too little, too late.

The Drifter's front wheel mounts the slope of the angled byke and Adam is launched skyward, using the Dead's byke and body as a makeshift ramp. In mid-air, he unleashes another stone from the sling, whirring above his head, and the stone finds its target.

Two down. Two to go.

Adam blasts out across the lava ground, in the opposite direction to the two Deads left. They brake and loop back. Adam does the same, wheel-spinning round so that he comes to face them again. He opens the throttle and roars towards them.

'WHAT ARE YOU GONNA DO!' he screams, loosing stone after stone. 'YOU CAN COME AT US AND KEEP COMING, BUT YOU CAN'T TAKE US!'

Each bullwhip crack reminds him of the barrage of blows that rained on Kane. They remind him of Frank's head hitting each step as he dragged him to his grave. And they remind him of Sadie's plea to him.

Adam! Do something!

The Deads see the intent in Adam and they check and swerve right, cutting up dirt tracks as they veer across the open black ground . . . away from Adam.

'I'M NOT ALONE!' he shouts at their backs. 'YOU HEAR THAT? I'M NOT ALONE!'

Adam comes to a breathless stop and sits astride his byke, staring after them. He's filled with a weird, heart-thumping thrill, an after-shot of adrenalin. But he has another creeping feeling in him. Revulsion. Horror at the violence.

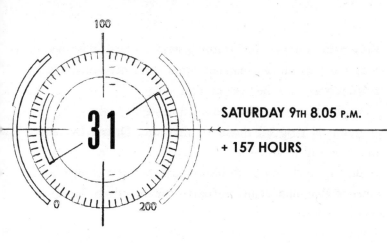

He rides into the night, watched by a gathering of indifferent airships. He rides until the Drifter – depleted of its store of heat energy – shudders and peters out.

He builds a fire to hold the cold at bay and kneads his stomach with a fist to stave off hunger cramps. He tips back his head to take one of his remaining hydro-pills. Then stares at the Drifter, at the flames reflected in its silver sides.

He sees himself mirrored there, behind the flames. A ragged-looking kid with a killing weapon gripped in each of his clenched fists. In one hand, a sling. In the other, Nate's blade. Kane slipped it to him in the infirmary.

He looks beyond the byke to the dim, moonlit plain. In the half-light, Adam can just make out the shadow of a mountain. A black hole cut out of the night. The dark smudge of El Diablo.

At first light, before setting out, he drains his canteen of water and throws it away. Then he stands looking at his

Race pack. Taking a few running steps, he hurls this away too, as far as he can manage. He doesn't need anything. Just his body and the byke and the sling.

Nothing between him and what he needs to do.

Adam is stripped down to the core. Driven by one thought only. Revenge.

But, as he climbs on to his byke, he senses a competing voice. Telling him to be careful. To remember who he is.

Not to lose himself.

In the shadow of El Diablo lies the final obstacle course – the remaining man-made challenge. One last test before a straight shoot home to Blackwater. Adam reckons there are at least half a dozen Riders between him and the winning flag. And one of them is Sadie.

What have they done with her? Is she bound? Gagged? Beaten?

Adam rides hard. Fuelled by rage.

In the sky above the course, a wake of vultures hovers – waiting for the carnage. Adam glances up at the airships and at the trykes, high on the slopes of the volcano, casting long shadows. They won't care about his personal circumstance. Or Sadie's. They are motivated by one thing.

Blood.

But it won't be my blood. Not today.

Adam shakes his head and catches sight of a flash of metal. A Rider, mid-course. He watches the racing line of the solitary figure.

The Rider is skilled and he manoeuvres his byke with artistry, but too fast. He's riding against time. Adam finds himself rooting for him. He doesn't know why. He doesn't know the Rider, he doesn't recognize his riding style or his dark blue byke, but the moment is stark and beautiful. A lone Rider, pitted against stone and dirt.

Adam looks up at the airships, wondering if they know something the Rider doesn't.

A sharp cry comes from the course and, without having to look, Adam knows what the cry means. But he does look. And hates himself for it. He sees the Rider fall.

The Rider drops backwards from his byke; at the apex of a jump, he plummets back with his arms upflung and . . . and, from his chest, thin lines extend.

Arrows.

Adam has heard of this type of sabotage. Sky-Base has rigged the final obstacle course with triggered arrows.

The trick with arrows, Frank told him once, is to ensure your racing line is pure. If a Rider veers from the optimal path – by inches – the arrows fly.

It was here, on the black slopes of El Diablo, where Frank lost his leg. Beyond saying where it happened, Frank never spoke of the incident. It was taboo. Like Pa's suicide, like Ma's death from the lung sickness before that. All taboo.

Adam arches his neck back and searches the sky for some purpose in all this. 'Where are you, Frank? You up there watching?'

Silence. Frank's echo doesn't inhabit the Drifter's metal skin.

Now Adam descends into the obstacle course. The Drifter purrs and he rides with his head up, watchful and aware. He engages the transfer engine and the byke ratchets up into a jumping position. He opts for goggles instead of helmet, with his filter mask feeding him clean air.

Stay light. Stay free.

The course is steep with furrowed lanes, fierce turns and six massive jumps.

He slips into the first narrow channel and concentrates on getting his racing line right, on taking every corner at the right angle, on keeping his speed well checked, not too fast, not too slow. Bursts of speed when he needs it. Control is the key.

He reaches the first jump in a hurry and he swoops up and leaps skyward. Down the other side. Beautiful. Perfect.

A familiar thrill runs through him. His vision becomes tunnelled. He sees nothing but the track in front of him, the next turn, the jump coming. He's back in the zone, riding by feel, unconscious to the world outside the course. It feels good. It feels natural. It feels like coming home.

He navigates the course with precision. Attacking the jumps, being cautious in the turns, taking the right line every time. No arrows shoot out from their secret channels. Not this time.

He powers up to the second to last jump. The biggest tabletop of the course and he sails over it without thinking.

He turns his front wheel in mid-air, floats, then plunges down the far side.

He's coming towards the last jump on the course when his instincts buzz. Something isn't right.

He keeps riding, alert. And then he hears the sound. Up ahead. Hollers and shouts . . . coming from the slopes of El Diablo.

Adam pulls up at the top of the last ramp. He's breathing hard and sweat streams down the small of his back. His riding suit clings to him. He sees them. Three dirt spirals climbing high. Three Riders coming out of the sun, careering down the lava slope like the devil's on their heels.

Time to haul ass.

With a last glance, he kicks down and goes. He flies down the jump and he's away. Flicks a look over his shoulder, sees nothing but dust. He flips a gear and the byke grinds. He's tired. He can feel the leaden weight of his legs.

He pulls off the track, strikes out for the desert. He looks back and sees one of them at a standstill.

ZZZLICK!

Something shoots past his ear. He swerves and ducks down. He's riding like a demon. Going as hard as he can.

ZZLICK! SSSHNICK!

Stones.

He looks back over his shoulder and there they are. Still coming. Still flying. Except the tall one, back on a rise, sighting him with a sling.

That's the last thing he sees before the pain hits. And then the world spins upside down and the sky turns black.

He moans and crawls on the ground. The Drifter, out of reach, lies with her wheels spinning. Adam reaches a shaky hand to his face. His mask is gone, ripped from his mouth. His goggles, incredibly, still strapped to his head. Teeth intact. Nose unbroken. When he moves, a pain knifes through his side. Bruised rib.

His temple throbs. Blood drips into his eye. He can feel the hot pulse of it running down his forehead, down his cheek. But it's OK – head cuts bleed.

He looks up at the three Riders circling him. One tall. One muscular. One on a white byke. All of them in gleaming Voddenite suits, their colours alternately black, silver and gold in the sun.

He tries to think. Tries to order his thoughts. His vision is blurred. A ringing noise jangles in his ear. A dull pain throbs at the base of his skull. It feels like his bones have turned to rubber.

Levi comes to a sliding stop with a back-wheel brake. The others follow suit. He lifts up his helmet visor and squints down at Adam. 'Who are you?'

Adam coughs and winces with the pain.

'Man asked you a question,' Red says, lowering his byke to its stand.

'Nobody,' Adam croaks, finding his voice.

'Well, that's all wrong,' Levi says. 'I know you. And you know me.' He swings off his byke and approaches Adam. With steady hands, he reaches down, unclips Adam's goggles and tosses them away.

Adam knows what's coming now.

Vengeance.

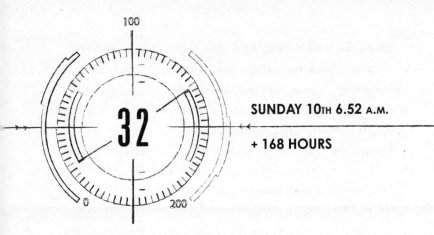

'*You!*' Levi stumbles back. He stares. And then a light comes on in his face. 'Of course. I knew we put him in the ground.' He smiles, squatting on his haunches in front of Adam. 'So ... if it isn't the Blackout Boy. Perhaps not broken after all. Beat up your friend, then stole his byke, I see.'

Adam says nothing.

Levi grins and stands, looking down on him.

'Round here we kill for stealing bykes,' Wyatt says, sneering.

Red steps forward, rock in hand. 'Want him dead *now*, Levi?'

A flicker of annoyance flashes in Levi's eyes. 'If I wanted him dead, he'd be dead ... Throw the damn rock away.'

Red pulls a face and grips the rock, white-knuckled.

'Throw it away, dumb-ass!' Wyatt spits.

Red glares at him. 'Call me dumb-ass one more time –'

Levi spins on them. 'Shut the hell up . . . *please* . . . for a goddamn minute.' He sighs and shakes his head. Then he looks at Adam. 'Don't ever say my life is easy.'

'Where's Sadie?' Adam rasps. He attempts to sit up on his elbows and flinches in pain.

'You've got it bad, haven't you?'

'Just tell me where she is.'

Levi smiles. 'I'll do better. I'll show you.'

Adam's hands are tied at the wrists and his waist is fastened to the byke frame. He's going nowhere. On his left rides Wyatt, leering at him. On his right, Levi, whistling some inane and repetitive tune. Red takes up the rear. They pass the burnt-out wreck of a byke. A charred carcass still grips the handlebars. Wyatt rides close and delivers a savage kick to the body.

Levi continues whistling. Adam turns away.

He hasn't seen living Riders for some time and he knows there's no one beyond the Scorpions now. If there were, they wouldn't be so relaxed. They wouldn't be taunting him. This is the leading group – he *knows* it – and there's nothing between them and the line.

They rise up the slope of El Diablo. The heat is oppressive. Then Adam sees something that makes his heart stop in his chest. Ahead, swimming in the heat haze, a figure lashed to a tree with ropes.

'SADIE!'

The full horror of what Levi has done descends on Adam. Running a few paces in front of Sadie, a red river belches and bubbles from a deep fissure. Molten lava.

She's too close. She'll burn.

He struggles in his seat and the Drifter angles and tips. He sprawls into the black dust and rolls, ignoring the pain. He gets to his feet and runs up the slope, but the rope is still wound to his waist, attached to the byke. He is jerked off his feet and slams hard on to his back. He groans and crawls upright, scrabbles through the dirt, stunned and dizzy.

Levi shakes his head and laughs. 'I can't watch this. Free the love-struck fool.'

Red pins him down with a knee and unties the rope. He stands and spins Adam round, unloosing the cord with a quick pull. Adam feels the rope burn. He gets up and staggers to the tree.

Sadie's arms are extended in front of her body, twisted over each other, and tied together. Her red bandanna is stuffed in her mouth. A rope, lashed to the tree, has been slipped through the knots that keep her arms pinned and it holds her at a slanting angle, away from the tree, leaning into the lava. Heat comes up in warping waves from the molten river. Sadie's eyes are wide. Full of rage and fear. Her cheeks are bright red.

Adam grits his teeth. Every cell in his body zeroes in on one task. Freeing her. He reaches for the rope and a stone whips through the air, missing his right hand by inches. He spins round and sees Wyatt, head down, sling in hand, loading another stone.

'Next one kills the girl,' Wyatt says, not bothering to look up.

'I'd leave those knots,' Levi says.

'She's your *SISTER*!' Adam yells. His heart hammers inside his chest. He feels like he's going to be sick.

'Here's the play,' Levi says. 'You'll stand your ground and you'll face me with that sling of yours. Kill me and you're welcome to liberate your girlfriend. But if I kill *you* ... well ...' He looks at Sadie, then down at the bubbling lava.

'And your thugs? They'll let us go on our way?'

'They'll do as I say.' He flicks a look at each of them. Red standing solid as a mountain on one side. Wyatt, whippet-thin and tall, swinging his sling. 'Isn't that so, boys?'

'Sure thing, Levi,' Red says.

'See?' Levi declares, throwing up his hands. 'Nothing to worry about.'

Adam glares at him. 'You killed my brother.'

Levi smiles and looks straight back at him. 'Toss the Blackout Boy his weapon.'

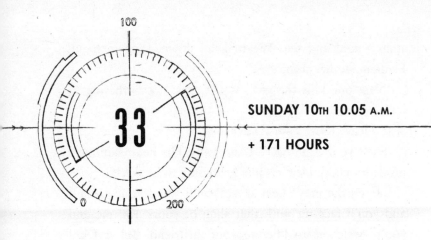

Adam looks at Red, to the left of Levi. Stocky, thick-necked, muscular. A forbidding sight, but, as far as his slingshot ability goes, he knows he has nothing to fear. Red's intentions are always plastered on his face. He'll advertise his move way before he lets the stone go.

He glances at Wyatt, standing on the right, legs apart, hands at the ready. Wyatt's ability is well known. To grow up in Blackwater is to know his speed. Wyatt is not subtle. His sling emerges, hell-fire quick, at the mildest provocation. Adam has seen the spectacle countless times. Each time Wyatt's opponent has fallen. Except once, when Wyatt's anger got the better of him. His weakness is his temper. Enraged, he's prone to wild and wayward throws.

Levi, on the other hand, is an altogether more complicated proposition. Adam has never seen him use his sling. All he has to go on is rumour. Stories passed from one Rider to another. But he knows the leader of the Scorpion Tribe is deadly. His face displays nothing. He stands in an easy, relaxed posture as though out for a casual stroll. But it's his eyes . . . his quick brown eyes that speak of danger.

Adam thinks back to Kane's interrupted lesson.

Sling won't work with anger. A sling needs tenderness.

He remembers Sadie pressed up against his body. Her satin skin on his skin. The hot pulse of her blood.

Hold a sling like you hold a woman. Loose. And strong at the same time.

He didn't know what it meant then. He does now.

He says nothing. Focuses his mind on the sling in his hand, and what is required of him.

The fingers on Adam's right hand itch. He thinks about the stone's journey: exploding out from the sling's cradle at the right moment, the top of an arc, when the powerful thrust generated by the cord's woven Voddenite is perfect, when the momentum will carry the stone to its target at a speed of about seventy yards per second, until it pummels right through flesh and shatters bone.

Kane told him a stone – shot from a Voddenite sling – can be more lethal than a pistol. And, in the right hands, more accurate.

Adam shuts his eyes and goes into a kind of trance, the way he does when he rides.

'I think he's set to black out,' Wyatt says.

'No,' Levi says. 'I believe you're wrong on that score, Wyatt. What we have here is someone changed into some other thing.'

'Some other thing, Levi?' Red asks.

Adam flicks open his eyes. He watches them. He doesn't move a muscle. Only his eyes move, from one Scorpion to the other, alert for a sign . . . a *tell*.

'I believe he owes us gratitude, brothers,' Levi says. 'See we fixed him. Gave him a reason to be alive. Took his ailment, and left him with nothing but hate.' Levi keeps his eyes steady on Adam. 'I think we may find him more formidable now.'

'S'pose he's gonna die all the same,' Red says.

'Like his brother died,' Wyatt laughs.

'My brother was a damn fine Rider,' Adam says with an even voice. 'Something you'll never be, Wyatt. Know why? Because you don't have the skill . . . but mostly because you're dumb. Dumber than Red . . . and Red's dumb as a pig.'

Wyatt's lip curls and his face turns puce. 'You goddamn . . . I'll show you dumb –'

'Wyatt, NO!' Levi barks. But Wyatt, at speed, has the sling in his hand.

Adam is hyper-aware, his senses alive, his instincts on fire. His right hand moves lightning-quick to the sling, he pouches a stone in one seamless movement, and then . . .

A dull knocking sound. A mallet-hitting-wood sound. Wyatt jerks his head backwards and to the side. Both arms fall limp and, when he winds his head back to them, a look of shock, of bewilderment, haunts his eyes. And, blue-black in the dead centre of his forehead, a plum-sized wound. Wyatt blinks, once, twice.

CRACK! A report echoes off the black volcano and all eyes swivel to the slope.

Kane. Standing at the top of the slope. Godlike and frightening in the harsh light. The terrain behind him black as night.

Levi stares at him. 'How the hell . . .'

Adam has a stone pouched, index finger through the loop. Cord ends between thumb and forefinger. He flicks his eyes from Levi to Red. Both are staring at Kane. Levi with his sling at the ready. Red still fumbling with his.

Wyatt is on his knees, surprise still etched on his face, he opens and closes his mouth like a gasping fish. He groans and tips face first into the dirt, throwing up a puff of black dust. It sinks on him and he doesn't move.

Levi turns, glances at Wyatt and looks at Adam. Adam's sling is aimed at Levi's head.

'Lower your aim.' It's Red. Adam glances at him, sees his predicament. Red, with his sling ready, is aiming at Adam, feet planted apart. But Red's hands are shaking and sweat streams from his forehead. His eyes flick from Adam to Levi, and always come back to Wyatt.

'WYATT!' he yells. 'Get up, Wyatt!'

'Wyatt's dead, Red. Wyatt's dead.' Levi says this with a serene expression, swinging his sling, down low at the hip, like none of this bothers him.

'You killed Wyatt!' Red chokes, looking at Adam. His eyes are blank. He's in shock.

'Take control of yourself, Red,' Levi says.

Down the slope of El Diablo comes Kane. He leaves Adam's byke, the Longthorn, where she stands and he comes on foot, his boots crunching. Even though his walk is ragged, he looks in total control. He's hard as bone, Kane.

Unbreakable. He moves through the dust with his slow Rider's gait and he kicks up a dark cloud as he comes. It sticks to his riding suit and his boots are blackened with it. Even at close range, he's difficult to distinguish from the terrain, as though he's a shadow snatched up from the sand.

In the glare, it's difficult to see the extent of his injuries, but his yellow eyes still blaze.

'Don't you ever die?' Levi spits at his approach.

'Did once,' Kane says. 'Didn't like it much.'

Levi studies him, eyes squinting. 'Who *are* you?'

'They call him Kane,' Adam says.

Kane shakes his head. 'But that ain't my birth name.'

A beat of silence.

Levi shifts his stance. He looks uncomfortable. 'Well, if it isn't Kane, what the hell is it?'

Kane turns his arm, pulls up his sleeve and displays something Adam failed to notice before.

A mark – not a tattoo – a raised welt on the inside of his forearm. The letter *P* burnt into his skin. An infamous slave brand – a Providence burn mark.

Adam remembers his conversation with Sadie.

He didn't just blame the slaves. He killed them. He took them – men, women, children – took them down to the river. He chained them and he drowned them. All of them.

Falsely accused of starting a fire. Chained and tossed to the river gators. Sunk to their death.

'Don't you see who I am? Kane's the name the Nakoda gave me. But the name I had when the Colonel sold me to them Providence Slavers . . . was Blood.'

PART 3

UNDER THE RED ROCK

Levi's expression doesn't change, but a flush comes to his cheeks. A band of white appears under the eyes. A sheen of sweat on his cheek. His mouth contorts into a grimace. It's there in his dark eyes, in the tight curl of his lips. Recognition.

He shakes his head. 'It's not true.'

Kane looks at him. 'It *is* true. My name was Blood. Joe Blood.'

Levi's mouth is set firm, like a line of wire. 'It doesn't matter,' he says. 'Nothing matters.'

Adam stares speechless at Kane . . . at Joe Blood. Levi, Sadie and Joe. He should have seen the resemblance, but no . . . Kane's scars hid the truth. Not even his brother and sister recognized him. Two brothers and a sister, ripped apart. The Colonel left his mark on his children. It made Sadie strong. It made Levi a psychopath. And it turned Joe into someone else altogether. Someone unfamiliar, even to his own kin.

A false night arrives. It begins to snow. Not real snow. Ash. Grey flakes drifting down from a cloud belching from El Diablo's gaping mouth, high above them. The floating airships disappear and the sail trykes dissolve into gloom.

Adam's sling is still directed at Levi's head. Red's sling is likewise directed at his head. Levi and Kane hold their slings at their sides. What happens next happens in slow motion.

Adam sees each frame of movement as though all four of them are underwater.

First – disrupting the scene – two Riders, Hawks by the look of their crimson jackets, come sailing past, swirling through the ash. They keep their heads low and they look neither left nor right. They don't even glance up at Sadie, hung on the rope. Anyone savvy enough to survive this far into the Blackwater Trail knows when to stop and when to keep going.

This intrusion of the Riders is a catalyst. Red swivels round to launch his stone, not at Adam, at Kane. Violence explodes all around.

Kane's sling blurs into action, loading and firing a stone before Red has even twisted halfway round. At the same time, Levi's sling has swung round and – a nanosecond before he releases – Adam fires his own stone. It sings through the air on a straight path. Red and Levi drop at the same time.

Adam steps forward in a daze, his ears buzzing. He comes to Red first and looks at the sightless eyes staring up. Dark blood flows from a circular wound above the left eye. Adam steps over him and keeps walking, to the crumpled figure of Levi. He lies with his face to the ground.

Adam stands over him, hands shaking, breathing hard. He tips him with his boot, the way he tipped Frank's body.

Levi flips. His arm flings out and lands with a loose thud. And he groans. He's alive. His chest rises and falls. On his cheek a bright smear of crimson blood. The cheek is blue-black already. The bone must have fractured where the stone hit. The skin under Levi's eye turns a deep red, then purple as Adam watches.

'Cut her loose,' Kane says at his elbow, handing Adam a canteen of water.

Adam doesn't waste any time. He runs across the ground to the tree and throws himself at the knots. He pulls away the rope attached to the tree first and hauls Sadie away from the lava. Then he plucks the bandanna from her mouth.

Sadie spits and sucks air. Adam works on the remaining ropes and gives her the water. She slugs it back. Hands him the canteen. Wipes her mouth with the back of her hand. 'Didn't need help,' she gasps. Her voice comes from her throat like a cough.

Same old Sadie.

Now she turns and looks at Kane and Levi. Her brothers.

They tie Levi to the tree. His eyes are shut. His head hangs limp, chin pressed into his chest. 'I should kill him,' Adam says.

An eye for an eye. Blood for the blood he spilled.

Sadie shakes her head. 'You're not like that.'

'Maybe I am. Maybe that's *exactly* what I'm like.'

'He'll die here soon enough.'

'No he won't,' Kane says. 'Airships will send a message to the Colonel. He'll free him.'

Adam looks up at a lone airship and then back at Kane. The brutal evidence of his beating is everywhere in his face. His bruised cheek. The darkness under his eyes. His swollen lip.

'When I left, you were –'

'Half dead?'

'I didn't think you'd make it.'

'Nakoda meds. In the package you brought up for me. Thunderbolt to the heart stuff.'

Adam notices Sadie staring at Kane. Her almond eyes carry a barrage of messages. He reads anger in them. Resentment. Bitterness. Joy. Love. Too many emotions to battle at once.

'You could've bloody told me,' she says. Her voice is quiet.

Kane looks at her. 'I wanted to. Woke up early, the morning after bunking in Adam's shelter. Aimed to come see you and make it plain.'

'But you didn't.'

Kane looks away, across the desert. 'Guess I didn't know how.'

Sadie watches him. 'We swam the lake the day before you left . . . Do you remember?'

Kane says nothing.

'I was five. But it feels like yesterday. We swam all day, until my arms ached and my fingers wrinkled. We drifted out so far, you let me hang on to your shoulders and you swam us back to shore. It was one of those perfect days. You called it a pearler. I'm not sure why – the sky was bluer than glacier ice. Then the next day you were gone.'

Kane shifts his weight. 'I'm not the same kid any more. I've seen things. *Done* things.'

'You ran away! Without a word. It killed Ma. She died of a broken heart.'

Kane shakes his head. 'I didn't run. Colonel came for me. Before dawn. Said he wanted me to see some business deal in Providence. Said I was a man now. I was *seven*. I didn't pack nothin, just took what I was wearing. Rode on the back of his byke. He rode your Stormchaser, back then.'

'I remember.'

'We got to Providence late the next day. Colonel took me out to meet some mean-looking devil. I had a bad feeling about it. Came up all of a sudden. I should've bolted *then*. But I didn't. Instead I watched the man I called Pa take a payment of cash money and shove me away.'

Adam stares. 'He *sold* you? You were just a boy. His *own* boy!'

Kane looks at Sadie, his eyes ablaze. 'Turns out I wasn't. Turns out Ma was already pregnant when the Colonel took her in. Then, eventually, after all them beatings, I guess Ma was gonna leave him. S'pose it all came out then. She told him. Selling me was his revenge.'

Sadie sighs. Long and deep. 'I . . . I had no idea.'

'I didn't neither. Not till then.'

She reaches out and puts a hand on his cheek. And, to Adam's surprise, he allows her to. 'You've been through hell,' she says. 'How did you survive?'

'I made a list.'

'A list?'

'All them who were gonna pay. The one who sold me, the one who branded me, the one who beat me, the one who worked me, the one who shackled me, the one who threw me in the river, and the one who let them do it. It's the list that's kept me alive.'

'And you took 'em all down?' Adam says.

Kane turns to him. His eyes are pools of fire. 'Came to Blackwater to kill the last.'

Silence. No one speaks.

Sadie drops her hand from Kane's face. 'Why haven't you?'

Kane looks at her. 'Oldest law we have. Anyone with enough base points secures a legal, one-way ticket to the Ark of Sky-Base. No matter who you are or what you've done. They *have* to send you up.' He taps the Plug in his head. 'No one can touch you. You start new up there.'

'What are you saying?'

'I'm saying the Colonel will pay his debt to me. But first I'll take my points.'

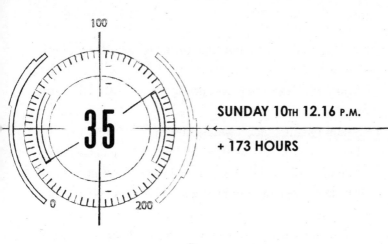

Adam worries a stone in his pocket with his right hand, looking at Levi, thinking about Kane's words. *The Colonel will pay his debt to me.* He knows Kane's right about Levi. They'll find him. The Colonel won't let him die like this. He'll get his son cut down. Or maybe he won't. Maybe he'll resent his son's failure and let him suffer.

He watches Kane and Sadie returning from across the sand. Coming back from hiding Levi's byke. Adam picks up Kane's canteen and throws a splash of water in Levi's face. Levi groans and lifts his head. He blinks his one good eye. Blood courses down his chin.

Neither boy speaks.

Levi winces as he shifts his weight against his bonds. The rope around his neck is tight and the more he struggles, the tighter it chokes him. He looks into Adam's eyes and perhaps he sees some change in them, something that tells of a hardening of purpose, or perhaps the rope choking him induces a sudden tightening in his guts, a spurt of panic. In either event, a vestige of fight leaches from Levi. Adam sees it go from his eyes.

'Untie me,' Levi croaks, putting up a show. 'No harm done. Not yet.'

Adam remains silent, watching him.

Levi looks at him with cold hate. His tone changes. 'All right, look. I didn't want to insult you, but we can settle this. I've got means. You know that. We'll work something out.'

Adam feels his pulse quicken. 'You killed my brother. You were gonna kill Sadie.'

'*What?* That's absurd. I'd never kill my own sister . . . It was just to . . . to scare you.'

Adam thinks about Kane and Sadie – brother and sister.

Isn't Levi their brother too? Wasn't his pa a mean bastard to him too?

'And your brother, Frank,' Levi says. 'He just . . . got in the way, is all.'

Adam feels his heart harden. He removes something from his jacket pocket. Holds it in his hand, turning it. Nate's ceramic knife.

Levi's eyes pop. 'Please, no. Not like this.'

Adam, without sympathy, watches his face contort. He presses the tip of the knife into the soft flesh under Levi's chin. Levi flinches. Adam nicks the flesh with a quick flick. A drop of ruby blood hangs, swells . . . and falls.

He lowers the weapon. Cuts open Levi's riding suit. Runs the knife down to his stomach, watching the way the point draws a thin line of seeping blood.

Levi's eyes track the knife's progress. He blinks and clenches his jaw. Sweat runs from him. Then his face turns white with fury. 'Go ahead,' he says. 'Kill me. Do it. Because if you don't I will hunt you. I'll spend everything I have to find you. I was a fool. I toyed with you. I should've ended you. I should've cut out your heart.'

Adam's fingers curl round the knife's handle. His grip is violent.

'Open your mouth,' he says.

'Why? What are you gonna do . . . you crazy bastard.'

Adam notes with satisfaction how Levi's dropped his condescending bravado.

'Open,' he repeats. 'Or I'll make this slow.'

Levi opens his mouth. His teeth are covered in blood.

Adam lifts the knife and wedges it sidelong into Levi's mouth. Levi clamps it in his teeth and stares at him with his one eye shut and the other hot with rage. Adam walks round the tree and unties Levi's hands. He binds them in front of him.

'You'll be able to cut yourself free. Just drop the knife in your hands.' He stoops to place the canteen at the foot of the trunk. 'Should be enough water to survive a few days. It'll take you a while to cut free. This is tough rope. And a while longer to find the bykes. But they're out there.'

Adam watches him, saying nothing more.

Then he turns to leave and never looks back.

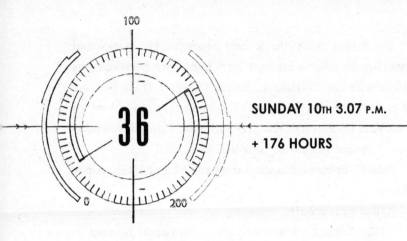

They blaze west across a blighted earth. Sadie riding the Stomchaser. Kane moulded to the Drifter. Adam back on his trusted Longthorn. The byke feels as comfortable as a worn-in pair of jeans. He *feels* the connection. Feels Frank's familiar presence in the machine.

The landscape shifts. The lava ground falls away and they swoop through a flat pan, shimmering white-hot under the sun, and they ride, elongating, shifting in the heat. No boundary lies here between earth and sky; the lines are fluid, indistinguishable.

By evening, they come to a valley with rust-coloured cliffs and powdery red sand. It's a warm, breezeless night and the sky is clear. They make camp. Build a fire and watch a pillar of smoke rise on the windless air.

'He'll come for you,' Kane says, his face lit by the flames. 'Not today. But one day.'

Adam nods. 'Let him come.'

*

The following day is long and punishing. Adam and Sadie trail Kane by some distance. The Drifter has too much pace for them. They come to a standstill in the dust and listen to their whirring bykes.

Up ahead, Kane slows. He looks over his shoulder, turns and rides back.

'Three of us and only one ticket to Sky-Base,' Adam says.

'That's a fact.'

'Will coming in second or third give you enough points?'

'Nope.'

'Then you need to win.'

Kane nods and stares into the dust.

'How many Riders ahead of us?' Sadie asks.

'Far as I can figure, just the two Hawks.'

'They'll be gunning as fast as they can.'

'That's right.'

'You're the one to catch 'em,' Adam says. 'You and that Drifter.'

'Yep. She can ride.'

'They're not gonna like you catching 'em.'

'Nope. Reckon they might put up a fight.'

Nobody speaks. Kane looks away from them and squints into the glare. 'When I saw you ride that day at the jetty, I knew then you were the one to beat. That's why I rode with you. Keep your enemies close, right?' He throws a crooked grin and glances at Sadie. 'See you on the line, sister.'

Before either responds, he gives a quick, two-fingered salute, pulls a fierce wheelie and cuts out across the hard-packed sand, tearing away from them, throwing up a plume of dust. More spirit and shadow than flesh and blood.

'There goes the Race winner,' Sadie says.

Adam nods. 'You can't beat what death can't beat.'

Adam and Sadie blast past two wrecks in the afternoon. Two fallen Riders, dead in the dust beside their carcass bykes. Hawks. The perfect circle of their stone wounds clear as day. They don't slow down. They don't stop. They keep going. And they don't see another byke until the finish line.

Dusk falls as they enter Blackwater Canyon. The same as when they left it, but in reverse. Soft river sand gropes their tyres and they hear the beat of drums . . . and a sound blurred in with the beat . . . a rising chorus of cheers. The Watchers have gathered to hail their survival, to draw them home.

High above them horns are playing. Ribbons take the wind and propeller down from the cliffs. Airships float in the hazy sky and the trykes sail up alongside them. Referees lean from the crossbars, cheering them on as they motor through the narrow channel.

Adam remembers the cries as he stepped up the line to shake the Colonel's hand.

One day. Long odds. Dead before the sun sets!

Yet they cheer for him. Blackwater allegiances shift like river sand.

'We did it!' Sadie cries over her shoulder as they round a bend and enter the last straight.

The air is hot and close and the sun throws golden light into the canyon, painting the walls so orange they are almost tangerine. Adam's eyes climb the walls to the top, where the multitudes are gathered. Where he would have been, summers before, with Pa and Frank. His eyes scan the crowd, the faces. He's waiting to see one man – Colonel Mordecai Aesop Blood.

'Aim was to win!' Adam shouts over the wind in his ears.

'Think about the cash,' Sadie hollers back. She's right about that.

All top-three placed Riders receive a thousand-dollar cash prize. Kane, Adam and Sadie.

Here come the motley crew. The referees, the Watchers, the GRUBs. The assembled masses erupt into a cacophony of noise as Adam and Sadie complete the final yards. Urchins run alongside them, throwing wilted flowers at them as they come to the line. Cheers echo from the canyon walls. Hooters blast and the drums beat.

Now the final approach. They cross together – side by side – sharing second place. Second place out of eighty-one Riders. Adam glances over his shoulder. The track behind him is empty. At last count, he remembers nineteen dead and fourteen presumed dead.

How many Riders left alive?

Here stands one of them now. The outright winner.

'Took your time,' Kane says.

On either side of him loom two GRUBs, with their cypherlike stares and their alert, metal fingers, ready to claw out fusion shooters at their robot whim. Their limbs clack as they walk. They come to a stop and stand straight-backed, like a pair of gate gargoyles, guarding their puny human.

Kane gives a lopsided smile. 'Like my new friends?'

'Wouldn't trust them far as I could spit them,' Sadie says.

Kane's amber eyes have lost none of their fire, but there's something else in them now. A flicker of hurt. Not physical pain . . . the pain of unresolved anger.

'You haven't seen the Colonel, have you?' Adam says, over the noise.

Kane shakes his head. 'He's gone.'

'He must be out there,' Sadie says. 'With Levi.'

Kane shrugs. 'Doesn't matter if he is. There's no time.'

'He'll pay for what he did,' Adam says. 'One way or another.'

'Maybe. But not by my hand. Not any more.'

The Debriefer appears in the dust, loping towards them. Ungainly and stoop-shouldered. He looks out of place with his white skin and his dark suit. He nods at the GRUBs and they jerk to life again. Instantly. The Debriefer stands there, stroking his thin lips.

'It's ready. We leave now,' he says, taking Kane's elbow. A gesture that seems more possessive than guiding.

'We'll see you,' Adam says, pointing to the sky. 'Up there we *will* see you. We've got two hundred base points each.'

'Yep. That ain't nothin.'

Sadie reaches out and grabs hold of Kane's hand, as if to draw him back. Tears brim in her eyes. Kane opens his mouth to say something. Then shuts it again.

The GRUBs force him away and, together with the tall Debriefer, they march him through a crowd straining forward to touch him. For the first time Kane looks vulnerable to Adam, escorted this way. He looks small, diminished somehow. A prisoner, rather than a victor.

Then he's gone.

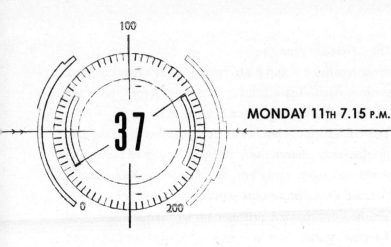

Adam and Sadie arrive at a ruined shell of a home. It squats under the red-rock cliffs, a forgotten corner of a nothing town on the edge of nowhere. They park their bykes at the well and Adam looks at the old oak, at the mounds of earth in the shadow of the tree's bone-dry trunk.

He stares at Frank's grave. The grave he dug himself. Frank, killed in a hail of stones. He thinks of his ma and her death by toxic skies. Dead before he knew her. Then Pa, whose mound of earth holds no bones. His true grave down at the bottom of Blackwater Lake. A death by water. Then he thinks about Nate. Lying dead in the desert.

Adam doesn't feel anger or bitterness. All he feels is emptiness. Above him the sky rumbles. A cold wind cuts through the hills. He turns to face his birth home.

A flash of lightning and thunder. It begins to rain. Huge drops spatter the porch and pummel the pockmarked walls. The cabin crouches on its foundations, absorbing the blows. Sadie takes cover under the oak. Adam looks up at the torrent, blinking, rainwater pooling in his mouth. He can't put his finger on the emptiness he feels inside. It's not just the graves behind him. It's something else.

He looks at the cabin and sees himself reflected in shards of glass and he realizes. It's because the Race is finished. And nothing will ever make him *feel* like that again. The Colonel was right.

You won't live more than you live in the Race.

Adam trudges through the mud, reels back the busted front door and plunges into gloom. A smell of earth and damp hits him. He pinches his nose and wades into the murk. Thunder breaks and raindrops clatter on the remaining sheets of corrugated-iron roof. Most of the roof has been peeled away, probably salvaged for other homes, leaving huge gaps for the rain to sluice in. Lightning flashes, revealing devastation. Shadows rise up and come at him.

Adam is engulfed in noise, shattering and crashing. He slams his hands to his ears. He tries to shut out the sound. The stones pound and they pound and they pound. But he knows the stones are in his head.

He makes his way outside to the shelter, and finds the trapdoor lock busted open. He descends the steps into earthy warmth. The air is close. Musty. The inside of a coffin.

His eyes grow accustomed to shapes. A spade. Broken barrels. The husk of chicken wire, throwing crooked shadows. In a dark corner, he sees some indistinct creature scurry low at the wall. Quick. Furtive. Then a blast of wind and a silent black shadow swoops past him. A keening squeak.

Another beat of wings and the dark shape gusts up into the shadowy support beams. Adam throws back his head and looks up. Moon-yellow eyes stare down at him.

Owls, roosting.

Outside the rain has stopped. Adam stands at the open door and blinks. The cabin looks unreal in the growing dark. Fake. A cardboard house. He could make it real again with the money he's won. Fix it up. Buy more chickens. Sadie and him. He takes a deep breath and thinks about their prospects – living here in Blackwater. Waiting for Levi to come.

How long do they have? A few moons? Days? Hours?

He picks up a stone. Turns it in his hand. Then he loads the stone in his sling – his hands an expert blur – and he hurls, surprising even himself with the ease and speed of the move.

First the bullwhip *CRACK*! Then the smash of glass. The remaining shards of a broken window shatter. Adam fishes out another stone, but he doesn't sling this one. Instead he turns and walks away. He knows he won't be back. At Frank's grave, he stops one last time.

'You were right about most things, Frank. All those mantras. All except the last one. *Trust no one. You're on your own.* You were wrong about that one.'

Adam swings up on to the Longthorn and looks at Sadie. 'We can't stay,' he says.

Sadie watches him. 'We should find the next Race. Keep boosting our points. Till we both have enough to make it to Sky-Basc. We'll survive. *Together.*'

Adam nods, but his thoughts float to the Nakoda. He thinks of children with long hair and valleys green with succulents. Moss-covered ground. Fields of coloured flowers. Juice squashing out of their stems like blood. Real freedom. Out in the wild. Where people don't just survive ... they *live*.

He rubs the smooth stone in his hand and he drops it in his belt pouch. Then he looks up beyond the cliffs and sees a white plume of jet stream climbing into a darkening sky. A departing solar rocket. He imagines Kane – strapped in – drifting off to sleep as the rocket soars.

A wind whips up and Adam shivers. It carries a winter chill.

'Where to?' Sadie says.

'There's only one place,' Adam answers, snapping on his goggles. 'Sky-Base.'

Acknowledgements

Huge thanks to my English teachers. Mike Stalley and Keith Savage (who was anything but).

The wonderful people over at Bath Spa MA Writing for Young People. All of them legends. Lucy Christopher. Nicola Davies. John McLay. Janine Amos. My fearless mentor, Mimi Thebo, who encouraged me to ramp up the word count. The lovely Steve Voake. If you ever experience a crisis of writing confidence, have Steve read your work out loud. He's a master at making the mundane sound magnificent (not that your work is mundane ... it's fabulous). The inspirational Julia Green. She epitomizes the heart and joy of writing and has a remarkable ability to recognize and hone talent. I guess I slipped the net. My writing group – Alex Hart, Blondie Camps, Clare Furniss, Helen Herdman, Lu Hersey and Sasha Busbridge – who *voraciously* guard against adverbs.

My agent, Stephanie Thwaites, and the team at Curtis Brown, especially Claire and Emma. Finding Stephanie was a goose-bump moment. I agree with everything she says.

My editors. Ben Horslen, whose ability to single out problems and opportunities is almost alien. Beverly Horowitz, with her astute eye for marketing. The irrepressible Tig Wallace, who is right about everything. And the tireless Puffin rights team, who sold *Stone Rider* to the world.

Working Title Films. For seeing the potential.

My brother. For reading drafts and not laughing.

My dad. For telling me to dream BIG.

My mom. For making me fall in love with words.

And Delphine. For being the most talented and beautiful human on the planet.

THE RIDER'S CODE

A MANUAL FOR RIDERS OF THE VODDEN CIRCUIT

Selected Extracts

THE ARTISTRY OF BYKES

A guide to the mystical art of byke riding and maintenance. Understand the volatile nature of bykes. Learn to get more from your connection and attune to the powerful echoes that inhabit your byke.

THE BIOMECHANICAL NATURE OF BYKES

Bykes (and this may seem like stating the obvious) are not just machines.

They may look like machines. They may even sound like machines (although this point is debatable – many attest to bykes sounding exactly like a purring or growling animal and some say they make an almost human sound). But they are not merely machines. Bykes are biomechanical entities.

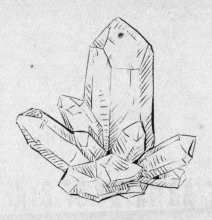

Diagram A. Voddenite

It is, of course, the Voddenite in the frame that gives a byke its biomechanical nature.

Voddenite. Possibly the most important discovery in the history of mankind (even outranking fire). No one truly understands the essence of this miracle stone mined from the Earth's mantle. But everyone knows its power. It forges connections. Between people and slings. Between Riders and bykes. It links them together with a living current that runs from one to the other.

In short, Voddenite imbues bykes with sentience.

From the Rider the byke draws life.

From the byke, the Rider draws strength, and a vestige of the machine.

It crosses over into the Rider's consciousness. You will become familiar with this feeling of otherness. Ride for a long time and you will feel the cold resilience build up inside you. But you must learn to master the sensation.

The trick is to let go. Don't fight the byke. Understand the byke. She derives her energy from the sun and the wind, but also you. The more precise and rhythmic your movements, the more efficiently your byke will ride.

If you remember nothing else from this manual then it ought to be this: A byke, like a horse, has personality. She becomes attuned to her Rider.

You cannot expect to coax performance from her at will (no doubt your many scrapes and bruises will attest to this). Winning a byke's trust and confidence requires sensitivity. A byke is changeable. She will react to your mood. And she will have moods herself. Sullen one moment. Spitting with energy the next. Learning to appreciate these idiosyncrasies not only ensures your connection with the byke is stronger, but makes you a far more accomplished Rider.

TROUBLESHOOTING

Given the brutal terrain bykes cover and the speeds they reach (up to 80 klicks per hour), they are prone to degenerate over time. Retuning by a qualified Bykemonger is required on a regular basis. You will find a list of registered Bykemonger stores at the back of the manual.

However, Bykemongers are not always available to get you up and running. In the event you are stranded in the Badland with no access to a Bykemonger (or even a lowly Greaser), you will be required to troubleshoot on the fly. Here are three of the most common problems and solutions:

1. **Transfer engine jam.** Bykes can shift form to suit the terrain. They can elongate on the flats for speed and lift higher to tackle extreme off-road conditions. But a common glitch of this manual versatility is that bykes are prone to stick in either mode. Unjamming the transfer engine requires unbolting the engager panel and recoupling the lever arms by hand. Take care not

to bolt the left lever into the right engager and vice versa (and try not to get your fingers caught in the cogs).

2. **Wheel puncture.** It is perhaps one of life's great ironies that while byke sentience can be achieved, you may still suffer the occasional puncture. In your Race pack you will find a standard wheel puncture set. The task is first to locate the site and dimension of the tear. This is simple with the murmur scope. Turn the byke upside down and work the scope over the entire spinning tyre. Place the funnel of the scope in your ear and listen for hissing. Once the fault is located, all you need to do is inject sealant directly through the rubber outer tyre. The sealant injector is designed to adequately flood the area with glue and not cause additional damage. The tyre will automatically pull air into the intake valve and refill as you ride.

3. **Gearbox malfunction.** Byke gearboxes are tough, but over time they can wear and break. Stripped gears and broken chain links will leave you stranded. Spare chain links are usually located in the byke seat panel. These can be grafted into the main chain structure with your fusion drill. Fusion drills charge as the byke rides, so don't forget to check the connection. Stripped gears can be unscrewed from the main rotor and replaced or sprayed with Vodden oil as a short-term fix.

STIR OF ECHOES

Since bykes are manufactured from Voddenite, their multitude parts can be prohibitively expensive. New bykes cost anywhere between $1,000 and $5,000, depending on the model.

It's for this reason that bykes are passed down from parent to child. It's quite possible the byke you're riding today has been handed down through four generations. And the result of this blood lineage is the echo.

Put simply, an echo is the imprint past Riders leave behind in the byke. Their feelings. Their character. Their strengths and weaknesses. The thoughts they might have had when riding. Conversations from the past. All these things, these moments, are held in the fibre of the machine, like DNA fragments.

But an echo cannot be explained. It must be felt to be truly understood.

Don't be afraid of the echoes stirring in your machine. Use them to your advantage. Allow them to guide you. They (mostly) have your best interests at heart.

It's your bloodline after all.

SLING BALLISTICS

Insights into the mechanics of the Voddenite sling as well as the skills required to master the deadly art of slinging. Learn to plan a strike, perform an expert swing and release at the perfect moment.

PLANNING THE STRIKE

In trained hands the Voddenite sling has remarkable power and accuracy. A stone shot loose from a Vóddenite sling will slice clean through a glass bottle 300 yards away.

It is most effective at a range of over 10 yards and can strike a target up to 500 yards away.

The longest Voddenite sling strike on record is 760 yards (this has not been legally verified).

At close range, quick-fire speed is essential, especially in a duel. But, at long range, many factors come into play before an accurate deploy is possible. At any distance over 300 yards you should have plenty of time to consider these. Don't worry: if your sling fails, your byke is your escape, unless darkness has fallen, in which case neither sling nor byke will prove reliable.

Slingmasters, generally speaking, have one rule in common:

PATIENCE ABOVE ALL.

It isn't just a rule. It's a mantra (and it applies equally to long-distance racing).

Understanding this precept is essential for sling wielding, given the sheer volume of factors that must be considered for an effective release. The following are priorities:

1. **Wind.** This one is vital. It requires awareness of subtle deviations in velocity and direction. Be aware: the prevailing Banshee is a northeaster and can reach gale force, around 40 klicks per hour. Enough to throw a stone well off course (some say enough to blow the feathers off a buzzard, although this is unproven and the author considers it rather unlikely).

2. **Sun.** Behind you, an advantage. In front of you, an enemy. This may seem obvious, but you would be shocked by the number of times a simple fact like this has been ignored by the rookie slinger. A grievous error. Keep the sun behind you.

3. **Terrain.** A glass bottle 300 yards away is difficult to see. In rocky, sun-drenched terrain, even more so. Now replace the glass with a moving target and position the target downhill or at the crest of a steep slope and the task becomes exponentially more challenging. It stands to reason that you should decrease sling speed for a downhill shot and increase for an uphill attempt. In addition, it is sensible to position yourself close to a well-sized boulder or tree, to shield yourself from potential return fire in the event that your planning is thwarted by a crosswind (or ineptitude).

Once these natural circumstances have been duly considered, the sling wielder is ready to take aim. However, it is advised (and prudent) to execute a rapid recheck of all natural factors.

Remember, *patience above all.*

PERFORMING THE SWING

The sling is constructed of a length of hemp, braided through with fine strands of Voddenite. It's important to note that while Voddenite enhances the sling's potential, the sling's true power is not technological: it lies in user skill.

One end of the sling has a loop and the other end is knotted. You operate the sling by slipping the loop over the ringfinger of your hand (right or left depending on your disposition) and the knotted end is held in the same hand, between your thumb and the centre joint of your forefinger.

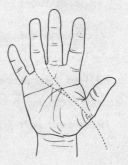

A stone projectile is then placed in the diamond-shaped pocket.

The advantage of stones is that they can usually be found when needed (although it is wise to carry at least three well-shaped stones at all times) and they are difficult to see in flight. Smooth and rounded stones are far more effective than any other shape.

Projectile sizes vary. Stones can be as big as buzzard eggs or as small as walnuts. In high winds select larger, flatter stones to maintain true flight. In humid weather conditions use a small stone (about ten grams and one inch in diameter).

The swing itself can be executed in three orthodox methods:

1. **The underhand method.** Stand side-on, right side away from the target. Point the pouch (with projectile) at the target with your left hand (if right-handed) and hold the other end near your head with your right. Now, keeping hold of both ends, rock your body a little right and then release the left hand and whirl the sling once underhand at the target.

2. **The overhand method.** Side-on again. Same stance. Point the pouch at the target and hold the sling near your head on the right. Keep the cords tight in your hand. When you're ready to fire, twist your body to the right, then jerk back left and whirl the sling once above the shoulders. Release high over the right shoulder, above your head. The arc of motion before release is high right to low left.

3. **The windmill.** The entire sling (with projectile) is whirled around three times horizontally above the head, before release. The first two revolutions are just to get the feel of the weight of the stone and to visualize the release. You must swing the sling as hard as you can on the final rotation. This style is best for long-range shots.

THE RELEASE

A perfect slingshot release is all about feeling. The connection between sling and slinger is an intimate one. It's a partnership. The sling must become an extension of one's own body.

Your task is to focus. You must zero in on the target.

Shut out everything else. Listen to your breathing. Listen to your heart thump in your chest.

Close your eyes and feel the hard abrasion of the sling in your fingers.

Now begin to swing your arm. Slowly. Then with gathering momentum.

It's all about rhythm, heartbeat and feel.

The sling, if wielded correctly, will become an extension of your arm, without you having to force the feeling. It will happen naturally. In the same way you feel the bond with your byke. This is the mysterious power and potency of Voddenite. It creates a force that can connect humans with elements, forging them into one entity, bonded in common purpose.

But partnerships are difficult. To partner with something (or some*one*) requires a sixth sense. It's like having a dance partner. You can learn the steps and rehearse until you're blue in the face, but if you have no feeling for your partner – no connection – the dance will falter.

It can be useful to imagine *you* are the stone – silent, waiting, endowed with kinetic force – ready to explode outward, at exactly the right moment. Use your intuition. Your instinct.

Now open your eyes. Focus on the target.

See nothing else. And sling!

If you have considered all factors and followed directions carefully, the stone will fly out at over 500 klicks per hour. Your expectation should be a direct hit. Anything else is failure. And, in the Badland, failure can be fatal.

Slung stones can bring down a moving byke. They can rip through armour. And they can crush a person's skull. One direct hit and it's game over.

GOOD LUCK AND MAY YOU LIVE TO SEE THE SKY!

In Conversation with
David Hofmeyr

Tell us about the inspiration behind *Stone Rider*

Stone Rider was born in a workshop with the world's greatest writing coach, Steve Voake. I submitted a piece that turned out to be the opening scene. Crossing an alien desert came a group of riders, like horsemen of the apocalypse. Only here, instead of horses, they were riding other-worldly *bykes*. I knew I wanted fear and adrenalin, dust and blood and vengeance. A primal story. I suppose it sprang from the Westerns I loved as a kid. The Dollars Trilogy. *Pale Rider*. *Once Upon a Time in the West*. But also something futuristic. *Mad Max*. *Blade Runner*. *Star Wars*.

What was your favourite book as a teenager, and which YA writers do you admire today?

Stephen King was a favourite in my early teens. In particular, *The Bachman Books*. I loved the darkness and the cool originality of his worlds. The short story, *The Long Walk*, has definite parallels with *Stone Rider*. I remember the feeling of the story. It stayed with me.

I admire so many YA authors today. Patrick Ness is a genius. Matt Haig writes with such humanity and wit and warmth. Nobody gets teenage angst better than John Green. My friend, Clare Furniss, knows how to move you from tears to laughter in a heartbeat. Sally Green's debut, *Half Bad*, is a masterpiece in character. Tim Winton's book, *Breath*, is exquisite. *Everything* he writes is beautiful.

Where and when do you do your writing?
I'd like to be one of those writers who wake up at six every morning, write for a fluid four-hour stretch, break for casual meandering and bullfighting, then another two hours in the afternoon and a further two editing in the evening. I read somewhere this is the optimal way to write. Clearly I am suboptimal. I work four days a week in Advertising, so I tend to write when I can. In the evenings and late at night. But I dream about my stories all the time and jot down scenes on the tube, the train or even at work during mindless conference calls. Don't tell my boss.

If you could meet one character from a novel, who would it be and why?
Harry Flashman. OK, not a YA character, but I challenge you to find a more original creation. His behaviour is riotous and ribald and never PC. Totally refreshing. I learned a fair deal from his creator, George MacDonald Fraser. I'm sure I'd learn a lot more from Harry.

Can you give us a clue as to what will happen next for Adam, Sadie and Kane?

A winter freeze descends and the desert turns to riven ice fields, snow-covered plains and creaking glaciers. Adam and Sadie will face unrelenting hardships and the terrors in their quest to reach Sky-Base. They will need all their skills as Riders of semi-sentient machines to survive their new ordeal. Kane cuts a lethal and mysterious figure. And Levi Blood and the Colonel prowl.

He just wanted a decent book to read ...

Not too much to ask, is it? It was in 1935 when Allen Lane, Managing Director of Bodley Head Publishers, stood on a platform at Exeter railway station looking for something good to read on his journey back to London. His choice was limited to popular magazines and poor-quality paperbacks – the same choice faced every day by the vast majority of readers, few of whom could afford hardbacks. Lane's disappointment and subsequent anger at the range of books generally available led him to found a company – and change the world.

'We believed in the existence in this country of a vast reading public for intelligent books at a low price, and staked everything on it'
Sir Allen Lane, 1902–1970, founder of Penguin Books

The quality paperback had arrived – and not just in bookshops. Lane was adamant that his Penguins should appear in chain stores and tobacconists, and should cost no more than a packet of cigarettes.

Reading habits (and cigarette prices) have changed since 1935, but Penguin still believes in publishing the best books for everybody to enjoy. We still believe that good design costs no more than bad design, and we still believe that quality books published passionately and responsibly make the world a better place.

So wherever you see the little bird – whether it's on a piece of prize-winning literary fiction or a celebrity autobiography, political tour de force or historical masterpiece, a serial-killer thriller, reference book, world classic or a piece of pure escapism – you can bet that it represents the very best that the genre has to offer.

Whatever you like to read – trust Penguin.